Rangers *of* Liberus

Book 1

The One with Magic

An ANNMAR CHRONICLES Book

Rangers of Liberus: The One with Magic – Book 1

Annmar Chronicles/ Truesource Publishing book

Rangers of Liberus: The One with Magic- Book 1 is edited by Carol Felder, J M Almgreen, and Audra Farris

The story is fictional and any resemblance to actual people, places, and certain facts associated with the characters created by Marcus Blake is purely coincidence.

Annmar Chronicles: Dallas Texas

Truesource Publishing: Dallas Texas

www.annmarchronicles.com
www.truesourcepublishing.net

ISBN : 978-1-932996-78-4

Printed in the United States of America
Published in Dallas, Texas

For More information on Marcus Blake go to....

www.marcusblake.net
www.facebook.com/themarcusblake
www.twitter.com/marcusblake
www.instagram.com/marcusblakeauthor
www.thatnerdshow.com

Table of Contents

Annmar

100 AG (After the Gods)

It is the first age in the World of Annmar. It is a dark time in Annmar where the gods are dead and magic has left the world. A world shaped by the creation of five gods where magic was prevalent throughout the land, it disappeared long ago. Now Annmar is the world made up of different kingdoms that are equally suspicious of one another. There are Kingdoms for Humans, Elves, Dwarves, Halflings, Fae, and Barbarians with free towns that do not come under the rule of any kingdoms. These towns such as Liberus are considered outsiders.

During this time, the Kingdom's of Anntheia and Belmere are constantly at odds with one another and battle for land and dominion over mankind in Annmar. The Elven Kingdom of Dorwinn, the Halfling Kingdom of Yorynn, and the Faerûn Kingdom known as the Emberwild all keep to themselves and stay out of the affairs of men. The Dwarven Kingdom of Guirinn maintains peace through Annmar with its merchant services to all kingdoms. And the Barbarian Clans of Skallvenn raid and plunder as with their nature throughout the land while always being at odds with different kingdoms in Annmar.

One hundred years after the Age of Gods, stories about gods and magic are merely myth. Most folks in Annmar do not believe them to be true. Even monks at the great Monastery of Lenntis who keep the written history of Annmar record these stories as myth. However, at this time, there has been an awakening. The time of magic may soon come again as the Kingdoms ready for war and vie for control over its power. A mysterious visitor will return and could fulfill a prophecy about the return of magic, but there are those who want to stop this and have the power of magic for themselves. The last 100 years in Annmar have been the Dark Ages, that time may soon be at an end.

TIMELINE

BG: before the death of the gods when the gods and man lived together.

AG: after the death of the gods and the beginning of the 1st age in Annmar

The Story of the Five Gods

In the beginning, the world was void and without form. It was desolate and undiscovered. And then one day, there were five gods who came into the world. Through their connection and their harmony within what we now call Magic, they gave the world life. Each god brought something unique to the world, each had their own influence, but it was their connection that brought peace and prosperity. The five gods occupied five distinctive points of the world which formed a pentacle, a symbol of perfect Harmony. It was believed that the gods came from a place called Eginon, some refer to the place as heaven in the common tongue. It is believed that if your soul was pure, this is the afterlife you would go to. There was Gennir, the god of magic, who was the centerpiece of the pentacle. She greatly influenced the use of magic in the world. Gennir created fairies, also known as Fae or Faerûn in the ancient tongue. Since the world was not without evil, a byproduct of Gennir's creation, Khronnes were born into the world.

They would be users of dark magic and creators of unholy spells. Dresda was the god of destiny whose influence and guidance to those who were to live great and noble lives would give birth to man. Or simply called humans in the common tongue. Of all the creations and races, men were destined to do great things, some legendary that would help shape the world. Dresda was there to help guide them in their noble acts that would maintain peace and prosperity in the world.

Cimis was the god of wisdom. He guided the wisest of all races in the world. They would be called elves and because of the guidance they received through the wisdom of Cimis they would also live five to ten times longer than that of any other race. In order to maintain peace and prosperity throughout the world, wisdom was one of the cornerstones. Elves and even Half Elves would become one of the noblest races in Annmar. For without them the world would surely descend into chaos. Eras was the god of tranquility and love. If there was ever a god that influenced and guided a peaceful existence, then it was Eras. Her influence gave birth to gnomes and halflings, simple folk who yearned for peaceful lives and non-adventures. They were content in their own homeland and found pleasure in simple things. What they yearned for most was good company and loved all things as long as it gave them tranquility. Eras was the second most powerful god; for tranquility and love is a powerful force. Living that kind of peaceful existence can lead to powerful magic.

Anion, the final god among them. He was the god of war and destruction. Brutal and hot-tempered at times, Anion was seen as a necessary evil to help balance the other influences of the gods. While Anion lived to rage war, most often, it was only done out of necessity. However, his influence would also give birth to warlike creatures and stubborn folk like the dwarves who never turned down a fight or a war they could join in. But Anion also had a lot of influence over man and was constantly at odds with Dresda. Their unity of opposites brought a common balance to the world and through their connection added a powerful harmony with the rest of the gods. Wisdom, destiny, magic, war and destruction, and tranquility and love are seen as the most powerful elements to maintain peace and prosperity. For thousands of years that's what these gods did for the races they helped create. The world grew plentiful because of the influence of the five gods. There were many languages throughout the land; many ancient dialects. But in the common tongue, the world the five gods created became known as Annmar.

Over thousands of years the world grew and became civilized. The population among the races grew exponentially. Advancements in technology and better everyday living increased peace and prosperity. The five gods were worshipped and respected as pilgrimages were made often to their shrines in the various places throughout Annmar. There was a harmonious connection between all races, war was unheard of. Everything that the gods wanted through creation was achieved. It was a Utopia. However, it was not meant to last. A darkness found its way into Annmar. It was a simple thing called jealousy as referred to in the common tongue. It was the jealousy of one god. After many years when the world grew into the perfect civilization, Anion grew jealous that other races worshipped the other gods. He wanted all to worship Him and only him. And through his jealousy and influence, war would come the world of Annmar. It started with the Dwarves who wanted more land and gold, they thought Man had too much land and gold while man thought Dwarves had too much.

War started with small skirmishes between dwarves and man over small partials of land that they both thought to be rich in minerals, especially gold. It also started with a war between Anion and Dresda, and their influence over the races they created. Eventually Anion killed Dresda and exerted his influence over man. Thus began the war of the five gods. It also brought war between the races of Annmar. The harmony that once existed between them faded away into the darkness that had crept into the world. One by one, Anion warred with each of the gods. After Dresda had died, Anion turned his attention to Gennir, the god of magic. The battle between them was fierce, but Anion killed Gennir and rid the world from the influence of magic. After she died, the world dove further into darkness. Magic had been the light and it showed the people that all things were possible, but without light, there could only be darkness and despair.

Cimis, the god of wisdom, and Eras, the god of tranquility and love, joined together to fight Anion, but he had grown too strong. With two of the gods dead by his hands, his power and influence over the world greatly increased. He was the most powerful god in Annmar, now, and so it would take two gods joined together to defeat him. Their battle would extend from one end of the world to the next. In a stunning and severe blow, Anion killed Cimis, but during the battle, he was severely weakened. This allowed Eras to gain the upper hand and eventually kill Anion at The Shrine of Nydar. It was a holy place for the gods. Legend has it, it was the birthplace of magic. With only one god left, the harmonious connection that had propelled the world into peace and prosperity was severed. The world had become ravaged by war between the inhabitants of Annmar. Eras tried to use her power to influence more tranquility and love, but without the connection between all the gods, it had faded too quickly from the world. There wasn't anything she could do for Annmar. It would take the power of the five gods to bring peace back into Annmar.

Era should have been looked at as a savior by those in Annmar. She should have been worshipped, but it was not so. Mankind, along with Oracles of Erinnity, had lost faith in the gods. For if any one of them could rise up and exert complete control over the world, and cause such destruction, then why did any of the races need the god's at all. They formed a plan and with the combined forces of all the races in Annmar, lured Eras to the shrine of Nydar for an audience and to pay respect the last god of Annmar. Led by the militant King Argas and the sworn Brotherhood that guarded the Oracles of Erinnity, in one swift moment, while standing by the altar at the Shrine of Nydar, they took turns stabbing Eras. She had been weakened in her battle with Anion and wasn't strong enough to fend them off. She was not powerful enough to stop them and so Eras died upon the altar. This caused a cataclysmic event throughout the world. Annmar opened up and oceans swallowed part of the land, thus separating five parts of the world from one another. What was once connected was now divided. And when the land opened up it swallowed thousands of inhabitants from all races of Annmar. The shockwaves from the event could be felt throughout every corner of the world. Overnight the world of Annmar was reshaped. Villages and kingdoms were washed away only to form new ones. At least half of the population died from the event.

The power of the gods was gone from the world. The light that had shone bright throughout Annmar disappeared and all that remained in the haze that surrounded Annmar was darkness. Now, light could only be seen in certain parts of Annmar. It was in the places where good still remained. Places where one could still feel peace, but they were small and hard to find. Over multiple Generations, nobody seemed to believe that the gods had ever been real or that there was once magic in the world. All knowledge of these things just became stories. They became myth and with them came the Dark Ages in Annmar. It was a time without belief. It was a time without knowledge. It was a time where fear gave way to suspicion. What few kingdoms remained within Annmar did not interact with each other unless it was absolutely necessary. When they did, it was usually brought on by war. After the last god, there was nothing, but destruction and despair led by jealousy and petty greed. For this is what ruled Annmar at the beginning of the First Age. The war of the five gods had destroyed the utopia that Annmar once was and perhaps could never be again. The world was created by the five gods. Their war reshaped the world and plunged it into darkness. But the story of the five gods would not end with their deaths. It lives on through their descendants and what they gave the world of Annmar. The story continues within the Annmar Chronicles and at the start of the First Age.

1

The night was restless. The three Rangers could feel it as they tracked something in the darkness during their night patrol. Rathgar was the first to say it. "The air is foul, can you smell it?" the other two Rangers Jaedann and Hanniah didn't disagree. Bad smells were always a good indicator to a Ranger that danger was lurking. They made their way through the heavily wooded area towards one of the small ports along the outer coastlines of Liberus. Jaedann stopped them and then bent down to look at the ground. It had been trampled on by what appeared to be a large group or herd of animals. Not by horses, but by heavy feet and bigger than a normal human. Finally, he saw it, crow feathers and small thorns around the outer edges. It wasn't natural, they had been made that way; a symbol for those who wore the feathers and their warlike identity. Jaedann showed Rathgar the feather. After examining it closely, he replied. "It's Barbarian, the Crowthornn clan to be exact."

Hearing that surprised Jaedann and Hanniah. Rathgar was not so easily surprised by the motives of the Barbarian clans since he came from one himself. He had once been a Ravennbeak until he had been cast out for loving the wrong woman and killing her husband in the Barbarian tradition of trial by combat when it came to settling disputes. He may have won the fight, but lost the woman he loved and his home. Now he was a Ranger on the outskirts of the world known as Annmar. Jaedann asked his friend Rathgar. "This is strange, Crowthornns don't venture this far to the coast, do they?"

Rathgar shook his head. "No, unless it is for gold…lots of gold."

Hanniah asked. "Then what else would they be looking for?"

"They're not looking for anything except people to pillage and murder. That's the only service Crowthornns sell to outsiders and I know for a fact, no Barbarian would hire them to venture this far west."

The three Rangers followed the trail left by Crowthornns. Rathgar figured it had to be at twenty of them, which equaled about a hundred Belmerien Knights in terms of ferociousness and fighting ability. But Barbarians were always more savage when it came to fighting and that made them more dangerous. The trail was leading to the coastline east of the Liberus, a trading town, and a small port only used by smugglers and blackmarket dealers. They were less than one mil (miles in Annmar) from the coast when Hanniah saw the smoke dance in the moonlight that that helped light the way. It was a full moon that night and gave off just enough light to see smoke rising above the tree line. She said to the other Rangers. "Look, smoke. Something's on fire." Jaedann and Rathgar couldn't see anything, but they never doubted her instincts. Jordan asked if she could climb a tree and see what was burning. Hanniah was very skilled at such things. She quickly scurried up one of the big redwood trees just enough above the tree line. Hanniah saw what was burning and said. "It is a small ship next to the broken dock. Crowthornns set it on fire." She could also see the Barbarians slaughtering people on the beach. They were not doing a good job defending themselves against the Barbarians raiding the area. Most of them were dead already.

Jaedann, Hanniah, and Rathgar sprinted to the small port, hoping to catch the Barbarians by surprise. As they reached the base of the tree line before the beach started, Jaedann stopped them. He commented. "They are mostly women, that ship is not a smuggler's ship. This is something else. why are Crownthornns interested in this ship."

Hanniah got annoyed as women were screaming while being hacked to death on the beach. She replied. "It doesn't matter, we need to stop this." Jaedann was going to say something, but quickly realized she was right, and they needed to help. They mystery if why the Crowthornns were there, could be solved later. He ordered Rathgar to go around and flank the Barbarians. He and Hanniah were going to use their bows and drive the Crowthornns towards his direction by shooting arrows at them while remaining hidden in the tree line. Rathgar smiled at the idea and even commented. "Great, my axes just got sharpened and need some blood on them."

Rathgar snuck around and flanked the croutons while still being hidden in the tree line. Hanniah and Jaedann stood side by side and got into position while also being hidden by the trees at the edge of the beach. They raised their bows. Steadied their arms and aimed. Arrows flew from the trees. Two Barbarians went down, then two more right after as more arrows came flying from the darkness of the tree line. The rest of the Crowthornns did not know what was happening and started to scatter. Jaedann and Hanniah shot two more arrows and killed two more before emerging from the trees. Jaedann's strategy was working, Crowthornns were running in the opposite direction toward where Rathgar was hidden. He came out of the tree line like a ghost and two Crowthornns did not even see it coming as his ax blades swiftly severed their heads. He swung the axes with precision and killed two more. The rest of the small barbarian army were trapped between Rathgar and his axes plus, Hanniah and Jaedann with their bows and swords, and the water they hated more. Sure, there were more of them than the three Rangers killing them with ease, but they had little chance as the Rangers took care of business. Rathgar didn't even get a scratch on him, but his newly sharpened axes were coated in Barbarian blood. Jaedann was out of arrows as the last Crowthornn came running towards him. He ducked and rolled behind him, pulling his sword out and slicing the Crownthornn down the back just to get him down. Then he finished the job by cutting off his head. They had killed all the Crowthornns except for one who escaped into the woods and ran away. Rathgar remarked that Crowthornns were cowards compared to other Barbarian clans, but he had never liked the Crowthornn clan anyway.

Most of the people who had been on the ship and had gotten off were found dead on the beach. As the Rangers were searching the area, Hanniah found an old woman still alive, but bleeding out. She was still conscious. Jaedann knelt beside her and asked. "Why did they attack you?" He was hoping that she had some clue to why these innocent people were attacked. The old woman replied as she coughed up blood. "You must protect here."

The Rangers looked at each other with curiosity and then looked back at the old woman. Jaedann asked. "Who?"

"The woman repeated. "Protect her, she is the one."

"Who is *her*?"

"The old woman gasped for air as blood filled her mouth. Then she grabbed Jaedann's arm and with last words said. "You must protect her with your life." They were ominous words, the kind that could send shivers through your body. The old woman died before she could say anything else, but her word left all three of them wondering who this mysterious girl was. The Rangers were confused, but that was to be expected. Rathgar spoke up. "Her, any idea who the woman was talking about? Is there anyone else alive?" They all looked around and could see that no one was moving on the beach. Hanniah suggested they check the small ship that was docked. Jaedann and Hanniah climbed aboard. They searched the ship, but found nothing of interest. Hanniah was the one who spoke up first. "I don't get it, there's nothing on this ship except the bare essentials they would need to sail, nothing of value."

She was right, there was nothing of value. The cargo-hold barely had anything in it, which made the entire situation even more strange. The ship had nothing that Crowthornn Barbarians would want. Then Jaedann heard a noise coming from the back wall. After looking closely, he spotted the hidden storage room, covered by barrels filled with fruit. He and Hanniah cleared away the barrels and opened the storage door.

Whoosh! An Arrow went whizzing by Jaedenn's head. His quick reaction knocked it out of the way. He an Hanniah saw that it was a young girl. She was frightened, but still tried to load another arrow in the crossbow and then she stumbled backwards, tripping over a boxed container. The girl fell, hit her head and knocked herself out. It was a bit amusing to Hanniah. She laughed and commented on it. "What was that?"

Jaedann softly smiled. "I guess we have a survivor. An unconscious one, but a survivor. Maybe if she comes to, she can tell us what the Crowthornns were looking for." Jaedann and Hanniah got the girl off the boat. To Rathgar's surprise, he asked. "Who is that? Is that girl that old woman was talking about?"

Jaedann replied. "We don't know, but she's the only one alive and may have answers to what really happened here."

"We're not taking her with us, are we?"

Jaedann nodded. "Yes, maybe Vorak can help her and I want to know why Crowthornns are venturing this far. Let us see what she has to say about it."

Rathgar grumbled. "She's dead weight. We should just leave her here for the Crownthorns. They'll just keep coming back until they get what they want. We should save the Liberus the headache…let he Crowthornns have her and they will be gone."

Hanniah shot him a dirty look. "We don't leave innocent women behind despite the half-wit notions of Barbarians, especially Ravennbeaks."

Rathgar was about to say something, but Jaedann interrupted. "It's best not to argue with her when she's mad. You tend to lose important body parts when you stoke the fiery wrath of Hanniah Bloodshout and I guarantee you'll miss what she takes from you." Rathgar didn't' say anything after that. The look by Hanniah was warning enough that the best decision was to shut up and go along. Jaedann put the unconscious girl over his saddle in front of him and the Rangers rode off into the night back to the trading city they had swore to protect.

2

The two men sat on their horses beneath the moonlight on a hilltop that overlooked a valley. The night was getting cold. Finally, Yvain asked the man next to him. "Sansonn, how long is this supposed to take? These Crowthornns should be back by now. I thought you said they could get the job done and quick?"

Sansonn chuckled. "Relax, they will be here. Sometimes, Crowthornns take extra time with the women after they are done pillaging…if you know what I mean."

Yvain gave him a dirty look. He did not like that remark any more than he liked Sansonn. Yvain considered himsElf a virtuous man and did not approve of such things. "Of course I do, but raping is usually a quick sport in my experience with the soldiers I have commanded."

"Not to Barbarians. Just like with food and drink, they take the time to enjoy what they consider the spoils of a good hunt."

In the distance they could see the silhouette of someone running through the trees up the steel hill. It was only one Crowthornnwhen there should be twenty. Yvain commented on that fact. The Crownthorn reached the top of the hill where they two men were sitting on their horses. It was the leader of the group and both men were gravely surprised to see only him. Sansonn spoke first. "Khonnd, where is the rest of your men."

He grumbled. "Dead, all of them."

Sansonn, stunned a what he was hearing asked. "Dead...how? Who did this to your kinsmen?

"Rangers. They shot arrows from the woods like cowards. And there was another Barbarian...I recognized his battle axes. I barely escaped."

Yvain replied. "Or you ran instead of fighting. That is the truth, isn't it?"

Khonnd growled back. "Crowthornns do not run from a fight...we only leave the fight to get more men if need be. That's what I am going to do so we can hunt these Rangers down and spread their insides throughout the valley."

Yvain did not like having to deal with barbarians any more than he had to. He did not trust them and believed they should only be used as fodder in a battle. He was about to say something snobbish and condescending, but Sansonn interrupted. "Khonnd, did you find it?"

"Everybody is dead. We killed them all before the Rangers showed up."

Yvain responded. "Then why don't you have the head. Our deal what that you bring the head of the   Elf."

"We found no Elf."

"Then you didn't get everybody."

Khonnd grumbled. "Maybe there was no Elf on that ship."

Yvain gave the barbarian a fake smile. "There was because someone a lot more powerful and certainly a lot smarter than you, saw it."

Khonnd grabbed the bridle of the horse Yvain was sitting on and in an angry tone replied. "Are you calling me a liar."

Yvain quickly pulled out his small dagger from its sheath and in a downward motion used it to cut off a few of Khonnds fingers. The Barbarian grabbed his hand in pain and was about to attack when Yvain grabbed his head and put the dagger to his throat. "I'm not calling you a liar, but you are clearly mistaken. If you want to see the rest of your gold and weapons, then you will gather a small force and find the Elf. And the next time I see you, you better have its head with you."

Sansonn said to Khonnd. "If the Elf is not among the dead, then the Rangers probably found it and took it back to Liberus, which means you will need a much larger army, but there should be plenty of wealth there to make it worth your while before you burn it to the ground."

Yavin sternly looked at Khonnd. "You have a week, after that I will find another clan to get the job done and we have plenty of gold to make sure the job gets done right." Khonnd was about to respond, but Yvain and Sansonn rode off before he could growl a final word. As the two men rode off into the night towards the village they were staying at, Sansonn asked. "If you suspect who you are looking for to be in Liberus then, why not just send your own army to sack the place. You would be within your right since there is no telling how many black-market goods from your kingdom flow through there every day. "

Yvain gave him a stern look as if to say, *how dare this man suggest such a thing*. He simply said. "Anntheia cannot be involved yet. If we send an army then other kingdoms will ask questions and no one must know our true intent. They must not know who we are looking for." Sansonn was confused. He was just a mercenary who brought people together for the right price. In order to be trusted and continually get business, it meant he could not ask too many questions. But this job had him overly curious, so naturally, he wanted to know more. Yvain shot down any further questions by saying. "We will not talk about this again. Just make sure this Barbarian clan gets the job done or you will suffer the same as them." Sansonn knew well enough not to press the issue and stayed silent for the rest of their ride back to the village.

3

The Rangers finally arrived back to the large trading town known as Liberus. The place carried on like a trading post with no permanent residents, only visitors, although at least a third of the folks and two generations there had lived in Liberus since it was first established over fifty years ago. Liberus even had it's own government and its own code of conduct that everybody who lived there or passed agreed to live by. There was a Magistrate and a small council that the people themselves elected. Something unheard of in a land with kings and noblemen, and hereditary titles. This is what made Liberus one of the best free cities to live in for those who did not want to live under the rule of a kingdom or had been banished from their homeland.

Liberus was buzzing with excitement when the Rangers arrived back. The place rarely slept as visitors entertained themselves through most of the night with drinking, gambling, and whores. And there was plenty of brawling between sailors looking to trade and merchants all to eager take their goods and give little coin in return. Some were friendly and just there to blow off steam, and some where more of a serious nature. Rathgar looked around as they rode in and to him it felt like one big party was happening without him. He commented. "From the looks of it, I will not be getting much sleep tonight."

Jaedann laughed. "How many women will there be tonight?"

Rathgar smiled. "At least there with plenty of ale in-between. "

Hanniah responded in jest. "Is that three at the same time or spaced out through the night?"

"We Barbarians always do things in threes. It's just a matter of how many times." Jaedann and Hanniah laughed at his thunderous enthusiasm. Jaedann told him that he could join the festivities and he was not needed for the rest of the evening. He and Hanniah could take the girl to the Cleric.

Vorak kept to himself. He enjoyed a nice ale every now and then, but as the cleric for Liberus, he was the religious prefect, the doctor, and record keeper. He spent most nights writing down the history of this place, the same kind of job he did in his former life. Vorak was startled by the knock at his door, but assumed it was important. It was Jaedann and he carried the unconscious girl in his arms. He explained to Vorak what had happened on their patrol and how they found her including how she knocked herself out. Vorak had him lay her down on the extra bed, he had in his cabin for folks who were sick or hurt. He asked. "Was anybody else hurt?"

Jaedann replied. "No, everybody else is dead. Killed by a Barbarian clan called the Crowthornns?"

Vorak was surprised. "That is strange…clans don't usually venture down to the coastal lands."

"That is what we thought too. But we need to talk to this girl. Is she going to live?"

Vorak did a quick examination. He replied. "Yes, she hit her head pretty hard, but she will wake up, eventually."

Vorak went to his mending table and made up a sticky substance out of herbs and moss. It was an ointment that would help heal the wound on the back the girl's head. She was wearing a hat that resembled something more like a bonnet and when it was removed by Vorak, her long beautiful light reddish hair fell down covering most of her face and chest. But Vorak, Jaedann, and Hanniah all noticed her ears at the same time as they were poking out of her long hair. Jaedann said it first. "Holy Fuk, she is an Elf." Hanniah looked at Jaedann, stunned, but Vorak took a closer look at the girl's eyes. "No…actually, she is a Half-Elf and what is even more strange, she has one blue eye and one green eye. Elves usually have piercing blue eyes or green eyes, having both is a sign, but I do not know of what. "

Hanniah asked. "How did a Half-Elf even get here? I didn't know there any around."

Vorak said. "They are not common, but you can find them in the port towns of the Elven Kingdom of Dorwinn. I believe a good majority of them live in some of the small villages on the edge of the Kingdom of Belmere."

Jaedann spoke up. "That is true, usually the bastard children of Belmere children and Elf maidens, but I don't think this one came from there. She came from west of here, from across the Sea. There were things on that ship that were not from Annmar and I believe they came with them from their port of origin; from across the Elmsonn Sea. So the bigger question is what is a Half-Elf doing across the sea and why did she came to Annmar?"

Hanniah responded. "That wasn't a merchant ship the Crownthornns raided. You don't suppose the crew were hiding her?"

Jaedann shrugged. Vorak finished putting the ointment on the girl's head and said. "We won't solve that mystery until she wakes up. There's nothing you can do until then. Go get some sleep or get drunk…I'll find you when she wakes up."

Jaedann was going to say something, but Hanniah stopped him. "Jaedann, let it go…it can't wait. In the meantime, buy me a drink. You need one too and perhaps we can blow off some steam." He was extremely curious about the girl, but didn't argue. They left to join the al the fun that would be raging until early morning, perhaps even until the sun came up. Hanniah remarked that other than a drink Jaedann could benefit from the soft touch of a good woman. Jaedann agreed.

4

There were multiple spots to drink and gamble in Liberus, but the most popular place was The Devil's Tavern. It was also the biggest.   The place even had a fighting pit right off the outside deck for friendly brawls and blowing off steam as Jaedann called it. Rathgar was in the pit giving his opponent quite the beating and taking even fewer punches when Hanniah and Jaedann walked into The Devil's Tavern. They were talking about the girl as they walked in and made their way to the bar. Jaedann said. "All I'm saying is this was not a normal raid by a Barbarian clan, there's something strange about that girl." The bartender handed each of then a mug of ale.

Hanniah replied. You're overthinking this…she's just a girl who got lucky and survived a raid. Before you claim that Crownthornns coming down this far is strange, barbarian clans venture further every year with their raids when they can't find enough plunder. It was only a matter time before they came this far.

Jaedann took a sip of ale. "I wish that were true, but I think you're wrong, I fear that this is a warning of some kind. Something bigger is coming our way."

"Did you see an omen because you do not strike me as someone who believes in those sorts of things?"

"No, just a feeling. It's like when you get restless the night before a big battle."

Hanniah took a sip of her ale. "And how would know that? Have you been in many big battles?"

Jaedann softly smiled. "Just like you, I wasn't always a Ranger. A long time go, I was a soldier."

"What army?"

"It does not matter, but when you're a soldier, you learn to read the signs and believe more in your instincts when it comes to big events especially that of war."

"The same as reading an omen."

"It's different. It is feelings based off of experience and not superstitions. To me, it feels like something bigger is going to happen and this wasn't some random incident. I don't know what it is, but I know it's coming."

Hanniah finished her mug of ale. "As long as it's not coming tonight, I don't care. I want to get drunk and ravished…and sleep way past the sunrise. You should quit over thinking this and do the same. You may need those things more than I do. Everything can wait until the morning." That's all she said as she walked off to find the fun she was looking for. Hanniah was a wild spirit and on most nights she needed to be tamed so she could feel like something new the next day. Jaedann in many ways was the same way. He just wasn't as boisterous about it like his fellow Rangers, but had his regular thing with with a fair haired maiden in Liberus by the name of Milley. She was the unmarried daughter of a merchant who traded in stolen and borrowed goods.

It was early in the morning and just a little past sunrise when the girl finally woke up. Vorak was asleep himself when he heard her screams. The girl had no idea where she was and the last thing she remembered were people with swords standing over her. Of course, she was scared, her screams were only normal. Vorak quickly woke and ran to the girl's bedside, trying to calm her down. He said. "Girl, it's okay...you're safe. You're not hurt...look at me, you're safe." She stopped screaming just long enough to ask. "Where am I?"

"You are at the Cleric's house in Liberus."

The girl was still scared. "I don't know what that is."

"It's a safe place, I promise."

"What happened to me?"

"I am not sure, except for the fact that you hit your head. If you want more answers then you will need to talk the Rangers who found you and brought you here." Vorak motioned to the other young girl in the room that served as his assistant most of the time. "Go find Jaedann and the rest of them, tell them the girl is finally awake. "

His assistant replied. "It is awfully early...I am sure they're all still drunk and passed out somewhere."

"Most likely, but trust me...they will sober up fast for this."

It did not take long to find the Rangers. All three of them were curled up with a companion, staying warm and getting past the hangover that had begun the night before. The news was like an instant wakeup for Jaedann, making him jump to his feet while barely getting his shirt on as he rushed to Vorak's building. Hanniah and Rathgar were both awakened in the same fashion and they both rushed from the people sharing their beds to Vorak's building.

The girl didn't say anything to all those standing in the room. In fact, she was so frightened that she was shaking. Vorak tried to calm her down by telling her that everything was okay and she could trust them. But trust is a funny thing when you were just attacked by Barbarians and then wake up to a room full of strangers who may just want to kill you all the same. How could she trust these strangers? Vorak handed her a cup. She inched away and didn't take the cup. He said. "It's just a broth with some herbs, it will make you feel better. You should drink it."

She had only asked one question until now, but she was starting to become more curious than afraid. "What is this place?"

Jaedann softly answered. "You're in Liberus. It's a small city outside the law of any kingdom in Annmar. It's essentially a trading town governed by the merchants who started it."

"You're not part of a kingdom?"

"No."

"Who are you?"

He reached out his hand to greet her. "My name is Jaedann Lionnshade, I'm a Ranger and help keep the peace around here along with my friends, Rathgar and Hanniah." She hesitated for a moment, but eventually took his hand to greet him back. She was still a little afraid, but Jaedann had a trusting face. Somehow, she felt at ease around him.

Jaedann asked. "So what about you…where was your ship coming from." She answered the question with a question of her own. "Where are the other people that were on the ship?"

Rathgar spoke up with a stern tone. "They are all dead."

The girl was frightened again after hearing the news. "Dead…they can't all be dead."

Jaedann replied. "It is true, you are the only one who survived. Do you remember anything?"

"We were attacked by some kind of warrior clan."

"They were a Barbarian clan called Crowthornns. But what I am curious about is what they were looking for, you did not have anything of value on your ship like gold or precious metals. And the ship had just enough food for a short journey."

The girl did not say anything for a moment, but finally replied. "I do not know…we were just attacked."

Rathgar said to her. "Barbarians don't come this far to the coast just to raid ships. They're an inland race. They were looking for something."

The girl replied. "I do not know."

Jaedann said to her. "I guess the captain of the ship did not tell you what was going on."

"What do you mean?"

"Rathgar is right, the Crowthornns were looking for something they thought was important, it was not just a simple raid, but perhaps the Captain or the rest of the crew did not tell you what they were really hiding."

She was a bit surprised to hear that and responded. "Hiding?"

"The crew had to have been hiding something for Crownthorns come this far, but maybe you do not know what it is, that is what I am trying to say."

She did not respond, but finally took a sip of what Vorak had given her. Jaedann asked. "Where were you going?"

"A town called Ellisar."

"I have never heard of it… what kingdom is it a part of?"

"Not sure, all I know that is where we were going."

Jaedann looked at Vorak. "Have you heard of this place?"

Vorak thought for a moment. "I am not sure. Perhaps it is somewhere in Guirinn, but why would a Half-Elf come by sea and travel to a Dwarvian kingdom?"

The girl seemed surprised by the comment. Jaedann could tell that she knew more than what she was saying, but didn't want to pry too much from the frightened girl. Enough tragedy had already beset her. Vorak suggested that she be prepared a bath and get something to eat. There would be time for more answers. The Rangers left. It was early in the morning and the sun was starting to rise above the treeline to the east of Liberus. The Rangers would be up in a little while anyway, so they decided to start their day. Rathgar suggested they get some breakfast and ale. It was how he normally started the day. All of them agreed and as they were walking to their usual breakfast spot, Rathgar asked. "None of you believed her story, right?"

Hanniah replied. "She hit her head and may not remember everything, but it will come back eventually."

Jaedann responded. "No, Rathgar is right. She is hiding something."

Rathgar grabbed his Ax. "Then let's get the truth out of her."

"We don't need the ax, Rathgar."

"My axe would say different."

"Easy big guy. She will tell us when she is ready."

"Why, when we can easily speed this whole thing up."

Jaedann smiled. "So that she will trust us. You always get more truth with trust."

"I trust that my ax can get the job done."

"And most of the time, I would agree with you. But let's try not frightening her anymore and see where that gets us. Also, she may be just like you, get a little food and ale in your belly, and it will quench your fear or your thirst for blood."

"Rathgar laughed. "I do feel better with food and ale in my belly so we will give it a try, but if it does not work, my ax will make it work."

Laughing at the comment, Hanniah said. "You are like a little boy with a new toy…a new ax and you want to kill everything."

Rathgar let out a thunderous laugh. "I'm a Barbarian, weapons always make the best toys, especially when you can use them to take someone's head off." All three of them laughed at the Barbarian's simple logic and he certainly was not wrong.

5

Vorak's assistant was preparing a bath in the big wooden barrel that had been fashioned into a tub. She was heating some water in a metal colander over a wood pile when Vorak brought a plate of food for the girl. It was some bread, fruit, and a little bit of venison. The girl couldn't remember the last time she had something to eat. She was famished and quickly started to scarf down the food, almost choking on it in the process. Vorak responded. "Slow down, you have plenty of time to eat and do not have to eat it all in one bite."

The girl smiled. "Sorry, I guess, I am really hungry."

"Did they not feed you on the ship you were on?"

"Not meat."

"We have lots of it, if you want it. This place is well supplied with meat between the forests that provide us game and the merchants that keep Liberus well stocked with goods."

"Thank You. That is very kind."

Vorak walked closer to her. "Do you have a name?" You never gave us one."

The girl clearly did not want to answer, but eventually gave her name "I'm Sernna."

"It's nice to meet you. I'm Vorak and as you can see, I'm the local Cleric." He pointed to his assistant who was still preparing the bath. "This is Lorna. She helps me around here. If you need anything, ask either one of us."

Sernna asked. "What's going to happen me?"

"You are safe here. Liberus is a place where all those who come are safe from the outside world. You can stay here if you want or we can find someone to get you to where you were going if it exists."

Sernna gave him a strange look. "You don't think Ellisar is real?"

"I am not saying that, but I have never heard of it and it doesn't sound like a common place. I would have to look at a map in order to find the place and it would have to be a map of the ancient world as the name is not of the common tongue. But we will help you get there. For now, get cleaned up."

She was grateful for the Cleric's generosity. It had been her experience that strangers were not generally that nice. Lorna finished filling the tub halfway. There was enough water to get her bath started. Sernna got undressed as Lorna was fetching more wood for the fire to heat more water. She got in the tub and the water was a nuke warm at best. It did not exactly make her feel warm compared to the brisk cold air that blew through the cracks in the wall of the cleric's building. Sernna shivered a little bit as she sat in the water. Lorna said to her. "You do not have to get in right now, I have almost got some more hot water ready."

Sernna ignored her and just sat there in the tub. She was frightened, at least a little bit. Sernna remembered hearing the screams when the barbarians attacked and started killing everybody on the ship. The screams haunted her. The water in the tub started to cool down fast. It made her shiver even more. She closed her eyes. Then she clenched her fists and all of sudden a tiny glow formed in the center of her palms. Sernna felt warmth. Her hands were warmer than usual. The glow was some kind of power that she had never felt before and it caused the water to heat up inside the tub. Her fear was not because of the place she found herself in, but what she had just done. It happened again and she could not control it.

Lorna walked back into the room with the tub and saw the steam rising from the top of the water. Lorna was shocked. She thought it was strange and commented on that fact with her question. "What happened? How did the water get warm?"

Sernna didn't want to answer, nobody would believe her. There was a part of her that didn't believe it herself. Maybe it was a dream! But Lorna didn't say anything else except. "Well, I guess you don't need anymore hot water. Enjoy the bath."

The bath was wonderful, Sernna had to admit. She felt rejuvenated. After she got dressed, Sernna walked back into the main room and found Vorak tinkering at on his workbench. He asked her. "Do you feel better?"

Sernna smiled. "Yes, I do. "Thank You for giving me a bath." Vorak smiled and nodded back. He also noticed some thing, she was wearing a necklace of some sort. It looked as if it had been forged in metal with a blue stone in the middle. It was in the shape of a Penntacle, an ancient symbol that had not been seen in Annmar for over 100 years. Vorak had only seen a drawing of the symbol in a book. He commented. "Your necklace has a curious design; I never saw anything like it before. What is it?"

The girl replied. "I am not sure, It was given to me when I was younger. I was told that it was my mother's." She put the necklace back under her robe and out of the way of prying eyes."

Vorak said. "Well, it's pretty."

Sernna was more talkative now since she was more curious about where she ended up. "What is this place called, again?"

"You are in the town of Liberus. It's more of a trading post than anything else, started by merchants who wanted a place where they could trade their goods at a good price and not be taxed by kingdoms who want just a little bit more than they need and require a license to trade in their ports."

Sernna softly laughed at the disdain in his voice. "These merchants, do they deal in what is referred to as black market goods?"

"You've heard the term?"

"Yes, my moth…the woman who looked after me taught me what it means?"

"I see, was she your mother?"

"I think so, but it doesn't matter. She's dead now."

Vorak gave her a look of sympathy. "She was on the boat, wasn't she?" Sernna nodded yes. Vorak continued. "I'm sorry, why don't you take a walk with me. I'll show you Liberus."

Sernna agreed. As they walked out of the building and into the main street, she asked. "You're not going to ask me more questions?"

"I know you're not telling us everything and that's okay. Everybody who comes here has a secret past and one of our rules is you don't have to share that past. If you want to share anything, that's up to you. Liberus is a refuge for lost and banished souls."

Sernna smiled. It was nice to hear. "Thank You."

"Now in answer to your previous question, yes, there are black market goods sold here. Most of them are necessary for the people who need them the most. Liberus is a place where goods can be smuggled, no questions asked" Vorak smiled. "You have something that needs to be smuggled?"

Sernna could see that he was being humerous with his last statement. She smiled back and said. "Not today, but I will let you if I need to smuggle anything another day."

Vorak and Sernna walked down the street. It was in the morning and the streets were bustling as the townfolk were getting up and starting their day. Vorak would visit different places as if he was a doctor making rounds. As the town cleric, he was the closest they had to a doctor. Sernna asked. "How long has this place been around?"

Vorak replied. "It's been some kind of port for probably 100 years. About 60 years ago buildings went up and people started living here, making it a permanent trading town. I think it was about that time, somebody called it Liberus.?"

"How long have you been here?"

"'I've been the cleric here for ten years." Vorak gave Sernna a curious look. "You are awfully curious about this place?"

Sernna nodded. "I have never heard of this place.

Vorak said. "Then you are not from Annmar, are you?"

"Why do you say that?"

"Because everybody in Annmar knows of the town that defies the rule of any kingdom and is the second largest port in the land. And I suspect that the ship you were on came here from the sea and not another port in Annmar."

Sernna felt nervous. How did he know that? "The look on her face gave her away. "I'm not supposed to tell you anything."

Vorak. "And you don't have to. As I said before, everybody around here has a secret past and you do not have to say anything. But you also don't have to lie."

"Can you I find transport here?""

"You can, for the right price. Do you have any money? Do you even know what the currency is in Annmar because not everybody deals in the same currency? Then again, you are girl and have a currency that is valued among all men."

Sernna got angry at the thought and then her impulsiveness got the better of her. She slapped Vorak for even suggesting it. Immediately she felt bad for what she did. Vorak was more surprised, but also smiled. "You got some fight in you…that's good. Now, I apologize, I only meant that some will expect that and you don't have to give it to them."

Sernna tried to smile and let Vorak know that she was sorry. "I have never hit a Cleric before. I cannot believe I did that."

"Nothing to be sorry for, it's not the first time I have been hit and by a woman."

Sernna softly laughed. "I don't know what kind of Ceric you are to be a hit by a woman."

"A Cleric who can be too honest at times." They continued to walk. Vorak said to the girl. "I should also tell you that if you decide to stay here then you will have to meet with the Magistrate. She meets with every newcomer to Liberus."

"She?"

"Yes, the Magistrate is a woman."

"That does not seem common."

"It is not. Her name is Thorsha. She and her husband came here about 20 years ago after being banished from Anntheia. Not sure why. But with his merchant contacts, he

tripled the amount of trade that came through Liberus. He
died about 10 years ago and she took over while also being
voted by everyone on the Council of Liberus to be the
Magistrate."

Sernna was impressed. "She sounds like quite a
woman."

"Thorsha is a force to be reckoned with. You may like
her."

Sernna nodded in agreement. The Magistrate
sounded like an incredible woman, but she had been taught
to be weary of strangers in a foreign land. Annmar was a
land filled with strangers.

6

Jaeden never liked talking with Thorsha. She was pleasant enough and always fair, but she was still a bureaucrat and he had a healthy distaste for them. Jaedann was too much of a soldier. Thorsha poured him some tea. He usually gave her a daily report. Most of the time it was not very interesting, mostly breaking up fights between rowdy sailors and stopping merchants from trying to steal from one another.

She asked Jaedann. "I hear you rescued a young girl last night."

Jaedann laughed to himself. "News travels fast around here."

"Yes, you should know that by now. I pay good money to know things first."

"And yet, you still want to get daily reports from me."

Thorsha smiled. "Perhaps I just like your company. And I hear that our new visitor is a Half-Elf?"

Jaedann sighed. He was trying to keep that a secret for as long as possible. A female Half-Elf in these parts was extremely rare. Some would say that it was a bad sign. Jaedann replied. "That is true."

"What is she doing here?"

"We are not sure. She just woke up not too long ago and either does not remember or is too afraid to say anything. But she is the only one left alive from a barbarian raid on the ship she was on."

Thorsha was concerned and rightly so. She took great pride in protecting the citizens of Liberus from cruel enemies and strange forces. "We need to know why she was on that ship near our port. Elves do not venture here and rarely do we see half-elves, which are usually men. A female half-Elf is a strange thing even for these parts."

"I agree and we will find the true meaning behind all of this. But I am not sure she can answer that question. I get the impression that she was kept in the dark for a reason."

Thorsha took a sip of tea. "And anyone who could tell us is dead?"

"Yes."

"Do you believe in omens?"

"No. I only believe in what I can see and what I can touch."

Thorsha softly laughed at his answer. "Well, I do believe in omens and this is not a good omen. Along with an orange moon a few days ago, I think something bad is coming."

"What would you like for us to do?"

"You need to find out more about the girl. Why is she here? Where did she come from? I do not care how you get the answers."

Jaedann shook his head, not wanting to believe what he was hearing. Was the Magistrate actually suggesting torture? "She is just a young girl, scared and probably confused. She will tell us what we want to know when she feels safe and can trust us. Just give her time."

"We may not have time. In my job, we have to prepare for the worst when it comes to the safety of the people.   I understand if you are reluctant to harm a young girl, but sometime violence is a must when it comes to the greater good."

Jaedann gave her a confident look. I do not have a problem with violence, but what you are suggesting is torture, I'm not squeamish about it, but it's been my experience that there are a lot more effective ways to get information from someone…like getting them drunk."

Thorsha laughed. "And I am sure bedding her would be considered a bonus." Jaeden nodded. "Yes, but that is not my intension." Thorsha asked. "What else is happening in Liberus"

"Nothing out of the ordinary. Although, Thadius Fimm keeps claiming that some of his goods keep getting stolen."

"Is that true?"

Jaedann laughed. "Not at all. Everybody else can outsell him because their prices are cheaper."

"I see. So this is a job for the Magistrate?"

"Unless you need Rathgar's ax that he's been itching to use some more to convince Thadius to stop telling lies."

Thorsha smiled. "Tell him to keep his ax sharp and I will let him know."

"Will do." Their meeting was over and now it was time to get on with the day's activities. They also needed to find out more behind the Crowthornn attack such as who was paying them. There was one man who would know the answer for his true currency had always been information. The problem was, only Rathgar truly knew him. Only Rathgar would be able to speak with him.   As Jaedann was walking out of the Magistrate's building, Rathgar asked. "So, what now?"

Jaedann replied. "We get on with our work, but I need to ask a favor of you."

"Oh, and what is that?"

"Speak with your friend, we need to know if somebody paid the Crowthornns to raid that ship. "

Rathgar was surprised. "Paid the Crowthornns?

"Yes, you heard right. It got me thinking, if the girl is what they were really after instead of gold, then maybe somebody paid them in gold to find her. If that's true, then we need to know who. Your friend would probably know."

Sansonn stood in the middle of the small hall of the Crowthornn's main building. It was their seat power. It may not have been that big, but there were powerful men who sat in the council chairs that faced Sansonn as he stood there waiting to speak. Hollgruk, who was the leader of the clan stared at Sansonn for the longest time. Then he spoke. "You come here asking for more men, why should we listen to you instead of taking your head for the nineteen Crowthornns that are already dead?"

Sansonn smiled. "I'm sorry for your men. We did not expect Rangers from Liberus to be there. But we have gold. Lots of gold."

Hollgruk gave him a disapproving look. "You think all we care about is gold? We would take your head just for sport?"

"So, I gather, but this time we offer more than gold. Raid and Plunder beyond any sport that could satisfy you."

"Go on."

"Instead of raiding a ship. I offer a town….I want you to raid and burn to the ground that festering trading town known as Liberus."

Hollgruk sat back in his chair. The rest of the council was not too keen on the idea, but Hollgruk saw the greater possibility even with his concerns. "The place is big and has many men who can fight. It would take a large force. Many would lose their life and deplete our forces."

"Maybe, but take all they have and you would be the richest clan in Skallvenn."

"But it would take damn near all of oue men to do it. At that price, it is not worth it. And what if we don't succeed?"

"100 men is all you need." Sansonn motioned for a chest of gold to be brought forth. It was brought by the Khronne who accompanied Sansonn, a race known to conjure the dark arts. The chest was opened up. Sansonn continued. "100 gold pieces to any Crowthornn who fights":

The mere mention of 100 gold pieces excited everybody in the room. It was enough to quell any concern that they could not succeed in raiding and burning Liberus to the ground. Hollgruk replied. "That is very generous, but we will need to purchase more steel if this is to work."

Sansonn smiled and pulled out a handful a gold. "We have plenty of gold, buy everything you need." Hollgruk and the rest of the council discussed the matter. They all quickly agreed. The money was too good not to and so the deal was made. Hollgruk sought a man in the great hall. His name was Marig the Black. He was a merchant, a tradesman, and cared more about information than money. He was known throughout the western lands of Annmar as a man who could get you anything. Hollgruck asked. "We need a large number of axes and swords. Can you get that to us in two days?"

Marig grinned. "I am always at your service, It shall be done."

"For the right price I assume?"

"Not as much as you might think. But I am curious about the strange visitor in your great hall." Hollgruk knew what he was asking, however, gladly dispensed the information to his friend. He could not afford to keep this kind of information from Marig and keep a fruitful business relationship. So a deal was struck, a bargain made. In a few days there would be a battle, who would be dead, and would be left standing was the only question remaining.

7

Everybody new that came through Liberus always paid a visit to the Magistrate. Thorsha made it her business to know everybody who stayed in her town. Something she learned from her late husband, to know all is to be feared by all. Perhaps it was a family motto by now, but she held it close to her heart. She poured Vorak and Sernna some tea. Sernna smiled after taking a taste of the tea. Thorsha introduced herself and explained her role in the trading town. She was head of the council and the judge that presided over all disputes or a trial if the dispute became really serious. Now that they were acquainted, she asked. "I welcome you to Liberus, but I'm curious, where do you come from?"

Sernna did not want to answer, but knew that she couldn't hide those details from the leader of the place she found herself in. After pausing for a moment, she finally answered. "I did notcome from Annmar, I came from across the sea."

"The Elmsonn Sea?"

"Yes."

"Where were you born?

"I am told I was born in a town called Kelna."

"But you don't believe that?"

Sernna paused. "I do not know for sure, but I was the only Half-Elf growing up. I guess the only Elf too."

Thorsha took a sip of tea. There was clearly more to the girl than just being a simple visitor. She was a mystery and as the Magistrate saw it, a dangerous mystery. Thorsha asked. "What is your destination?"

"A place called Ellisar"

"I am not familiar with the place." She pointed to Vorak. "I assume our good Cleric told you that transportation could be purchased to get you where you're going."

Sernna smiled. "He did, but I have no money."

"No, I did not think so, but we have a rule here in Liberus. Those who stay contribute to the life of this place. They earn their keep because everyone who stays has a role in keeping this place alive. You are no different if you stay, but you can earn money to find transportation."

"Thank You. I do not know what I would do."

Thorsha smiled at the thought. She could see the girl was still too young and innocent to really know anything or at least that's what she thought, but she had to ask, "Do you have any skills?"

"Sernna did not want to answer. To answer that question would reveal a secret that was too dangerous to tell. Sernna could not say anything. Whatever answer she had was frozen in her silence. Vorak could tell she didn't want to answer so he spoke up. "Whatever skills she has or does not have, it makes no difference, she can work with me."

Thorsha was a bit surprised. "You already have an assistant, do you not?"

He smiled. "I can always use another assistant. "

"Very well."

The three of them finished their tea. As Vorak and Sernna were about to leave, Thorsha said to the girl. "I hope you understand that while everybody's past is their own and they do not have to share it, we also have a code of honor in Liberus…no lies. We only ask that you don't lie when asked a direct question. You don't have to answer of course, just don't lie."

Sernna replied. "I understand. She could sense that the Magistrate was suspicious of her. Perhaps it was smart of her. And when they were walking out of the building Sernna commented. "Someone in your position must know everything about the place they govern or the people they rule in order to rule."

Thorsha smiled. "When you're a leader, to know all is to be feared by all."

Sernna smiled back, agreeing with the Magistrate's philosophy. Who could argue against it? But just like Thorsha, she mostly distrusted people.   And to her credit, that was the smartest thing she had done since waking up in Liberus. Sernna thanked Vorak for the work despite not knowing exactly what she would be doing. She was suspicious of Liberus as it was filled with all kinds of men and women, rogues, merchants, cutthroats, slaves, and whores. But she understood the need for such a place and how hard it could be to fit in. Sernna would have to do the best she could for now.

Rathgar stared at the narrow path that led into the heavily wooded area. It was perfect for an ambush. His friend always took extra precautions because his loyalty was only money and information. A man like that garnered a lot of enemies so it was reasonable to be extra cautious. Rathgar did not dare venture onto the narrow path. He called out.

"I am Rathgar of the Ravennbeak clan, here to see Marig." Four guards camouflaged by the woods made their presence known. One of them asked. "What business do you have with Marig?"

Rathgar held out his coin pouch and said. "I am here to purchase information. We are old friends, tell him that Rathgar is here to see him."

One of the guards walked up the path and brought Marig back with him. It was true, they were old friends. After all, it was Marig who gave him his first ax when he was a young boy barely strong enough to swing it. Marig had been friends with Rathgar's father and after he died made sure that Rathgar was looked after. He had been a teacher and a father figure to Rathgar, more than a friend. Marig came down to the edge of the path. Normally, he would smile when he saw a friend, but when seeing Rathgar, he gave him a stern look. "Rathgar of clan Ravennbeak, but not anymore. Why would I see an outcast like you?."

Rathgar laughed. "Are we not friends anymore?"
"What do you think?"
"I think for the right price, we can be."
Marig laughed. "I think you're right. It is good to see you, old friend. Come on up and let us drink a pint of Ale. We will tell old stories and then try to figure out which ones are lies." Rathgar walked up to Marig and the two men embraced. Nobody in Liberus knew that they were friends and all that Jaedenn knew was that Rathgar had a friend who seem to know all the comings and goings of Annmar because he dealt mainly in information. From time to time Rathgar would seek out Marig to find out what he knew. It was usually under grave circumstances. Jaedann had his own suspicions after the Crowthornn's raid and the arrival of Liberus' new guest. It was time to find out if something

else was coming. There was and as it turned out, Marig had those answers.

The two men got caught up and had a few laughs over some ale. Finally, Marig asked. "So, what brings you here? From the looks of your ax, you're not here for steel."

Rathgar laughed. "No, my ax is just fine and it's been battled tested. I'm here for information."

"Ah, the true currency. What do you want to know?

"Did you hear about a raid on a ship the other night?"

"You are talking about a raid from a band of Crowthornns."

Rathgar was surprised. "So you did hear about it."

"Of course, a raid like that does not stay a secret in these parts. But what they were looking for, that's the mystery."

"They were looking for gold and plunder as they always do."

Marig softly laughed. "That would be true if they had not already been paid in gold."

Rathgar with a look of shock, said. "If they were paid in gold, then by whom?"

"That's the right question to ask."

"Don't play games."

"No, games, but people rarely ask the right question. The deal was brokered by Sansonn Yonnvadr."

Rathgar thought about it for a moment. "That name sounds familiar. He's part of the Rogues of Hamlinn?"

Marig nodded. "His specialty is brokering deals between powerful men and mercenaries. Sometimes brokering a deal between a Kingdom and fighters that are not their own army. He also gets things for people that they cannot get themselves. We have crossed paths once or twice."

"So, somebody else paid for the raid?"

"Yes, but not just one, a second raid too."

Rathgar was even more surprised by what he was hearing. Who would pay for such a thing? He knew one thing, if someone was paying so much gold for more than one raid, what they were hunting was very important. Rathgar asked. "How do you know all this?"

Marig confidently smiled. "Because I was there when Sansonn paid for 100 Crowthornns at 100 gold pieces each."

"What!"

"I happened to be doing some business in Hunnvasik when he went before the council and I am friends with the Clan Leader so he invited me to the great hall."

"You really do seem to know everything. But who is the benefactor of these raids, the real enemy behind it all?"

Marig took another sip of ale and then took out a gold coin from the pouch on his desca. He flipped it to Rathgar. "See for yourself. Recognize the coin?"

Rathgar looked the coin over. It was familiar. The symbol was the daggered sun inside a ring or better known as the Light of Annmar. Rathgar said. "This is Anntheia gold."

"Yes, are you that surprised?"

"A little. How did you get it?"

Marig chuckled. "Who do you think is providing the steel for their next raid. Sansonn Yonnvadr did not flinch when I told him my price. He just quickly handed over the gold."

"Fuk the god…if Anntheia is behind this then what they are looking for is important and highly dangerous to us."

"So, it seems. Do you know what they might be looking for?"

Rathgar shook his head. "I have an idea. Do you know where the next raid is going to be?"

Marig nodded. "I do, but the price for that information is what you know."

Rathgar rolled his eyes. "You are always dealing in information."

"Because you know that it's the true currency of the world."

"You may be right. We found a girl, a Half- Elf to be exact. She was the only one left alive."

Marig was now the one surprised. "That is very interesting. Rarely do Half-Elves venture in these parts, but a female Half-Elf…that is something we don't see around here. I wonder why she's here?" It had been said before. Marig was not the only one who saw the strangeness in these events or of the girl's appearance in the land of Annmar.

"We do not know. Now where will the Crowthornns raid next?"

Marig looked at him directly. "Liberus is where they will raid next."

Surprise draped over Rathgar's face. "Fuk the God's. This is no Joke?"

"Afraid not."

"How could you be a part of this?"

Marig laughed. "You think I am committing some great crime. What is the one thing that I have always been…neutral. I will do business with anybody, especially with war."

"You would see the place you do a lot of business in be burned to the ground, does that not take away from your business?"

Marig nodded. "Liberus has been burned down and built back up many times. As long as merchants trade goods in that port, then Liberus will always survive."

"You really don't have any loyalty to anything, do you?"

Marig softly laughed. "What did I teach you years ago. Remaining neutral will often keep you alive, while loyalty will often get you killed. I survive because I'm neutral and will do business with anybody. Maybe you should question your own loyalty…are you really loyal to a trading town with barely any law, just common courtesy to keep it alive. Or is being a Ranger of Liberus just a job because you have no other place to go?"

Rathgar paused for a moment. "There is a special place in Gruvara for you."

"That may be true."

Rathgar grabbed His ax and started to leave. Marig asked. "Where are you going…back to Liberus to warn them."

"What the fuk do you care?"

"Have you not asked yourself why I am telling you this."

Rathgar paused again. "No, why do you tell me?"

"So that you can do something about it."

"What do you mean?"

"If the Crowthornns succeed or not, does not mean anything to me. I have already been paid. But if they are defeated and Liberus survives, then I still make money."

Rathgar smacked his fist on the table nearby. He was angry. "Why must you play both sides?"

"Because I will make money either way. Now listen up. I know for a fact that there is a small camp of Ravennbeaks to the Northwest of here. If you take the western road back to Liberus, you should come upon them. They could be convinced to help you."

Surprised by the suggestion, Rathgar replied. "I don't see how since I have been banished. They won't listen to me."

"They will not do it for you, but they would for the gold they can take from the Crowthornns. Perhaps 100 pieces for each Crowthorn they kill."

Rathgar walked towards Marig. He was blood boiling mad. "Why do I have the feeling you planned this all along? This plan is fuking mad."

Marig smiled. "Is it? The more mad the plan…the more money that can be made."

"You are a fuking shittheel, you know that!"

Marig laughed at the comment. "I do now, hurry Rathgar, you have a day and half to get back and defend your home. Do not waste more time here." Rathgar grabbed his ax and quickly found his horse. He rode hard and fast through the narrow path and headed Northwest. He did not like it, but agreed with Marig, they could use the help of some fierce warriors even if they were Ravennbeaks to save Liberus from a raid that would most likely see most of the people killed and Rathgar could not have that in the town he had grown to love.

8

The sun was starting to set over the sea by Liberus. The day was was almost over and that included Jaedann's rounds. Everything was safe in Liberus, at least for now. Jaedann grabbed some food and a bottle of a drink made special only in this place. He had dinner plans with the newest guest of Liberus. Hanniah was curious about what he was doing. As she followed him to Vorak's place, she inquired about his plan. Jaedann suspiciously smiled. "I think we should get some more answers from the girl."

Hanniah was taken back with surprise. "Your plan is to wine and dine her!"

"No, I have something else in mind." He showed her a rather large jug. Hanniah smiled. "Ah, I see, you're going to get her drunk."

"Yes, and it's easier than torture."

"Yeah, but not as quick."

"Also, not as fun as the drinking game we are about to play."

Hanniah laughed. Even she could not disagree with his observation."

When the two arrived at Vorak's place, they found the Cleric teaching Sernna about the herbs and potions that he had in his workroom. He was teaching her the science of things, an education that she had never known before. Jaedann greeted them and offered the food and alcohol. Sernna was happy to see him and asked. "What is in the jug?"

Smiling again, Jaedann replied. "It's a special beverage of Liberus. It's only made here. We call it Ruminn. I could have brought you wine, but from what I hear, you will be staying for a while, so you get our special drink."

That brought another smile to Sernna's face. "Thank You. I have never had it before. Is it bitter?"

"No…this drink is made sweet with natural sugars that are found in the surrounding hills. It's the largest area in Annmar that produces these sugars. It also allows for good trade out of Liberus into Annmar."

"Fascinating. I cannot wait to try it." Jaedann got some cups from Vorak and poured her a drink. She tasted it and her eyes lit up. Sernna enjoyed it and asked for another cup. For the next hour, Jaedann, Hanniah, and Sernna ate and drank. Jaedann and Hanniah told stories about some of the people in Liberus. Most of them were humorous stories that made Sernna laugh, something that she had not done since waking up in Liberous. With each story, Sernna had another drink of ruminn and with each laugh became more boisterous than the next. She was getting intoxicated.

Jaedann spoke up and asked Sernna a question. "Did you meet Chay Rollant today? He was one of he local merchants."

Sernna said. "No, I did not."

"He is an interesting character; a good businessman with fair prices, but how he ended up here is a funny story."

Sernna took another sip of ruminn. "This I must hear."

Jaedann took a sip of rum as well. He was not nearly as drunk as Sernna.

"Chay was a wanted man from a town called Garigill. He was accused of cheating a Lord who just did not want to pay for the clothes he had ordered for his mistress. There was a bounty put on his head, so naturally he fled and came here. But when he arrived, he was dressed as a woman, a short, plump woman named Ottie."

Sernna was stunned, but laughed at the same time, replied. "He did not. How long did he keep it up?"

"Thinking it was the only way no one would recognize him because according to him, he was a well-known merchant, he stayed a woman for a week before he was found out."

"How did that happen?"

"It's hard to hide a beard, he couldn't get shaved every day."

"I hear that's true."

"I asked him why he did it, he told me that a friend said to disguise himself as a woman and change his name. I cannot say for sure if that's a good friend or not, but he made it here alive."

Sernna had another sip of ruminn, she was almost out again. "Yes, he did. It was good advice. The woman who took care of me said the same thing except for dressing as a woman."

Jaedann poured her another cup of ruminn. "Did you change your name?"

"Yes, I had to. Nobody could know my real name in Annmar. The woman who took care of me told me that." Hanniah and Jaedann were both stunned at the Sernna's revelation. Jaedann responded. "Most people, here are not known by their real name…even me. What is your real name?"

She took a big gulp of ruminn. "Deva Mirarel."

Jaedann was beyond shocked.   Even Vorak who was in the back and overheard the name as extremely surprised. It was a familiar Elven name. The name of a prominent house in Dorwinn, the Elven Kingdom. There was certainly more to her story with a name like Mirarel and in time maybe they would all learn the whole of her story. But why was she here at the edge of Annmar? Why had she been living across the Elmsonn sea? Hanniah was going to ask the girl another question, but Sernna or Deva as she just revealed felt lightheaded and passed out.

As Jaedann and Vorak helped the girl back to bed, It was Vorak who asked what they were all thinking. "Did we just hear that name right…Mirarel."

"Yes, " Jaedann replied.

"This is a bad omen… a Half-Elf from that house is a dangerous thing."

"We don't know the whole story yet. I think we should know it before we make any judgements."

Vorak replied. "I do not disagree, but this is a bit strange?"

"I agree and we will talk to the girl when she wakes up. Let us get the rest of her story before we do anything."

"Okay, but I also want to send some ravens to people who may know of any secret births from the Elven Kingdom."

Jaedann nodded yes. He saw the advantage of finding more from those who were in the position to know such things. The girl may not even know her own true story. It was a dangerous mystery, that much they all knew for sure.

It was suspiciously dark as Rathgar rode through woods baring northwest. He came over a hill and saw the burning light of the fire in the distance. He found the small troupe of Ravennbeaks. He approached slowly and when he was about twenty yards, he shouted out. "Who is the leader that sits at this fire?"

There were nine of the them and they all quickly sprang to their feet with axes and swords in their hands, startled by the stranger stealthily approaching their fire. One of them shouted out. "What devious beast would sneak upon our fire?"

A voice shouted back. "I am Rathgar, son of Grelrok."

The other voice replied. "Come into the light." Rathgar approached until the nine Ravennbeaks could see him. Finally, the voice gave his name. "I am Krulf, son of Hanngull. I lead these men and you are not welcome at a Ravennbeak fire anymore."

Rathgar nodded. "I understand, but I need your help."

Krulf looked at his men and started. He said to them. "You need our help. What incredible balls you have to ask that since you are banished from our clan. We should kill you where you stand." In fact, two of the men pulled him down from his horse. Rathgar did not resist, but he replied. "You have that right, but hear what I have to say first."

Krulf paused for a moment deciding if it would just be better to slit his throat or let him speak. Krulf replied. "Speak and if I do not like your words, then I will kill you."

Rathgar looked at him. Understood! I offer you blood and gold."

That peeked the interest of the nine Ravennbeaks. Krulf answered. "Go on."

"In one or two days, 100 Crowthornns will raid the town of Liberus, we need your help to defend the town."

"Nine of us against 100 of them, the blood will be ours at those odds."

"It won't only be you fighting, but you will be the strongest among us and we need you to each kill four or five to even the numbers with the small force we have at Liberus. And I know how much you hate Crowthornns."

Krulf laughed at the part of his speech. It was true, Ravennbeaks hated Crowthornns more than anything, a hatred that went all the way to when time began. But he had to ask. "What about the gold."

"Each Crownthornn has been paid 100 gold pieces and most likely they will have their gold with them. For each Crowthornn you kill, you get to keep their gold. You can be rich men by the end of the battle, so I offer you the chance to kill your enemy and take their gold."

Krulf let out a big, boisterous laugh. "I must say, that is a great deal of blood and gold, and what we have been looking for."

Rathgar smiled. "Then join me and save Liberus."

"I don't give two shitts about your town, if I had the men, I would raid the town myself. We will do this for the blood and gold."

"That works too."

Krulf laughed again. "Then sit by our fire and let us drink to the spilled blood of our enemies and the gold that we will steal from them." That is what they did. Rathgar drank the rest of the ale Krulf had brought with his fellow Ravennbeaks and then they spent the rest of the night telling tales of warriors. It had been a long time since he drank with members of his own clan since he had been banished. Rathgar felt as if it were a homecoming and it brought a joy to his blood lust heart.

9

Jaedann woke up early, the sun was barely over the edge of the trees that faced the east when his eyes finally opened. He and Hanniah had finished off the Ruminn and passed out themselves while in the chairs they had been sitting in at Vorak's place. He splashed some water on his face and packed his horse. Hanniah saw that he was about to leave and asked him. "Where are you going without me? If you are starting your patrol early, we should get some food before we start."

Jaedann nodded, but declined. "No time for food and you will be on your own today."

"Why, where are you going?"

"I am going back to that ship to find the logs or any journals that might give us answers, something that we didn't see before."

Hanniah gave him a strange look. "You think there will be some secret journal that might tell us the girl's tale."

"I do. If she was watched over by someone and not of House Mirarel, and then told to change her name, then maybe they kept a journal and hid it."

Hanniah winced at the idea. "I don't like it. She does not need to be here and this should not be our problem."

"It will be our problem if somebody more dangerous than Crowthornns comes looking for her. We need to know more about her beyond her real name and what she has told us." Jaedann climbed on his horse. "I will be back by nightfall. Don't question the girl when she wakes up. We will do it together." Hanniah nodded yes, she may not have liked it, but agreed. Jaedann hurriedly rode off towards the forest outside Liberus.

A few hours later, Jaedann found the ship still docked at the small port. Nobody had found it yet and the beach was still covered with dead bodies. The port that the ship was docked at was a smugglers' port so very few knew about it, but that did not mean that somebody could not have found the ship and picked it clean. Jaedann hoped that what he was looking for was still there. He got onto the ship and made his way to the captain's room. They had taken the captain's log with them the other night. It had the usual notations about the voyage like their point of origin and what happened daily, but nothing that really told the Rangers about the girl, Jaedann searched around the captain's room and there were not anymore logs, but there was a separate sleeping quarters next to the captain's room. It had two beds in it and a small table made for one person to sit at, but that was it. Jaedann walked the small room looking for some kind of drawer or perhaps a hiding spot. Nothing. Then Jaedann stepped on a loose board. He pried it open and found what he was looking for. There were two full size thick books bound together by horse twine and hardened animal hide for the covers. He flipped through one of them and from what he could tell somebody had been writing in it for eighteen years.

Jaedann was trying to read through it when he heard a commotion on top. He put the books in his satchel, drew his sword and made his way to the deck. There were a few men on the ship and it looked as if they were trying to steal it. One of them, holding a small sword, panicked when he saw Jaedann. He lunged for him and tried to stab him with the sword. He was not successful when Jaedann parried and then swung the sword from left to right, slicing the man's throat. The three other men paused for a moment, looking at each other and trying to decide who was going to strike first and while the other two followed. Jaedann facetiously smiled at them. "You can lay down your swords right now or die right here. Your choice!"

The men looked at each other again and finally one of them lunged, but before he could even get close to the Ranger, a man shouted out as he was climbing on board the ship. "Stop this madness or die where you stand." Jaedann was a surprised to see the man. It was Thadius Fimm. He said to the Ranger. "Jaedann, my apology, we didn't know you were here."

Jaedann, annoyed at the man who climbed onto the ship, said. "You thought you could lay claim to an empty ship without the Rangers knowing about it."

"I did not know you had been here or that the ship was under your possession. There was no posting about it at the Grand Hall." Thadius looked at the dead man. "I suppose he struck first."

"It would not have mattered as I am an enforcer of the law in Liberus. That alone gives me right to kill him for being here. Now, what right do you have to take this ship?"

Thadius paused for a moment and then finally spoke. "No one had claimed the ship and I found it first, that should give me the right."

"Perhaps, if you were outside of Liberus…this Smuggler's port is a part of the town as designated by the merchant's treaty ten years ago and approved by the Magistrate. You should know that."

Thadius looked around the ship. "Am I in trouble?"

Jaedann smiled. "No, you can have the ship on a few conditions."

"What are they?"

"First, you make no more complaints that your goods are being stolen, we know that's not true and with a second ship, you can increase your business." Thadius shook his head at the idea, but didn't really have a right to argue. Jaedann continued. "Second, if I ever need a ship for passage somewhere, you will give it to me without question. Third, whatever I found on this ship is mine and you cannot claim it later, not matter what."

"Did you find something of value?"

Jaedann shot him a stern look. "It does not matter. What's mine is mine and the price is, you can have this ship. Do we have a deal?" Thadius looked at his men as they were still holding their swords, waiting to strike. Maybe they could have killed Jaedann, but that would almost certainly lead to their own deaths. It was a calculated risk, but not one that he was willing to take when he was being given the ship anyway. Thadius nodded yes and asked his men to put their swords away. But he was still curious as Jaedann was leaving the ship and saw the bulge in his pouch, he asked. "Whatever you found, was it worth killing my man?" Jaedann stared at Thadius, contemplating the question and whether it was worth answering. He didn't answer, he simply nodded, yes. For it was the truth, what he found was easily worth a man's life.

Jaedann took the eastern road back to Liberus. He did it for a reason, hoping to catch up with Rathgar if he might be on the way to Liberus. He knew how long it should take for Rathgar to go see his friend and be back. About two days total. And he was right for the most part. Jaedann happened to come up behind Rathgar and the rest of the Ravennbeaks he had with him. Krulf was the first one to hear Jaedann's horse come out of the woods onto the path. Instinct made him pull one of his homemade hatchets and throw it at what he thought was a stranger trying to sneak up on them. Jaedann was quick enough to draw his sword and knock it away. Rathgar finally saw who it was and yelled, "Hold it, it is my friend Jaedann. He's a Ranger of Liberus."

Krulf replied. "So you claim this sneakery of a man is your friend?"

"Yes, brother…no need to kill him…at least today."

Jaedann rode up and greeted Rathgar. Then he said. "I thought if I came this way, I might catch you on your way back. Looks like I was right."

Rathgar nodded and then asked. "What are you doing out here?"

"Checking the ship to see if there was more information about our visitor other than what was in the Captain's log." He showed Rathgar the bounded journals. "Somebody has been writing down the girl's story for the last eighteen years."

Rathgar was a bit stunned. "Why? Is she someone important?"

"She might be. Her name is Deva Mirarel."

Rathgar paused for a moment. Even a Barbarian like him had heard the name Mirarel. He responded. "Is that House Mirarel in the Elven Kingdom…it cannot be, right? It must be a mistake?"

"Perhaps. And perhaps these journals will tell us if it is true or not. Now tell me why are you with some other Ravennbeaks? Are you still not banished?"

Rathgar smiled. "Yes, but we are going to need their help for what is coming. They are here for blood and gold. I brought them to help save Liberus."

"Save Liberus? What is about to happen?"

"I found out from my friend that a hundred Crowthornns are marching this way intent on raiding the place. Each of them was paid 100 gold pieces."

Jaedann was shocked. Who had that much gold to buy a Barbarian clan? Rathgar flipped the gold coin he received from Marig to Jaedann. "Do you recognize the seal?"

"Fuk the gods," Jaedann replied in anger. "Anntheia gold!"

Rathgar said. "Does not make sense. Why would Anntheia buy a Crowthornn army if they just want to burn Liberus to the ground? Why not send their own army?"

"It is not about Liberus. I think it's about the girl and no one in Annmar can know their true intent, so they hide it by using barbarians to raid the place. " Jaedann had learned many years ago when he was a soldier himself that a kingdom's true intent towards another place would not be known until such time as they wanted it to be. "How long do we have before these 100 Crowthornns arrive?"

"They picked up their new steel last night so by nightfall at the earliest or the morning by the latest."

Jaedann nodded. "Then we must prepare. I will ride ahead and warn the town, try and put some kind of defense together. I want you to take the northeastern road and come in behind them. If we are lucky as they begin to raid, all of you can strike them down from behind, catch them by surprise."

Krulf did not like the plan and said so. "I do not kill my enemy in the back; I stare into their eyes when I drive my blade into their heart."

Jaedann gave Krulf a deathly stare. "Then you can turn them around and face them as you kill them. But with so many of them and so few of us, we need to catch them by surprise." Krulf was about to say something when Rathgar intervened. "Jaedann is right. Coming in from behind and surprising them is a wise move." Krulf was still not happy, but did not argue with Rathgar. Either way he and his fellow Ravennbeaks would still get their blood and gold. Rathgar nodded at Jaedann, agreeing with the plan. It was a good plan, one that could very well succeed if time was on their side. Jaedann took off in a hurry since he was the faster rider. Getting back to Liberus before Crowthornns arrived was not the problem. Figuring out how to defend it against some of the fiercest warriors in Annmar would be. Liberus had no army of its own, just merchants and sailors with a moral code to do right by each other. But now they would have to be an army in order to survive and it was a long shot at best.

10

Jaedann made it back to Liberus just as the sun was starting to set. He had made it in time before 100 Crowthornns would raid the place. There was no army and not even any natural defense of the trading city. It had always been left alone because too much business went through Liberus that it was considered an essential town by most people in Annmar. As Jaedann warned the Magistrate, her first thought was whether anything could actually be done to defend the place. Most of the fighting men were for the most part useless by the time it got dark as the nightlife in Liberus had already started. The Ale and Ruminn was flowing heavy and most of the men would be passed out by the early morning. If somebody was going to attack Liberus, then this would be the perfect time to do it.

Liberus did not have much in the way of swords. At least it did not have enough to defend 100 Crowthornns, but the one thing they did have was a large number of arrows. The Rangers of Liberus saw to it that there was an abundance of arrows. And another thing that Liberus had were buildings and a couple of towers to keep track of the ships that were coming into port. Jaedann thought, if they could control the high ground with enough archers, they might be able to take out a good number of the Barbarians as they came raiding through the town. Those who had swords could try to take them one on one, but at the end of the day they were still outnumbered when it came to warriors. It was the best plan that Jaedann could come up with using the resources of Liberus. Meanwhile Vorak had his own homemade weapons that could be used to defend the town. As a cleric, he was good at making medicines, but also something that could be deadly, which they referred to as Godsfire. He created a highly flammable liquid from certain oils found in the soil and put them in containers with cloth as a fuse. If you threw them on somebody like a bomb, they would catch on fire. The idea was to create these and throw them from on top of buildings onto the Barbarians who were running through the streets. But the biggest problem was they only had so much time to make these small bombs from Godsfire. They only had about two hours to prepare before the Crowthornns reached Liberus.

Finally, it happened, the night became still and the cool air warmed from the torches that the Crowthornns were carrying as they reached the edge of the city. An archer in one of the towers was the first to spot them. The Crowthornns were not even trying to hide for they wanted to be seen and strike fear into the citizens of Liberus. The barbarians came in two groups. Half of them came into the town from the east and the other came from the northwest in an attempt to surround the place. The idea was to hit the town from both ends and meet in the middle killing everybody along the way. Jaedan did not anticipate this strategy, but as they came in raiding, Jaedann was able to split the archers so they were firing in both directions and have Godsfire bombs for the Barbarians coming from both directions as well. But they were limited in their supply and had to pick their targets carefully. He hoped that Rathgar and his fellow Ravennbeak we're not far behind.

Jaedann was in one of the towers and Hanniah was in the second one at the end of the main street. The buildings were so close together that men could leap from one building to the next and the towers were connected to a building by a ramp so people could easily get inside the tower. When Jaedann saw the Crowthornns enter the town, he looked at the young boy standing next to him. Even the young boy had been drafted into serving Liberus and defending her against raiders. The boy's father was one of the biggest merchants in Liberus. Jaedann said to him. "Boy, you have the most important job tonight. You will make sure that no archer runs out of arrows or die trying. You must run back and forth across the rooftops as fast as you can with no delay. As long as we have arrows, we have a chance. Do you understand?"

The boy was scared, but mustered a small amount of bravery and nodded yes. It was time, the battle had now begun. The Crowthornns were here and without hesitation, ran though the town trying to kill everything in their path. The magistrate had most of the women including the prostitutes locked in the main hall. Even prostitutes were considered essential in a place such as Liberus. The Great Hall was locked up as well, but that didn't stop some Crowthornns from trying to get in. Jaedann gave the signal and the archers concentrated their shots on any Crowthornn they could see. Jaedann swiftly killed the first two Crowthornns coming down the main street from the east. Hanniah did the same with the Crowthornns coming from the west. She was actually better with a bow than Jaedann. Crowthornns would try to get inside buildings and find people they could kill or gold they could steal. Sometimes they would be ambushed by someone who had a sword and could slice them as they came through the door.

It was a frenzy of blood as Crowthornns rushed through the streets and killed those who could not find a place to hide. Vorak was on the roof of his own building. He had a prime spot when throwing the Godsfire bombs that he had created. They could get more than one of the Barbarians to catch on fire if they were standing close enough to each other. Lorna and Deva were standing beside him. Their job was to help craft the bombs and make sure he didn't run out of materials to make Godsfire. At first the people of Liberus were succeeding in stopping the Crowthornns. Vorak killed at least ten of them as they came running by his building, but the Crowthornns were learning to dodge the arrows and worst of all, had their homemade hatchets that could be thrown and hit someone. The man Jaedann was standing next to, took a hatchet to the chest as Jaedann was shooting an arrow. It startled Jaedann and then it got worst. The young boy who had been running back and forth making sure the archers had arrows told Jaedann that they were almost out. Jaedann reached behind to the quiver and found only two left. He nodded and then shot them both killing two more Crowthornns. Then Jaedann ran across the buildings towards the tower that Hanniah was in, telling the archers to pick their shots and make them count. Jaedann reached the other tower and told Hanniah it was time for a new plan. They would need to go into the streets and take down the Crowthornns one by one. Hanniah didn't like the plan, but their swords and knives were the only weapons they had left.

Finally, they heard it. The sound of a horn. It was Rathgar's horn. He had arrived from the east and he and his fellow Ravennbeaks caught the Crowthornns on the edge of Liberus by surprise. There were twenty of them taking up a rear position. The Ravennbeaks cut them down quickly and then they entered the city to find more Crowthornns they could kill. They weren't hard to find. Jaedann along with Hanniah would fight in the streets until they met Rathgar in the middle. At least that was the plan. There were plenty of Crowthornns still running through the streets. As soon as Jaedann would kill one, another one would be trying to take his head off.   Crowthornns were also trying to climb on top of the buildings and kill the remaining archers. Jaedann and Hanniah pulled arrows out of dead bodies to replenish their supply and then they each shot any Crownthornn they could see climbing onto a roof. Jaedann killed three and Hanniah killed two. There were still too many Crowthornns running through the streets. It was chaotic and hard to know how many were left despite the numerous bodies that were piling up in the streets. A man came up to Jaedann and Hanniah and told them that Crowthornns were trying to burn the Great Hall down with the Magistrate and most of the women in it. At the same time, Jaedann saw Rathgar as he made it through the crowd of mostly Crowthornns. He was smiling as his swung his ax wildly killing everything in its path. It gave Rathgar true joy. Jaedann looked at Hanniah and said. "Take some men and stop the Crowthornns at the Great Hall, I will fight with Rathgar to end the bloodshed in the streets."

Hanniah nodded. "I am on it, but I need no men to stop some Crowthornns from trying to kill the women of Liberus." Jaedann smiled back, not at her bravado, which he always found charming, but knowing that she was such a fierce warrior and capable of killing many men without anyone's help. That is what he loved most about her.

Rathgar met Jaedann in the streets. Jaedann was the first to speak. "It is great to finally have you in the fight. Your timing is impeccable!"

With feistiness in his smile, Rathgar responded. "What are you talking about, I always show up just in time to kill my enemies."

"Glad you're here. There is still a lot more of these bastards to kill. Any ideas on what to do next."

"We kill everyone we find. You go up the street, I will do down and then we will meet on the other street. And let my fellow Ravennbeaks have their way with them."

"Deal…now let us kill some Crowthornns!" And that's what they did. Jaedann moved through the Chaos of the streets and with his sword, sliced open any Crownthornn he could find. Rathgar did the same and found plenty of Crowthornns to bloody his ax. The other Ravennbeaks were like men possessed when it came to killing Crownthornns, all of them were still alive except one. The tide was turning and most of the Crowthornns were dead now, but they had killed plenty of Liberus' citizens too.

Hanniah made her way to the Great Hall. She found five Crownthornns trying to chop down the main door to the building while another one was trying to set fire to it. Hanniah grabbed some arrows out of dead bodies and fired them one by one, killing three of the Crowthornns. She started with the one who was trying to start the fire. The other ones, startled by the arrows coming at them, came after Hanniah with their axes. They all swung wildly and Hanniah was able to easily duck and come underneath their weapons while using her own sword to gut them open with three swift and precise blows. She was superb with a bow, but just as deadly with a sword. Even better than most men. Two of the Crowthornns while trying hold their guts in place tried to swing their axes at her, but Hanniah easily parried them away before delivering a death blow to the Barbarians standing before her. It was a good kill. She knocked on the big door and yelled her name so the women inside knew who it was. The Magistrate came to the door once it was opened and asked. "Did Liberus survive?"

Hanniah smiled. "Almost…we have killed most of them, but there are some still some left in the city. We are hunting them now."

The Magistrate was relieved. "Thank the gods. Looks like Jaedann's plan worked."

"It did, better than expected. The Crownthornns were caught by surprise and didn't know how to defend against archers. But if you will excuse me…I have more of them to kill." Now the Magistrate and the other girls were safe, Hanniah ran off to find the other Rangers.

11

Only a small handful of Crownthornns remained after their raid on Liberus, but they were scattered. The Rangers and the Ravennbeaks hunted them down one by one. However, a few, angered at the cleric who had been using Godsfire, stormed his building intent on killing Vorak and his assistants. Vorak was out of the materials to make it anyway, but he was not that bad with a bow. While he was not a warrior, he was a fair shot and could hit his target even under pressure, something he learned as a monk, believe it or not. They did have to hunt for their own food after all. Five of the last Crowthornns ascended onto the building. Vorak shot one of the with an arrow from his balcony, but another one through his hatchet and hit Lorna, However, she did not get hit with the blade. The Crowthornns throw was off and she was knocked out when slipping trying to dodge it and it her head. Deva was scared as she ran to check on Lorna. She asked. "What do we do now?"

Vorak pointed an arrow towards the door in the floor and said. "Lock the bolt on the door. That should keep them from getting up here and then we pray they cannot somehow climb the walls. Hopefully, we will get rescued soon."

The banging on the door continued and with each bang, it increased Deva's fear that tonight was the night she would die. She had never been in a battle before. She had never seen a man die. Her fear crippled her to where she could hardly move. Finally, the banging was not as loud and Vorak saw why. Three Chrowthornns were below the balcony trying to get up there and not get hit by an arrow. Vorak could not even get a shot off. Deva got behind him near the edge of the balcony as they both knew that the Crowthornns would soon be on the balcony and kill them.

Jaedann had made his way over to Vorak's building, trying to make sure they were still alive. As he was running up the street, he saw the Crowthornns trying to climb to the balcony. As he had done before, he grabbed a few arrows out of some dead bodies, aimed and shot two of them. The third was already on the balcony so Jaedann couldn't shoot him in time before he threw a small hatchet at Vorak. He dodged it enough only getting grazed in the arm, but he accidentally knocked Deva over the railing and she fell to the street. Luckily, she fell on two dead Crownthornns and did not injure herself, but she clenched her fists as a defensive reaction. And then came the biggest surprise, her fists glowed like fire and when she opened her hands, fireballs shot from them. The first two were shot upwards as she was aiming up without realizing it. The fireballs struck the Crowthornn on the balcony and sent him bursting into the building wall. Vorak and Jaedann both saw what she did. Surprise would be an understatement. It was more like fear of what she could do after seeing a power that had not been in Annmar for 100 years. Deva was shocked, she knew she had powerful abilities, but never before had fireballs shot from her hands.

The last Crowthornn who had been inside trying to chop through the door on the top floor to the balcony came outside to see what was going on. He saw Deva and came after her with his ax as she was still lying on the ground. Fear grabbed hold of her again, but she didn't cower out of fear. Deva pushed her hands forward and shot two more fireballs at the Crowthornn coming towards her. He too was pushed back into the wall of the building, breaking it as he was killed instantly. Jaedann stood there for a moment, not knowing what to do, but then he helped her up and got her inside Vorak's place, hiding her before anybody could see what she could do with her hands. He was beginning to understand why somebody would be looking for her or worst yet, want her dead.

Deva was shaking, frightened to her core, and not only of what she has just done, but what Jaedann and Vorak would do to her. Would they see her as something evil whose true purpose was to destroy their world with her power? She did not say anything, waiting for someone else to speak. Vorak was coming down the latter to the balcony when Jaedann's stern tone, asked Deva. "What in the name of the gods was that?"

Deva frighteningly replied. "I do not know. I have never done that before."

"But have you done anything strange like that in the past and do not lie to me?"

"Yes, but nothing so dangerous or powerful."

Jaedann paused for a moment, trying to make sense of everything he just saw. "You have been able to do these things, but did not tell us, why?"

"I was told not to by the woman who took care of me."

"Your mother?"

"No, she died giving birth to me."

Vorak was standing in the room next to Jaedann. He asked. "Do you know anything about your father?"

"Only that he was an elf."

Jaedann looked at her. "What else have you done other than shoot fire from your hands?"

"I have made snow levitate and threw it far away."

Jaedann rolled his eyes. Normally he would not believe such trickery, but he could not unsee what he just saw from Deva. "Did anybody else know that you could do these things?"

"Only the woman who took care of me."

"What you can do, does it have a name?"

Deva did not answer. She did not have an answer for there were no words to describe it where she came from. However, Vorak did have an answer or a theory at the very least. He responded before Deva could say anything. "It's magic...the power of the gods."

Jaedann gave him a strange look. "Magic? More like myth."

Deva was curious of Vorak's answer. He replied back. "It's easy to think that. Magic has not been seen in this world for over 100 years. Most people think it's myth or just stories about all powerful gods."

"I guess a Cleric has to believe in the story of the five gods and magic. I have been given no reason to believe in gods or magic."

Vorak nodded at Jaedann conceding to his point that he didn't have a reason to believe, but on the other hand proof was always in the eyes of the beholders and Vorak responded in kind. "You saw what she did...would you call it something other than Magic?"

Jaedann gave him a dirty look. "Perhaps there is not a word for what she did, but I am not going to give way to superstition. "

"Jaedann, this isn't superstition, what we saw is real. Don't be the fool who refuses to acknowledge the truth."

"I am not debating philosophy or religion with you...we have bigger issues here."

Deva finally spoke up. "Enough with the bickering, both of you...you are not the ones cursed with these abilities. What are you going to do to me? I was told that I would be killed if anybody in Annmar found out what I could do, so what happens to me now."

Jaedann replied. "It's true that some men may want to kill you for what you are. I suspect that's why the Crowthornns were paid with Anntheia gold to kill you. I may not know what to do with you, but I assure you, your death will not be at our hands unless you give us a reason why you should die "

Deva tried to smile. She was thankful, but also had to ask. "Can I stay in Liberus?"

Vorak replied in a kind voice. "Stay, child you are safe here, but I think it would best to stay out of sight so no one finds out what you can do. We will keep your secret." Vorak looked over at Jaedann who agreed. Deva was relieved, but still had a small amount of fear, mainly for the fact that she could now create fireballs with her hands. Jaedann started to walk out and finish what remained of the battle. Vorak stopped him and said. "We should talk when all this is done. There is a prophecy you should know about." Jaedann paused and starred at Vorak for a moment. He may not have liked the idea of prophecies, but he was smart enough to take them seriously. He simply replied. "Okay, I will hear you out...but after we have killed every last Crowthornn in Liberus."

12

King Lancelynnn of Anntheia was not very superstitious. Like many in Annmar he did not even necessarily believe in the gods, they were just stories to him, but he believed in power and most of all, maintaining that power. Anntheia had the largest army, the largest navy, and they were the biggest kingdom in Annmar. For King Lancelynnn that was the epitome of power, and he would do anything to keep it. When signs told him that there was one who could bring magic back into the world, he saw the balance of power shifting. If magic was real, those who controlled it or destroyed it would be the most powerful. The king ventured to the lower corridors of the great palace of Wimbornn, the capital of Anntheia. He went to see Azigronn, the Khronne who lived in the palace. Khronnes were conjurers of dark magic when there was magic in the world. They practiced in things that were deemed unnatural. And they were also known as oracles and soothsayers. Khronnes were thought to have disappeared along with the gods in Anntheia, but the truth is, they lived in secret and worked for powerful men who wanted to control the future even if they did not use full magic as they once did 100 years ago.

Azigronn was in the laboratory in the basements of the palace. Azigronn did not even look up when the King entered the room when most people would. The Khronne said. "Your highness, what news can I bring you today?"

King Lancelynn was annoyed. "You are too bold. Don't you know that you should be standing when a king enters the room?"

"Perhaps it is you who are too bold, your highness, for seeking a sorceress of the dark arts. What would the Lords of Anntheia say if they knew?"

"Does it make you feel powerful to stand up to a king?"

"I am already powerful."

"Powerful enough to stop me from slitting your throat or taking your head."

Azigronn smiled and liked to play mind games, especially those that annoyed powerful men and women. Azigronn kept on even footing with Lords and Kings. "Do not worry your highness, I know that you are the King and I am but a servant so how may I serve you today? And please excuse my playfulness; we Khronnes have a wicked sense of humor."

"What news do you have of this mysterious person who has magical ability?"

Azigronn pulled from a shelf, a big bowl and then threw chicken bones in it. Then Azigronn poured some kind of potion on the chicken bones and stirred everything together. When the potion and the bones rested in one place Azigronn looked at the shape of everything and read the signs that came forth from her mixture. Each shape, each color, and each smell represented a symbol. Put them together and they told the nature of the things, past, present, or future. Khronnes could see what was happening far away when reading the signs. A minute passed and Azigronn replied to the king. "A girl has arrived in Annmar."

The King was surprised. "A girl…are you sure?"

"Yes, a girl and she is in a southern coastal town…most likely, Liberus."

"So, the rumors are true? Magic has returned."

Azigronn looked up at the King. "I have never believed in rumors, only what I can see. But it appears that you were right to act upon those rumors."

"What else do you see?"

"That it will take more than barbarians to stop the prophecy."

King Lancelynn was annoyed by the Khronne's answer. "Are you speaking of the prophecy about the one who will bring magic back into the world?"

"Yes, the very same that has you worried and why you employed my services."

"Can you see if she is still alive?"

"I believe so because something happened…something unnatural. I see blood by fire, but from a power that has not existed in 100 years."

The King stood up and began pacing around the Laboratory. "Liberus should be burnt to the ground by now and all of its citizens dead."

Azigronn softly laughed. "If only it were that easy. But the girl will have to die a certain way, death by fire, in the same way that the last god, Eras was put to death."

The King was a bit surprised. "Why fire?"

The Khronne smiled. "Fire cleanses the impurities. It is the only way to destroy magic."

The King paused for a moment. "Is she still in Liberus? Can you be sure of that?"

"I can only be sure of what the signs tell me, but it appears that she is still there, for now!"

King Lancelynnn sat up and started to walk away. He needed to send a raven to put the next part of his plan into action. Azigronn gave him a grave warning. "Your highness, beware, she will not be easy to kill and you are not the only one looking for her. A mysterious power rises in the west; something Elven that will protect her and you will not be able to defeat it. You do not have much time to find her." The king had an ominous look on his face, but he took the warning to heart. Not out of caution, but more out of fear.

The battle was finally over and every last Crowthornn was dead. The Ravennbeaks who were still alive went around and picked the Anntheia gold right off their bodies. Some of the buildings were on fire and there were more than just a few citizens from Liberus who were killed during the battle. Jaedann walked through the streets to survey the damage. Deva stayed out of sight while Vorak tried to put his home back together. Rathgar finally came out from the outskirts of town and had a present of sorts for Jaedann and Hanniah who was standing beside him now. He had a prisoner. Rathgar walked the man towards the other Rangers and then threw him to the ground at their feet. Jaedann and Hanniah were both bewildered a little bit. Rathgar said. "I present to you Sansonn Yonnvadr. We caught him with the leader of the Crowthornns as we came up behind."

"Who is he?" Jaedann asked.

"The man who paid the Crowthornns to raid Liberus and the ship we found days ago. I thought he might be worth keeping alive."

Jaedann nodded. "Good call. I bet he has a lot of answers."

"My ax would agree." Sansonn looked up at Rathgar with an uneasy feeling."

"Only as a last resort my friend. We will take him before the Magistrate and see what he has to say." That's what they did and Sansonn was all too happy to be spared Rathgar's ax blade. There were too many questions to be answered and they all knew that he probably had those answers. Horsham along with some of the other girls were cleaning up the Great Hall when the Rangers brought the prisoner before her. She was a little surprised as well, but demanded answers. There had always been an uneasy peace between Liberus and Kingdoms of Annmar. The city of trade was a necessary evil that everybody in Annmar tolerated. Sansonn was sat down and even given a cup of Ruminn. He gladly took it. After a few sips Thorsha started questioning him.

She spoke. "I understand you are responsible for paying these Barbarians to burn our city down."
He didn't want to say anything, but Rathgar nudged him along with the butt of his ax. Finally, he spoke.

"Their intent was not to burn the place down, but to kill everyone here. But you know how Barbarians get carried away in battle." He gave Rathgar a dirty look. Rathgar hit him again with the ax.

"Why do you want to kill everybody?"

"I don't care about you, but those who paid me wanted all of you dead."

"And who paid you?"

Sansonn didn't say anything for a moment. Then Jaedann pulled out an Anntheia gold coin. He dropped it before the prisoner and said. "Anntheia gold, we know who is behind this, but we want a specific name."

"There are many names I can give, but only one that truly counts."

Jaedann asked. "And what name would that be?"

Sansonn gave him a deathly stare. "The King."

Thorsha and the Rangers all had the same look of surprise. The King of Anntheia, would he be so bold! Why would he now want to kill everybody in Liberus? What purpose would it serve?

Jaedann was the first to respond. "King Lancelynnn! If that's true, then why is he paying Barbarians to burn the city and kill everyone. Is he finally making a move to destroy the second largest port in Annmar?"

Sansonn didn't say anything; Rathgar hit him again with the butt of his ax and told him the next time, he would just take some fingers. Sansonn replied. "He does not care about Liberus, only somebody who might have come here."

"Who?"

"An Elf or Half-Elf, but somebody with Elven blood. That is all l know." Jaedann looked at everybody else, shocked, just like the rest of them at what he was hearing. This was the kind of thing that could start a war between kingdoms for if one innocent girl was worth the King of Anntheia destroying a city, she must be somebody important.

"You did not ask why they were looking for this Elf or Half-Elf."

Sansonn with an irritated tone replied. "I do not ask those kinds of questions, when I am paid, I do the job and that is it. But the amount of gold that was paid to kill the Elf, I would say they're royalty."

Thorsha responded. "It is of no consequence now. Your plan failed. Liberus still stands and the Barbarians you and your king hired are all dead."

Sansonn laughed. "You think this is over, you are not prepared for what is coming next. The King will stop at nothing to find and kill this Elf, even risk going to war with the other Kingdoms and that is why you should be afraid. If the Elf is still alive, all you need to do is give the Elf to the King and this place will still exist for years to come."

All of them gave each other a strange look at Sansonn's ominous warning. Then Rathgar hit him again with the ax. "Whatever happens next, you will be dead first."

Thorsha looked at Jaedann. "Is there a reason the King might want our new visitor?" He had a good guess, but did not give away what he really knew about the girl. He replied. "Give me some time to find out. She may know more than what she has said."

Thorsha nodded. "I have to discuss these matters with the council. If she is a threat, then we need to be rid of her."

"We don't know what she is, yet. But we owe it to one another to find out before any hasty decisions are made."

"Then go, but she needs to be brought before the council."

Jaedann started to walk out so he could find Deva. Rathgar, looking down at Sansonn. "What about him?"

Jaedann looked at Sansonn and softly laughed. "We have cells around here; throw him in one of them. He can rot there for all I care." Rathgar was all too happy to oblige his friend Jaedann, but taking Sansonn's head would certainly be more enjoyable.

13

Elves are a peculiar folk. Reserved and most often serious. They are the seer of things long gone and things to come. Their life spans lasting five times as the average man, they have seen the history of Annmar more than any race. And they often know of things happening before most in Annmar. Illrunn of the house Tyriall in Dorwinn stood on the big balcony of his great home waiting for his son Arunn. House Tyriall was one of the oldest houses on the Elven Kingdom from the time of magic and gods. As the Lord of House Tyriall, Illrunn sat on the Elven high council. He was almost a hundred years old.

Arunn was late as usual. He finally appeared before his father. There were no formal greetings between most Elves; they got straight to the point. Illrunn said. "Thank You for coming son. It is good to see you."

Arunn smiled. "And you father."

The reason I sent for you is I have a scouting mission for someone I trust most of all."

Arunn was intrigued. It was not often that his father asked him to go on a scouting mission. Arunn was more on the adventurous side and Elves were not supposed to be adventurous, but he wanted to see everything in the world of Annmar. His curiosity stretched even beyond the seas outside of Annmar so he asked. "What do you need to me scout, father. I have had heard rumors about a stranger in Annmar. Someone dangerous and that could upset the balance of power in Annmar"

Illrunn nodded. "There are always rumors and signs of such things. People look for them to try and explain prophecies that they think will make sense of the world around them. I have heard the same rumors, but do not put much truth in them."

Arunn was a bit surprised. "You are not asking me to find this person even though it may be just a rumor?"

"No, if these rumors or signs prove to be true, they will reveal themselves in time and like all who search for wisdom in Annmar, they will seek out the Elves."

"Then what I am to scout?"

Illrunn showed his son a small parchment that came with a raven. "Four ships from the Rogues of Hamlinn were seen setting sail from the Island of Oakheart. The Rogues never sail more than one ship in the same direction, it is strange to see four ships sailing together as they usually keep their ships separate to avoid losing their small fleet. I want know why the four sailed together."

"And you want to me to find out?"

"Yes, they were seen sailing west so you will go to the port at Easthavenn. See if the ships make port or turn south and if they keep sailing west. We must know their true intentions."

Arunn nodded. He and his father may not have gotten along for the problems between fathers and sons could be found even among Elves. "I will ride immediately, but what do you want me to do after I have spotted them. "

"Send a raven letting me know of their whereabouts and then stay there until further instructions."

"You are sure that you don't want me to investigate the other thing?"

Illrunn smiled at his son's curiosity and eagerness to do the right thing. It was the one noble trait that he liked about his son especially when he became annoyed at his other traits. "If the time comes we will deal with that too, but it is not today."

Jaedann made his way back to Vorak's home. He was hungry and knew he could find a meal there, but more importantly he was wanted to check on Deva. She must still be scared. When he walked through Vorak's door, he found Deva helping with Vorak's wounds. He asked. "You hurt bad?"

Vorak smiled. "Just a few scratches and I am not dead so I am one of the lucky ones." Jaedann smiled at the comment and then gave a sincere look to Deva. "What about you, how are you?"

She tried to smile. "Better, I guess, but still…

Jaedann interrupted. "Scared…you're still scared?"

"Yes, what is going to happen with me?"

"You will get a hot meal, maybe take another bath, and then get some sleep. Tomorrow is a new day and we'll figure out a new plan."

"One where I am still here?"

Jaedann smiled at her again. "Yes…you're not going anywhere." Deva was happy to hear that and the smile on her face was proof. It had been a while since she had actually smiled. But still, she did not know if she could completely trust Jaedann and Vorak with her secret. They seemed honorable, but most only had honor when it suite them. They could easily giver her up or send her away if they thought their own survival was worth more than her life.

Jaedann turned and looked at Vorak. His sincerity turned to more of a serious nature. "Now tell me about this prophecy that you seem to think is important."

Vorak replied. "All prophecies are important to someone. This one may be important all of us." Deva excused herself, wanting to leave the men alone, but Vorak stopped her. "No, you should hear this too." Now she was extremely curious while at the same time feeling scared. Did this have something to do with her? Vorak started to prepare some food, mainly sausages and cheese. It had been a while since any of them had eaten. Vorak gave them each a plate and then he started to tell of what he knew. "About 80 years ago someone wrote down a prophecy telling of those who would bring magic back into the world."

Jaedann replied. "Magic, a prophecy about magic. You cannot be serious."

"Jaedann Lionnshade, I know you are not a believer, you are too much of a soldier, but maybe you can be a little more open minded after what we saw her do earlier tonight."

Jaedann nodded. "I have always thought stories about magic were simply just stories as many people do."

"I know as most people do, but what if its real just like the gods. The prophecy simply states that there are five, called the Penntacle, who will bring magic back into the known world. Five of different races, each one representing one of the five gods."

"How do you know of this prophecy," Jaedann asked, "I have heard most wise tales throughout Annmar, legends and stories from all kingdoms, but nothing about magic coming back into the world."

Vorak softly laughed at his cynical comment. "I doubt you would have heard of this one and definitely would not have read it anywhere. It is known only among monks and high priests."

"Well, I was not always a cleric…I was at one time a Monk in Lenntis."

Jaedann was stunned. He never saw Vorak being a Monk at one time and certainly did not see him as someone who would have learned at the great Monastery of Lenntis. It was very prestigious for Monks to train there. He said. "You were a Monk? How did I not this about you all these years?"

"We all have a past and we all have our secrets. You are no different, I know you were a soldier, but I suspect that you were much more than that."

Jaedann laughed. Vorak was right of course. "So that is where you read this prophecy?"

"Yes, and I know for sure that it is only written down in two places, Lenntis and the Great Library of Cornnith in the Elven Kingdom of Dorwinn. If would be easy to dismiss if it were not for the fact that only few have read it and its secrecy is of the highest order. That's why you do not hear stories about godlike beings bringing magic back into the world."

"Why is this important to us, after all, it just seems like a story Monks would tell to make the world sound better than it is?"

Vorak looked at Deva. "Because I think she may be one of five." Deva was shocked to hear something like that. She knew that she has strange abilities, but Deva thought she just had some abnormality. How could she be a part of prophecy? Deva replied. "This cannot be magic, it is something strange I do from time to time. I am not a part of any prophecy."

Vorak said to the frightened girl. "I understand if you don't want to believe it, but that does not make it untrue."

Jaedann spoke up. "So Vorak, you believe in this prophecy?"

Vorak nodded. "As a Monk we were always taught to think logically with anything we read. I cannot say that I truly believed when I first read it, but now, after seeing what Deva can do, I believe in it more than I did before."

"Okay, let us say that it is true, what happens if it is?"

Vorak looked at Deva. "I think we are already starting to see the aftereffects of a magic user in Annmar. I believe a war is coming because there too many in Annmar that do not want magic users in this world. And your life put us greatly in danger." Deva had a sinking feeling in her stomach. She was scared before, but it grabbed hold of her to where she could not move. Jaedann was about to reply when Hanniah rushed inside, not even bothering to knock. She looked at Jaedann. "You need to come with me now. The Magistrate called an emergency council meeting to make a decision about the girl." Jaedann knew what that meant. He knew that she did it on purpose to avoid his input. Hanniah and Jaedann rushed out of the room and headed to the Great Hall.

14

The council meeting had already begun when Jaedann and Hanniah burst through the doors. In fact, after a short deliberation, they were ready to vote. There were five members on the council including the Magistrate, Thorsha who also represented the tie-breaking vote if necessary, very rarely did she have to be the tie breaker in any vote. The rest of the council members were made of merchants, one of them being a brothel owner. The council was startled when Jaedann burst through the door making Thorsha reply. "What is the meaning of this, we are in an emergency council meeting." Angered, Jaedann said. "I see that. It is meeting that the Rangers were not invited to, especially the head Ranger such as myself. And you know it is customary that a Ranger be at these meetings." "But not required," Thorsha angrily replied. "We don't need the Rangers to have a council meeting."

"How convenient that you choose to acknowledge that now. I have been to almost every council meeting since I have been a Ranger of Liberus and when I was not here, another Ranger was here in my place. But I guess you did not want me here when voting on the fate of the girl we found and brought back to Liberus." Thorsha replied. "It does not concern you. You have no vote here. And I've seen the way you look at her, your doey eyes when it comes to her would only cloud your judgment."

Jaedann had to laugh at what he considered

nonsense. "Oh, I see. That is what you think this is about, I never took you for being stupid because you could not be more wrong. What exactly is your move regarding the girl?" Derninn, one of the merchants in Liberus who sat on the council spoke up. "We were just about to vote on whether to give her to the King of Anntheia and broker peace with him regarding Liberus?"

Both Jaedann and Hanniah rolled their eyes at the council, not wanting to believe the treachery they were hearing. Jaedann responded. "I see, is that what we do now? Give up a citizen of Liberus to their enemies."

Thorsha with a stern tone, said. "We have to do what is best for Liberus. You heard Sansonn, King Lancelynnn will stop at nothing to kill her. Better her than the rest of us."

"I also never took you for a coward."

"Be careful of your next words, Ranger…I still have the power to have you killed."

Jaedann nodded, acknowledging her power. "Liberus has always had a code. Every citizen is protected, we do not turn them over to their enemies. That is the very foundation that holds this place together when it is made up of criminals, cutthroats, and bandits masquerading as traders and merchants."

"These are extenuating circumstances, whatever the reason, if the King wants her then she must be dangerous. She must be wanted for something."

"We are all wanted in some kingdom. We have all been banished from our homelands and ended up in the only place that would have us. She is no different. Why should she be treated differently? If we give her up then anyone of us can be give up to our enemies." Jaedann looked directly at Thorsha. "Even you Magistrate. I wonder what the price is on your head these days."

Thorsha slammed her hand down on the table. "The difference between me and her, is no one will send an army for me. What happens when they send an army to destroy the city and kill everybody. Barbarians are one thing, but an Anntheian army, we cannot defeat them and we should not try over one girl. Besides why do you really care?"

"I admit that she must be important if King Lancelynnn wants her, but the real question is why. Also, I am from Belmere, it has been my experience that whatever Anntheia wants is usually bad for the rest of Annmar. But if you insist of trading the girl for what you think will be peace with Anntheia then you might as well trade me in too."

Thorsha gave him a strange look. "Are you wanted in Anntheia?"

Jaedann laughed. "I'm sure you could get a good price for my head there considering how many Anntheians I have killed, but the bigger price on my head is in Belmere and my last name is not Lionnshade. It is Barrenn. "

Thorsha like everybody else in the room was stunned when he said that name. Hanniah had the more shocked look, but it was Thorsha who spoke first. "Barrenn, as in House Barrenn of Belmere… as in King Jornnus Barrenn."

"Yes, he is my brother."

"Then that would make you…"

"A prince."

Hanniah asked. "If you are a prince then why is there a price on your head?" Jaedann looked at her. "Because I tried to kill my brother and now I am banished from my home. He would like nothing more than to see me dead. And before you ask, it is a long story." Jaedann looked back at Thorsha. "You can vote and give her up, but where does it end… who else is given up…me, you…any of you. And if you are afraid of an Anntheian Army then we send for help. We have plenty of friends in Annmar who want us to keep going, they need us in order to trade their goods and would love to defeat an army from Anntheia,"

"I am sorry, It is too risky to let her stay."

Jaedann stared at her for a moment. "Then what's the point of having a code in Liberus. Why govern ourselves at all, just let every man be for himself?"

"Moving words, but we still have to vote." Thorsha and the council took their vote. Jaedann was not going to stop them no matter how moving his words might be. They voted and to his dismay, it was unanimous, they voted to give the girl to Anntheia. Jaedann stormed out of the Great Hall. He didn't give the council time to decide his own fate as a banished Prince of Belmere.

Hanniah followed him out the door. Jaedann looked back at her. "We need to find the girl."

"Hey there, hold on." She stopped Jaedann from the fast pace he was making as, trying to get to the girl. He stopped, giving her a curious look. She asked. "Why did you not ever say anything about who you really are?"

He replied. "I do not know everything about you. We all have a past life."

"Sure, but I am not royalty. I am not in line to be a King."

Jaedann softly laughed. "I was never going to be the king of Belmere. I am too much of a soldier. I never even wanted to be a prince. I always saw myself more as a Genneral."

"What happened, why did you get banished?"

Jaedann paused for a moment. "That is a story for another time and definitely with lots of Ale, but right now we need to find the girl."

Hanniah was stunned, hearing Jaedann say that. "Why, are you now giving her to the Anntheian King?."

"Fuk no, we need to find her and get her out of Liberus so they cannot give her to Anntheia." Hanniah was a little confused. She was just a young helpless girl…what did it matter if she was given to the King of Anntheia so she asked the question. "Why do you care, really, you may not be able to tell the Magistrate, but you can tell me. After all, she's just some girl we found. "

"I wish that were true, it would make things easier."

"What are you talking about?"

"She might be a Mage."

Shock washed over Hanniah's face. Could it be true? "No…impossible, they have not been around for a hundred years if they even existed at all."

"It's hard to believe…not saying I really do believe it, but I saw fireballs shoot from her hands and kill some Crowthornns. Maybe this is why the King wants her. Either way, she cannot stay here." Hanniah nodded in agreement, even though she didn't completely understand what's going on. They went back to Vorak's place, thinking Deva would still be there. When they arrived, they found only Vorak. He had sent Lorna and Deva out to get some badly needed supplies. Jaedann knew that Thorsha would probably send her own guards to retrieve the girl because she couldn't trust Jaedann and the Rangers to do it. And she was right to not trust Jaedann. Although, he was a man of honor, he was too much of a soldier and followed a code especially when helping those less fortunate. Jaedann told Vorak what had just happened while they waited for the girls to arrive back. He was shocked and angered just as much as they were by the vote and what the Magistrate was going to do. But as Jaedann was telling the Cleric what happened and how they needed to find Deva, the girls arrived back and heard the men talking.

Lorna was about to walk in when Deva stopped her. She wanted to hear what they were talking about after Jaedann mention her by name. Deva heard most of what they were saying, but started to get afraid when the conversation turned to finding her and giving her to the King of Anntheia. Lorna asked her. "What are they talking about, why would anybody want to give you to the King?" Deva did not know what to do at that moment. It was becoming too dangerous for her now. She made an impulsive decision and grabbed Lorna, covering her mouth in the process so no one could hear her scream. Her hands started to glow with fire and in one swift move, she turned Lorna's head to fiery ash, killing her instantly. She did not mean to kill her, just to knock her out so she could escape. But Deva did not know the limits of her own power. Scared, Deva moved the body and hid it in some bushes next to the building and then she disappeared into the night. Deva had to get out of there, the one thing she knew for sure is that she could not hide anymore in Liberus. The best place for her now was far away from anyone that knew of her. The town was still in a bit of a frenzy trying to clean up from the battle and put out any remaining fires. She stayed in the shadows as she snuck throughout the city, but then she finally found a stable. Fortunately for her, there was one horse in there. Deva had only ridden a horse once and she was not a very good rider, but she remembered enough from when she was a child to put some kind of saddle or blanket over the horse and then grab the horse's mane to direct the horse where she wanted it to go. The horse was actually gentle and not afraid of her. Deva got on the horse and rode off slowly, hoping no one would catch her. She went in the direction that had the fewest people who might see her. She went north.

15

King Lancelynn sat at the head of the king's council table reading a raven's note brought to him by his Spymaster, Emericc. He was known as a Master of War, but Emericc's true talent lay in knowing secrets and getting information first so he was better known as the King's Spymaster. The note did not bring good news to the King. He read it over and over, not wanting to believe the news. How could it be? Emericc had gotten the news first. Dismayed, the King responded to the note. "This is accurate, all of them are dead?"

Emericc replied. "Yes, your highness and the city is still standing. Some buildings were burned, but very few deaths occurred in Liberus except the Crowthornns."

The King was angry. "Fuk the gods. How did a town with no natural defense, defeat 100 ruthless barbarians?"

"It appears that someone devised a plan to use archers on top of buildings and were able to shoot most of them as they ran through the city and then a small group of barbarians known as Ravennbeaks flanked them from behind."

The King was surprised to hear that. "That sounds like a soldier's strategy."

"Yes, your highness. I am told that the Rangers of Liberus are very resourceful."

"It sounds as if they are more than simple Rangers, perhaps one or two of them were soldiers at one time, would you not agree?"

"It appears that way."

"But it does not matter. They may be able to defeat some Barbarians, but can they survive a legion!"

Emericc was taken back by the last part of the statement. "Your Highness, do you have some plan that I am not aware of?"

The King looked directly at his spymaster. "Send word to Genneral Owaynn. He has the nearest legions to the Liberus. He is to march his two of those legions to Liberus. I want that city burned to the ground and no quarter given, no mercy shown to its citizens.

Emericc was shocked. It was a bold move, too bold in fact. "Your highness, I urge you, not to do this. It will be seen as an act of war."

The King rolled his eyes at the notion. "You think the other kingdoms would risk war over one little trader's town that lives outside the law of any kingdom! I think you underestimate what the rest of Annmar would do."

"Maybe not all of them, but I think Belmere would and our relationship with them is uneasy at best."

The King laughed. "You would be surprised by King Jornnus' response to us destroying Liberus. This is one of those times that my spymaster does not know everything."

Emericc was overly curious by that statement. He was the master of information and this was something he did not know and so he asked. "Is there something I should know about King Jornnus? I feel like I am being left in the dark on purpose."

"A King's prerogative, my old friend. In time, you will know what I know on this matter."

"At least let me send some of my assassins to kill the one you're looking for. They can be in and out before anyone there knows anything."

The King put his hand on Emericc's shoulder. "Not this time. I need a show of force…a warning to the rest of the kingdoms not to interfere with Anntheia's affairs no matter what part of Annmar they are in."

"Even if the other kingdoms do not know what those affairs may be?"

The King smiled. "Especially if they do not know. But what one does not know is what they fear the most." The King was partially right on that matter. This was a time when he needed more fear than curiosity from the races in Annmar. He finished scribbling out his note with instructions to Genneral Owayn. He gave it to Emericcc for it to be sent by raven immediately. After the Crowthornns defeat at Liberus, time was of the essence for King Lancelynn. He walked out onto the balcony of the big room. He stared up at the sky. Normally the sky was bright from all the stars that covered Annmar, but not tonight. The moon masked the light with a crimson red… a blood red. There was a blood moon tonight. The King commented on it to Emericcc. "I have never seen a blood moon before."

"I have not either, your highness. Do you know what it means?"

"It is a sign, I know that much…a sign of a new beginnings. I fear that a great evil has come and it is shrouded in magic!"

The King's spymaster gave him a strange look. He thought to himself, was magic and evil the same thing? For most men of power in Annmar, the answer was yes.

Vorak was staring up at the sky, waiting for the girls to return. His stare lingered at the blood moon as his heartbeat increased. It was true, he was a little nervous for he was a man who believed in signs. A blood moon was not necessarily a good sign. Jaedann saw the moon too and since he had never seen one, he asked about it. Vorak told him that it was a sign and that the last time a blood moon had been seen was when the last god had been killed and magic disappeared from Annmar. How strange that a blood moon would be seen on the night Deva shot fireballs from her hands and used magic to do it.

Jaedann asked. "The blood moon, is that part of your prophecy too?"

Vorak found the comment amusing. "It is not my prophecy, just a prophecy foretold about how the world would change. But no, there is no mention of a blood moon. However, I read something once about a blood moon in the Tales of Vorstol the Sorcerer. He speaks of the blood moon appearing when new magic would come into the world. It is magic that had never been seen before. Now it may just be a story, but all stories are based on some truth."

"So you are saying the moon appeared because of Deva?"

"Perhaps, but one thing is for sure, everybody in Annmar has seen the blood moon and those who believe in signs will know that a great change has come to the Annmar. Some will see it as danger, which means more people will be looking for her. You may not want to believe it, but you should be warned nonetheless."

Jaedann looked at Vorak. "I believe there will be more blood before we find some semblance of peace, but that is just the soldier in me talking."

Vorak nodded. "Or is that a Prince talking?"

"I guess you heard."

"I did."

"And?"

"And I don't care. I don't know you as Prince just as a Ranger and an honorable man. That's all I need to know for we all have a past that we are trying to escape from. I was dismissed from my order because I loved a woman when I was not supposed to."

"I did not think loving a woman could stop you from being a monk."

Vorak smiled to himself. "You do not get to be a monk anymore when you make love to another man's wife. That sort of thing is forbidden, but love can make any man forget his vows to the gods. Love is death to the oaths we make."

Jaedann agreed. "So is vengeance, which for me was the case when I tried to kill the King I swore to protect."

"I am sure that is an interesting story and a deeply tragic one too."

Jaedann smiled. "It is, but one that should be told over Ale or Ruminn. Both men laughed at the thought. Ruminn or Ale could always make a story better, especially a tragic one.

By morning the girls had not returned and the Rangers were looking for them throughout Liberus. It was strange, they should have been back by now. Thorsha would send her own guards out to find the girl as well. She did not trust Jaedann and why should she! Jaedann returned to Vorak's home, checking to see if the girls had finally returned. That's not what he found. Vorak had been searching around the building when he found Lorna's body in the bushes. Jaedann walked up behind him and they were both surprised by what they had found. A body with no head. Jaedann spoke first. "What happened to her, how did she lose her head? It does not appear to be cut off. "

Vorak took a closer look. Not cut off…burned off. There's ashes around her like from a fire."

"How?"

"What if Deva instead of shooting fireballs from her hands, touched Lorna's face and burned it. She appears to have the ability to create fire with her hands."

"But why?"

"That's the real mystery. You think she is running?"

"Would explain why she cannot be found. But why run off unless…" Jaedann looked at Vorak with a sense of concern and finished his statement. "Unless she overheard us talking last night about the council wanting to give her to Anntheia and got scared thinking her only option was to escape."

Vorak nodded, agreeing with Jaedann's assessment. "But where would she go? I cannot think of anyone in Liberus who would hide her except us." Before Jaedann could answer, Hanniah walked up behind them. She was flustered and confused, she could not understand why one young girl was causing so much trouble. Jordan asked if she or Rathgar had found her.

Hanniah answered. "No, we have not found her, but Chay Rollant complained to us earlier that the last horse he had his stable was missing?"

Jaedann replied. "Missing, as in, it ran off during the battle."

"I asked the same thing, he says no. He is complaining that somebody stole the horse."

Vorak gave the both of them a concerned look and said. "Deva!"

Jaedann nodded. "She must have taken it and rode off in the night."

Hanniah saw the body. "What happened, did the girl do this?"

"We do not know." Jaedann was about to say something else when two of Thorsha's guards came walking up. They were not actual soldiers, just swordsmen she hired to protect her and worked independently from the Rangers. They were good swordsman, Thorsha always found good swordsman and these two just happened to be Sellswords. Jaedann knew he could take them, after all, besides being a Prince, he was a pretty fierce warrior back in the day. He just knew that it would be more a challenge than he was used to and today was not the day to fight them. Lying to them would be easier and faster when it came to finding Deva. And that is what he did when the two guards asked where the girl might be. Jaedann told them that the girl was seen at the southern end of town. The two swordsmen luckily did not say anything about the body, they just left for the southern part of the town.

Jaedann had Hanniah take him to talk to Chay Rollant about the stolen horse. Chay wanted the Rangers do something about it, but they did not have time for that. Jaedann looked at the horse tracks. They were heading north. That's where he figured she went and it was a safe bet she did not know where she was going. She just rode off towards the first direction she could find. Jordan looked at Hanniah. "I need you to do me a favor."

Curious, Hanniah replied. "What is that?"

"Tell Thorsha's men when it's discovered the horse was stolen that the girl went southeast."

"Why?"

Jaedann pointed in the direction of the horse tracks. "Because she went North and I don't want anybody finding her but me."

Hanniah understood what we he was getting at. She agreed,but had to ask. "Why find this girl, if she left, then she is not our concern anymore."

Jaedann nodded. "Any other time, I would agree, but if Deva really is a Mage then somebody like her falling into the wrong hands would be dangerous and lead to war that people like us cannot win. Whereever she is supposed to be, I want to make sure she gets there safe."

"Is that the Ranger or soldier in you speaking?"

"Both…just because we are Rangers does not mean we don't have honor and try to do the right thing in this fukked up world." Hanniah smiled. She liked Jaedann, maybe even loved him, but he was too much of a soldier. She on the other hand did not believe in having this much honor. Hanniah only believed in surviving and being of service somehow other than a whore, which is what most men would only want her for. But she could fight and that made her valuable in a place like Liberus. She would always help Jaedann including his cause despite not necessarily believing in it herself.

Chay also kept the Ranger's horses fed and groomed. Jaedann climbed on his faithful steed and rode north, following the tracks of Deva's horse. She had maybe half of day on him and it would be hard to find her quickly even for a Ranger. So when Jaedann reached the woods North of Liberus, the strangest thing started to happen. It started to snow. It never snowed here. They were too far south. Was this another sign, a sign of bad things to come? Jaedann could not say for sure, but the snow did not bother him. Jaedann Lionnshade was a Knight of Belmere where true soldiers were made in winter and forged from the harsh snows in the Mountains of Bellmora.

16

The snow was starting to come down hard as the three elves arrived in Easthavenn. Snow was not uncommon even in the southern ports of the Dorwinn, but just like in Liberus, this was different. It was as if a blizzard was rolling through, covering everything in white and making it clean. Easthavenn was a bustling port filled with cutthroats, pirates, merchants, and Elves, always full of life and adventure. It was the most southern port of Dorwinn and it connected the outside world to the Elven Kingdom. It was a place for outsiders and Elves to trade their goods and partake of the lively commerce afforded to all parties in Dorwinn. The Elven kingdom for the most part was closed off to the outside world. The thing about Elves in Annmar is they were very isolated as to not have their elegance and wisdom tarnished by the darkness of a world without gods and their power. Easthavenn, like a few other ports was the kingdom's connection to the outside world. It was also a place that was looked down upon by highborn elves because the port was rich in brothels for those who would pay good money to fuk an elf as well as Lowborn Elves who sought more adventure and strayed from the core values of Elves such as the seekers of wisdom and grace. However,

Easthavenn was necessary for commerce between the Dorwinn and the rest of Annmar.

As Arunn, Malonn, and Saida strolled through the streets of Easthavenn that were covered mostly in white, they did not see many people. Folks stayed inside the taverns and inns trying to keep warm. Saida responded. "This feels strange. When I have been here before, the place has not been so quiet." Malonn, the more robust of the Elves, he was taller and bigger than the typical slender frame of an elf, replied to Saida. "Everybody is inside somewhere getting drunk or fuked: what else would you do when there is snow and it is cold outside? All three Elves laughed at his assessment, for he was not necessarily wrong.

Arunn said. "Let us find a tavern with a nice fire and get some ale. Let us see if we find any Rogues of Hamlinn who have made port." That is what they did. The Gray Bear Tavern was the biggest in Easthavenn and where most sailors who were not from Dorwinn frequented. Everybody mainly kept to themselves. The three Elves drew stares from those inside. The Elves were clearly highborn and did not come here often. They found a place at the end of the bar which extend around the corner of the tavern. It was more private. Arunn looked around and did not see any sailor that could be from the Rogues of Hamlinn, but they could be taking care of other needs first. There were rooms on the second floor of the tavern where they could find an Elf to bed down with. And for most sailors, there was no greater prize than bedding an Elf. Meanwhile Saida was curious about something else.

Looking at Arunn, she asked. "I do not believe that everything is a sign like most elves, but the snow is strange, do you think this is a sign or merely uncommon weather?"

He replied. "First a blood moon, now more snow than we have seen in years, yes, I think it's a sign."

"But a sign of what?"

"That the world as we know it about to change forever. I believe something extraordinary is about to happen just like my father does."

Before Saida could say anything, a few sailors walked over. Curious about the female Elf and a little drunk, they wanted to have a go with her despite the fact that she was not a whore. The sailors surrounded the Elves and then the first one reached for Saida's breasts, turned on and mesmerized by her beauty and shapely appearance. He said as he reached for her. "Hello love, being an Elf and all, how would you like to have a real man fill you up inside?" Arunn and Malonn were about to intervene when Saida swiftly swiped his hands away and put her dagger close to his crotch with the blade right below his tool. She replied. "I don't know. How would you like to lose what you think makes you a real man?"

The sailor said. "I like Elves that are feisty." He reached for her again and this time she did not give him warning, Saida sliced upwards, cutting off one of his testicles. The other sailors tried to go after her, but both Arunn and Malonn put their swords to the sailor's necks while Arunn said. "Take another step and will be your last. Take your friend and go back to your table if you want to live through the night." The sailors did not press the issue. They took their friend who was in agony as he tried to hold his bleeding scrotum in place. Arunn and Malonn smiled at Saida. Smiling back, she responded in kind. "Why are men so dumb and never look for the blade below their tools when trying to fight or grab a woman that can actually defend herself?"

Arunn said. "Because most men are easily distracted by a beautiful woman, especially an Elf and never think to look down. It makes them an easy target."

They finished their ale. They did not see any Rogues of Hamlinn so Arunn led them to the top of a building nearest the shore. Arunn pulled out what Elves referred to as a spyglass. It was not a common item in Annmar, but common among Elves. It gave them the ability to see things that were a long way off. It was a handy tool, used mostly among sailors. Arunn did not see any ships out in the sea. Maybe they had not passed because they were not passing this way. Or perhaps they had passed already. The elves decided to stay no more than three days and see if the Rogues of Hamlinn ships would come by this way or make port in Easthavenn. Three days is all Arunn would give it before traveling south. On the third day one of the ships made port as the Elves found some of the sailors in the Gray Bear Tavern. Saida asked when she saw them, "now what do we do?"

Arunn smiled. "If they're here then they must be going to Liberus as my father said. We must get their first and warn them. I know someone there who can help."

Deva was lost, but then again, she did not really know where she was going anyway. All she knew was that she needed to head north. Deva did not know why, but north is where she was supposed to go. She had been traveling for almost two days now and she was hungry. Deva thought she might have found a town by now, but the snow was making it difficult to see anything. She had only seen snow once in her life, but never so thick. She had never felt so cold. The horse that she took was having trouble breathing. They had rested, but the horse was not used to this kind of weather as they traveled through a heavily wooded area. Just short of another mil, the horse finally collapsed and fell dead. Deva was frightened, what was she going to do now? She was too cold, but kept moving forward, struggling through the huge snow drifts.

Deva tried to create fire with her hands just like before, hoping that it would warm her up. She could not do it and unfortunately, she could not control it. As she made her way through the large trees and over a hill, Deva did not discover a town, but a large hut. It looked as if somebody had been there before and recently. She did not care for she needed to get warm, so she made her way there. Deva walked inside. There was no fire, but wood to make one. Deva also found bread. It may have been a little stale, but it was still bread and she was hungry. She gulped it down quickly, almost choking from eating it too fast, but it tasted good as anything would after not eating for two days. Now Deva tried to make a fire. She did not know how, but again, tried to create fireballs from hands. Nothing. Still, she could not do it. That's when she heard something at the door. It was men, perhaps the previous occupants. Deva did not have time to hide before they walked in. They were actually Barbarians, Crowthornns to be exact. And they were just as surprised to see her.

One of them said. "Hello girl. You are a nice surprise. Here to keep us warm!"

Another Crowthornn replied. "Look at her, she is an Elf. I have never had an Elf before."

Deva was even more scared now and tried to run. She did not get past the Crowthornns, one of them grabbed her. Deva tried to fight back, even biting the hand of her captor. He took the butt of his sword and hit her over the head, knocking her out. They would have their fun with her later. The other Crowthornn said. "When she wakes up, I get the first go." The Crowthornn standing the next to him said. "If there is anybody that will go first, it is I." The one with the sword, replied. "It does not matter who goes first, we will all have a chance with the girl, but we only get one time with her."

One of the Crowthornns replied with an angry growl. "Fuk the gods on that. Why just once?"

The one with the sword said. "Because she will fetch lots of gold if we sell her to one of the whore houses in Witchhold. Brothel owners will pay more gold coins for an Elven whore. They are not common, but they will not pay much if she is damaged."

The other two Crowthornns got excited at the notion. While raping was a source of pride when it came to spoils of war or capturing a top prize like the girl they just found, they loved gold even more. Crowthornns loved gold enough to forgo the many times they could have a pretty thing like her. They had caught a good prize with Deva and selling her to a brothel would be worth more. She had good reason to be afraid because a girl sold to a brothel in Witchhold was the worst thing that could happen to a girl and her only escape would be death after she had been used up by thousands of men. That would be the cruelest of fates for someone like her.

17

The Accuriann Legions of Anntheia were positioned on the border of Anntheia just outside of the Cosonn Rivers. Their Genneral was a great war hero, loved by everyone in Anntheia and greatly feared by the enemies of Anntheia. He was what some might call old and after nearly 40 years as a soldier that may have been true, but even now he could easily kill multiple soldiers that would attack him at once. His name was Genneral Rulf Orwaynn, a legend among the army. He even taught King Lancelynn when the king was a young prince and was sent to Anntheia's war school. Like all legions in Anntheia, they were named after the providence the came from. Half of the legions had been sent to the border to quell barbarian attacks; about 45,000 men in total along with artillery and cavalry. It might have been overkill for simple Barbarians, but the King of Anntheia wanted to send a message. He was a cruel king and wanted to see the Barbarian clans burn.

Genneral Orwaynn was eating dinner when the raven with the King's message arrived. He was surprised to see it.

It was not the kind of order he would expect to get and it was certainly out of the ordinary. He called his second in command, Commander Tolbernn Rogier to come into his tent and read the note. The commander and had a strange look on his face. He asked. "Genneral, this cannot be real."

Orwaynn nodded. "Strange as it may be, it is real, it has the King's personal seal."

"But Genneral, sacking a town, even Liberus would be an open declaration of war."

"I know. Now I am inclined to follow security procedures and send a raven to confirm the order, but I want to know what you think. Would you follow these orders or risk losing command by asking to confirm a King's order if you feel it was sent falsely?"

Commander Rogier thought about it for a moment. "I would confirm the order."

"That may be the smart thing to do, but when you do not have the luxury of time on your side because this order says to sack the city immediately, which means that we cannot wait to confirm anything, it has to be done soon to go along with whatever the King's strategy may be. In this instance, we follow the orders and if we are wrong, then we ask for forgiveness later. Time is either your most important ally or enemy in war. And it's snowing, which means we will not be able to move the army as fast. We could be stuck in the middle of storm without supplies with men who are starving and are too weak to fight." The Genneral grabbed a piece of parchment and dabbed a quill pen, he wrote an order for Commander Rogier and then handed it to him with the seal of the Kingdom of Anntheia. He said. "Take this with you, you will need it if anybody asks where you are going."

The commander gave the Genneral a strange look. "Where I'm going?"

"You will take two of our legions, roughly 5,000 men and march towards Liberus. You will also take 4 of our ballistas. You can take care of this task. I will not move the whole of our forces just for one little trading town. A small force can burn it to the ground. If anybody asks, then you tell them you are on King's business to stop an open rebellion. This should provide you safe passage based on the Treaty of Kingswatch."

Commander Rogier nodded. "Other kingdoms are not going to like this, especially Belmere, aren't you afraid this will lead to a war? Not just with Belmere, but all Kingdoms since everybody seems to get some of their goods through Liberus?"

Genneral Orwaynn smiled. "Every King's action can lead to a war, but it is usually the common sense judgments of those Kings that find a way not to have to go to war and send thousands of their subjects to die. All we can hope for is that our King has the same judgment in this situation, but we have our orders."

The Commander nodded to confirm the orders,but had to ask. "Genneral. I did not mean to speak out of term when it comes to our King, but do you think sacking Liberus is a good idea? What do you think?

Genneral Orwaynn thought about it for a moment. "You should not speak out of term when it comes to our King, we are here to carry out orders. But this one time, I will say what I think. This is a terrible move by our King. It will lead to war…eventually. But then again Anntheia is always at war with someone. That is how we extend our empire. Perhaps it is time to deal with that wretched trader's town once and for all. Maybe we take control of the area and have a foothold in the west. It would be very advantageous for Anntheia. So I have faith in my former student and we should trust that the King knows what he is doing. Me, I was built for war. I say let's get on with it before I have the unfortunate grace to die in a bed.

Commander Rogier laughed. He shared the same thoughts. The Genneral dismissed him, but before he left, told the commander that he and his men should get some rest. They would leave at dawn. And more snow was coming so there was not telling how long it was going to take. There was only one main road to move an army towards Liberus from where the legions were positioned. Heavy snowfall could easily block if they did not move fast enough. Time was their biggest enemy now.

Jaedann followed the horse tracks as far as he could before the snowfall covered them up. He hoped that he had made up a lot of time when trying to find Deva. He was hours behind her, but Rangers were good at making up time when tracking someone. Even though the snow had covered up the tracks, he could still find imprints in the snow where a horse had traveled. There were also broken branches in the trees within the heavily wooded areas that the girl had traveled through. For the most part she kept straight north even on rocky terrain. It was cold and Jaedann's horse was having a hard time breathing in the cold air. He needed to get out of the snow and find some place warm or his horse would die. But mostly he was worried about Deva, she was not accustomed to the cold weather like he was and she could very easily die.

Finally, he saw it. A dead horse. It was Deva's horse that she stole. He recognized Chay Rollannt's brand on it. It looked as if it had frozen to death. He continued North down a hill about a mil. There were still signs that someone had traveled this way on foot from broken twigs on the trees and to small imprints on in the snow. These tracks were fairly fresh. Jaedann came to the edge of the hill and saw the hut. He saw the smoke, somebody was in there, but there was a stable area without any horses. Jaedann thought to himself, it had to be Barbarians. They did not travel by horse, it was too loud and their enemies could easily hear them so they traveled by foot. Jordan tied his horse up in the woods and put a blanket over its back to keep it warm while he went down and inspected the area.

The Crowthornns were cooking stew when Deva finally woke up. It was the smell of the stew that woke her up, for it smelled bad. She screamed in fear,but was gagged as well as being tied up so she didn't make that loud of a sound. Although, it was enough to get the Barbarians attention. They got excited for she was awake and they could have some fun with her. One of them said. Hello love, look who's awake. Just in time, we were getting mighty lonely. I am going first. "The leader of the small clan said. "Take her outside to the stable while we eat. Do not wear her out before we get to have a go" The Crowthornn took her outside as she kicked and screamed saying to her. "Pretty thing, you will scream even more when I fill you up." He then took her to the covered part of the stable and tied her up to a post. Then he stood behind her and tore her robe enough where he could get underneath and lifted it almost over her back. Next, he tore her leggings and pulled them down until her ass showed in the moonlight and he could get a good angle to have his way with her. Deva was trying to fight him off, but his strong hand pinned her up against the post has he undid his belt and pulled his leggings down revealing his manhood.

Jaedann saw what he was about to do. He was already close to the hut near the stable area, not too far from the Barbarian. The Crowthornn was too busy trying to get with Deva to notice Jaedann sneak up behind him. Jaedann was very good at being stealthy and making sure no one would hear him. Just as the Crowthornn was about to enter inside Deva, Jaedann with his sword drawn and with a mighty force, swung the sword forward and around in one motion, taking the Crowthornn's head clean off his body. Deva didn't see it and was trying to block out what was about to happen as the body hit the ground. Jaedann grabbed and immediately took the gag out of her mouth, but also putting his hand over her mouth to muffle her screams. He held her to comfort the scared girl and then whispered into her ear. "Deva, it's me, Jaedann, look at me, don't be scared. You do not have to be scared anymore. I'm here and you're okay now."

Deva was shaking. She couldn't stop shaking, but seeing Jaedann instantly made her feel better. He helped her cover herself as she pulled her leggings up and tried to put herself together from the assault she just experienced. Then she said to Jaedann. "There are two more in the hut."

Jaedann smiled. If Deva was talking, she was feeling better. He replied. "Okay, I need you to something. I am going kill them, but I need you run to my horse in the woods and distract them." Deva gave him a strange look. She didn't understand, but after getting her clothes back on she did what he said. Jaedann spoke again. "One more thing…scream when you run." Jaedann then picked up the Crowthornns head and walked to the front of the hut. He threw the head inside so the other Crowthornns would see it. They were stunned at the site of the head and then heard the girl scream. Both of them came running out of the hut and saw the girl running towards the woods. One of them shouted. "Fuk the gods, what happened to Clawbekk?

Jaedann was standing near the stables and was out of their line of sight as they came out of the hut. With his bow, ready to fire an arrow. He answered. "The same thing that is going to happen to you fukshitts." They both charged Jaedann. He fired one arrow and hit the first one coming towards him. Then he quickly fired another arrow and hit the second Crowthornn. The arrows knocked them down and while they were on the ground trying to get up in the snow, Jaedann pulled his sword out, walked over, and before the Crowthornns could attack, swung and sliced them both open . Then he took their heads clean off, killing them instantly.

Deva was still running and getting tired doing so. Jaedann let out a strange whistle, the whistle called the horse out of the woods. He whistled again and it stopped by Deva. She was caught off guard by what just happened, but figured the horse was for her to ride so she climbed on. Jaedann let out another kind of whistle and his horse, who he called Stormcloud because of his grayish colors that gave him the same color as the sky and clouds during a storm, came riding back towards the hut. He was also a bit fierce like a storm and that's one of the main reasons Jaedann loved riding him. When the horse with Deva on top got back to Jaedann, he said. "You are more lucky than these Crowthornns, if I had not found you when I did, you could be lying here dead after they used you for pleasure." Deva, still in shock over nearly being raped, but manage a smile towards Jaedann. She did not exactly know what his intentions were, but responded. "I'm glad it was you who found me, Jaedann Lionnshade." He did not say anything, just looked at her for a long moment. There would be plenty of time to talk later. But also for Jaedann, this was the first time he truly saw her beauty as the snow was coming down again. Deva was extremely beautiful with her hair let down, but it was her eyes that drew him in and could capture any man's heart.

18

After two days the snow was still falling. The streets of Liberus were covered in white and citizens were having to shovel it out of their doorways to keep from getting blocked in. It was hard to move around with all the snow so most people just stayed indoors. Rathgar took a big gulp of ale as he looked out Vorak's door. He and Hanniah were having dinner with him. Vorak also had something to share with them. He wanted to tell them about the prophecy or at least what he knew about it. Rathgar responded in gest at the mention of it. "A prophecy about magic users, you think this girl is some kind of Mage? Are you sure you saw fireballs, maybe she threw something!"

Vorak sternly replied. "I know what I saw, Rathgar. The girl could not throw fire and a Crowthornn across the room, she's not that strong. As for a prophecy, I don't know for sure. No one is absolutely sure when it comes to prophecies, belief in them is based on faith."

"Do you believe in this prophecy about magic coming back into the world?

"I do."

"I believe it is all horseshitt. They are just stories to make people believe that this world is better than the dark pile of horseshitt it really is."

Vorak laughed. "I know why you would think that, but I have seen too many things even before the girl to know that magic was once real and will be again.

"Oh, that's right, you were a monk at Lenntis. How did you stop being a monk, the full story?"

Vorak poured himself another cup of Ruminn. "This story is going to take a drink. There was a nobleman from Belmere that would come to the vineyards of Lenntis and stock up on wine for his cellar. He was married to a young woman, half his age, who did not love him. It was an arranged marriage. The woman's parents wanted her to have a better life and married her off. The nobleman would stay a week each trip and we would talk each and every day she was there. She was magnificent…kind and beautiful, passionate and full of life. So, naturally, I fell in love with her. I could not help it and so I forgot my vows. I laid with another man's wife."

Rathgar laughed. "It is always a woman that makes us betray our oaths. Why would it be different for a celibate Monk."

Vorak took another sip of Ruminn. "You are right, it is no different for a Monk and a Barbarian when it comes to love. She consumed my every thought even at the expense of the gods."

Hanniah asked Vorak. "Have you even been with a woman before her."

"No, she was my first. She wanted to leave her husband, her title, and her whole life just to be with me. I arranged for us to leave the next time they came to get wine. He found the note I left her about my plan. The nobleman wanted me dead for being with his wife, which was his right. But the order took pity on me and just banished me. I can never be a Monk again, but I can still find work as a Cleric."

Hanniah asked. "What happened to the woman?"

"The nobleman had her executed for laying with another man as was his right under Belmerien law. I guess it's a better fate than what happens to most women who are unfaithful to their husband. They usually end up working in a brothel. Belmere takes oaths very seriously."

"Fuk the gods. It is too cruel fate."

"Yes, it is. I have often wondered if those who break their oath even for love are destined for tragic things."

Rathgar replied. "Maybe the world is just a shitt place and we are not meant to have true love." Vorak raised his glass to agree with Rathgar and said. "You may be right." Rathgar raised his glass and they both took a sip of what they were drinking then Rathgar replied. "Now, what is the prophecy you speak of. How does it work?"

Vorak gave Hanniah and Rathgar a serious look. "There are five who will bring magic back into the world. They are called a Penntacle for it will take all five of them working together in perfect harmony to bring magic back into Annmar…full magic, meaning all the powers of the gods that anyone could possess. They will be of different races, each of them will represent one of the gods. Each one of them will possess magical abilities that they may not be aware of or can even control."

Hanniah asked. "So you mean one will be an Elf, one will be a Human, one will be a Dwarf, and one will be a Halfling?"

"Yes, or one will be a Fae because the gods had dominion over different races. Five different races for five different gods, that will be the Penntacle."

Rathgar asked. "The girl, she is the Elf in this prophecy, I suppose. But she is an Half-Elf, does that matter?"

Vorak answered. "I think she is the Elf in the prophecy, but perhaps it is about having Elven blood so it does not matter that she is only a Half-Elf. However, she may come from a powerful Elven house so perhaps that has something to do with it."

Hanniah asked. "If this is true, will the five know about each other?"

"I do not know. I would not think so."

"So they have to find each other?"

"I suppose so."

"If they find each other, what happens next? Magic just comes back."

Vorak laughed at the last part of her statement. "I do not think it works like that. I suspect they will go to a special or powerful place, perhaps perform some kind of ritual, but I do not know what it is or where they would go."

Rathgar was getting angry. "This just sounds more and more like a bedtime story. No one knows for sure that magic even existed."

Vorak looked at Rathgar, disappointed by his lack of belief. He asked Rathgar. "Do you believe in the gods."

"Barbarians have lots of gods."

"But do you believe in the five gods?"

"Yes."

"Then why is it so hard to believe that magic was real and can be again?"

"Just because the gods may have been real, does not mean they were not simply men and the stories over the years made them out to be gods. They are just stories, nothing more."

Vorak softly laughed. "They are just stories until they become real just like prophecies."

Hanniah spoke up before Rathgar. She didn't want to hear an argument between a cleric and a barbarian. "Okay, if this true about the girl, what happens to her? She is in danger and will have to be protected and we cannot do that here. Where would she have to go?"

Vorak thought about it for a moment. "Provided Jaedann can find her and that she is not given to Anntheia, there is a place where I think she could hide until she is ready to fulfill her destiny."

Hanniah was extremely curious and had to ask. "Where is this place?"

Vorak smiled again. "A hidden city where she can hide in plain sight."

Deva was still cold as she sat by the fire in the hut. She tried fiercely to get warm by the rubbing her arms and chest. Jaedann brought more wood for the fire. He did not t want too much smoke coming from the hut and to attract unwanted visitors, but Deva had to get warm. Elves and even Half Elves had fair skin and were not akin to the cold as humans. Too much cold could kill them. Jaedann was not about to let her die.

Deva finally asked. "Why did you come after me? To take me to Anntheia?"

Jaedann shook his head. "I guess you did overhear

me talking to Vorak about what the council in Liberus wanted to do with you. That's why you ran off, am I right?"

Deva got angry. "Yes and yes. So I guess you captured me and now taking me to Anntheia?"

"No, I came to find you to get you out of Liberus. You are not going to Anntheia, no matter how much the King wants you. I am here to take you somewhere safe and protect you."

"Why?"

"I do not know what you are. Maybe you are a Mage. Maybe you have some kind of destiny that will change the world as we know it and possibly in a good way. But whatever you are, you need to be protected and that means hiding you. It is clear that you have abilities, which makes you dangerous and vulnerable to those who would want to exploit them for their own gain. You are also an innocent girl who does not deserve to be handed over to a vengeful king. That is why I came to find you."

"I thought you were just like them and wanted to send me away."

"No Deva, I am not like them. The council is scared. Scared of what happens next if we don't turn you over because Anntheia won't stop coming after you, which means you are a danger to them. Maybe you are a part of a prophecy as Vorak says."

"I do not care much about prophecies. I just want to get to where I am supposed to go. "

Jaedann smiled. "I can understand and maybe that is part of the prophecy, it does not matter whether you care about it or not. If it is true, then you are a part of it whether you want to be or not. That is all I know. This is Vorak's area of expertise. However, if you want to know more, I will help you find out more about this prophecy."

Deva was still shivering so Jaedann put his cloak

around her and then held her to keep her warm. "Here, come close, body heat will get you warmer faster than a fire. "Hesitant at first, she leaned in close and let Jaedann warm her up. Jaedann softly smiled for hair smelled like fully bloomed flowers even in the hard fallen snow. That was his first thought, even beyond her beauty. Jaedann was a bit taken with her, he had to admit to himself. He had not been this taken with a woman since his late wife.

Jaedann said. "I suppose you have not eaten since you left Liberus, is that right?" She nodded yes. "Well, we have some stew here. It does not smell good, but its food and it we will keep us alive. Perhaps some wine will make it better." He poured his small pouch of wine in the cauldron that was next to the fire and then he put it back over the fire to cook some more. After a few minutes Deva and Jaedann ate some of the stew. Both of them winced. It was terrible and the wine did not make it much better. But they ate the stew anyway. They were both famished and needed their strength.

After a while asked. "Where do we go if I am to hide from everybody?"

Jaedann thought about it for a moment. "There is a place, I believe, would be perfect. A place where you can blend in and no one will ask questions. It is a hidden city in the trees."

"There is a hidden city in the trees?"

Jaedann laughed. "Yes, a hidden city in the trees. It sits between the kingdoms of Dorwinn, Yorynn, and the Emberwild and it is a place for outcast Elves, Halflings, and Fae. Half-Elves too so you will fit in perfectly.

"What is this place called?"

"The Cohnnwood."

"Thank You for taking me there."

He smiled. "Do not thank me yet, we still have to get there and we cannot make it without this much snow coming down. Plus, I think we are being followed." Hearing that shocked Deva, but mostly scared her, although, somehow she knew Jaedann would take care of her no matter what. She felt, somehow, someway, he would always be there for her. The thought made the fear go away. But outside the hut on a hilltop by the edge of the woods, stood an unwelcomed visitor. It was a Khronne, the same one who had been with Swanson and the Crowthornns. She was from Anntheia and went by the name Vazigronn. She was an assassin sent by Emericcc Tabenn, King Lancelynn's Spymaster.

19

The snow relentlessly fell for weeks, not letting up and blocking roads with six meter snow drifts. Nothing could move, especially men on horses. And an army definitely couldn't move anywhere on the Carrann Road leading from Anntheia through the Kingdom of Skallvenn to Liberus. Commander Rogier's two legions and the catapults were stuck and entrenched many mils from Liberus along the Carrann road. They had not been able to move and supplies were running low. They already had to slaughter some of the horses for food. After weeks entrenched along the large road, the legions were finally able to start moving again, but they were a long way from their final destination.

Meanwhile, Deva and Jaedann had not been able to leave the hut for weeks. The snow was too thick and Jaedann's horse could not make it through the snow drifts so they stayed until it stopped snowing and finally started to melt away. The horse even had to stay in the hut with them for a while just to keep warm. Food was scarce, but Jaedann always seem to know where to find game. Plus, being from Belmere and growing up in the cold, he knew how to ice fish. On most days he could get fish from the river nearby. They may have only eaten once a day, but they were able to eat thanks to the resourcefulness of the Ranger. Jaedann was also able to teach Deva a few things about survival. He taught her how to hunt. He taught her about herbs that had healing properties. He taught her how to be invisible. He was teaching her how to be a Ranger. She had to learn some skills for she had not had a magical incident since the night of the battle in Liberus. Deva was beginning to wonder if she could even do it again. She would keep trying, but nothing would happen.

Finally, it stopped snowing at the hut Jaedan and Deva had lived in for weeks. The snow started to melt and they were able to go farther north. In was early in the morning. Deva has used Jaedann's bow to shoot down some doves so they could have a meal before heading out on their long journey. Jaedann commented that they were tasty. After they ate, Jaedann got the horse ready and then asked Deva. "Are you ready to leave?"

She nodded yes. "I think I'm going to miss this place. Maybe not the smell, but being here with you felt good. I felt safe."

Jaedann smiled as he climbed on the horse. "Good and you are right the smell was not always pleasant, but what do you expect with a hut made by Barbarians who are not exactly known for their cleanliness. Although, I would never tell Rathgar that." Deva laughed. Jaedann reached out his hand to pull Deva up. "Now get up on the horse, we got a lot ground to cover." She did just that and they started north.

Deva asked. "How will we get to this hidden city? Are we staying in the woods?

"We are not too far from the Carrann Road, the main road through Skallvenn. There are lots of traders who travel the road to get to different kingdoms. We can probably find someone to travel with who won't ask questions and will allow us to blend in. Someone who is going to Dorwinn or

Yorynn. If we are being followed, we might able to escape their sight if we blend in with fellow travelers."

They traveled for about a day before they came to the Carrann Road. It was still heading in a northerly direction before it would turn in different directions. It was also still covered in snow, but only a little so they were able to move along the road. The air was starting to get warmer after the snowstorm began to disappear even as they traveled North. Deva asked. "Do you think we will find any fellow travelers today?"

Softly smiling, he replied. "Hopefully, this road is usually busy with the it being one of the main roads in Annmar, even after a storm." As luck would have it, they did not have to wait long. Towards the back, they heard whistling. A man with four horses and two big wagons carrying all sorts of goods was coming up on them. By his whistling, he was a lively fellow. His wagon rode up to Deva and Jaedann and said. Hello, fellow strangers. How goes your travels?"

Jaedann replied. "Hello yourself, fine sir. Two wagons, I would guess that you are a traveling merchant."

He smiled, "Right you are. Gerabald is the name. Purveyor of fine goods is my game. You want it, I can get it. Now that the snow is cleared, I am on my way to some of the towns and ports in Yorynn and Dorwinn to do business that is long overdue. And what be your business fine sir?"

"Heading north to find work as a swordsman."

"You have the look of a Ranger, not a Sellsword.

"I've been that too."

"Who is your pretty friend?"

"A shipwrecked girl that I am getting back home, but the rest is her business."

Gerabald nodded at Deva "Very wise of you to keep such business to yourself. Well, if we are heading in the same direction then you can travel with me, even give your horse a rest by riding on my wagon. We will swap services, if you protect me with your sword from any cutthroats that might want to steal from me then you can have a ride, a fire to sleep by, and food to eat until we get to where we are going."

Deva curiously looked at Jaedann, not knowing what was going on. Jaedann nodded at her and then replied o Gerabald. "That sounds like a good deal." They got off the horse and Jaedann tied his steed to the back of the Wagon. Deva got in the front part of the covered wagon while Jaedann sat next to Gerabald. The merchant asked. "Do you have a name, sir?"

Jaedann answered. "I am Rolannd and this is Sernna." Deva had an ominous look on her face, but then she realized that Jaedann was giving the man a false name like she did with him at first to protect them from any overly curious party. The three of them traveled for most of the day when the conversation turned to where they had all been throughout Annmar. Deva did not say anything. She kept her business to herself. Gerabald asked Jaedann.   "So you're a Sellsword and a Ranger, interesting combination! Where did you train if you don't mind me asking?"

Jaedann nodded. "I don't mind at all. I learned how to be a Ranger in a town called Bronnwhich. That is where I am from. My father was actually a Ranger who hired out to the military."

Gerabald thought for a moment. "Bronnwhich. That's up north in Belmere, correct."

"Yes, it is" It was an actual real place in the Kingdom of Belmere. A Town under the lordship of House Fensenn. It was a place where scouts and Rangers actually trained because of the heavily wooded area and mountains that surrounded Castle Fensenn. Jaedann had actually been there and wasn't going to give the man false information about a place he had never been to. It would not be wise to do so."

Gerabald replied. "I think I am familiar with the place, but have only been there once. As a Sellsword, have you ever been to Dragonnshead? I hear all the best sellswords come from there."

"I have been there." Another truth from Jaedann. He did hire out as a Sellsword from there for a little after being banished. He continued. "And yes, the best swordsmen generally come from there."

"Is it as tough as they say?"

"Definitely and then some. I consider myself pretty good, but I did not want to fight some of the swordsmen that come from there."

Gerabald laughed. "Where have you worked?"

"Here and there. Mostly port towns along the cost."

"I do a lot of business in places like that. Surprised we have not run into each other or shared a pint of Ale."

Jaedann laughed. "With so many ports, it's hard to keep track, especially with the Tavern wenches."

Deva gave him a dirty look, but Gerabald thought it was funny and shared his sentiment. He said. "I agree fine sir. Liberus is my favorite place to visit. The women are fine as silk, curvy with great bit tits, just as I like them. And the local drink they have, Ruminn, it's usually my best seller. I do not know how they make it, but it is good and will make you easily forget all your troubles."

"That it does. I have had many a rough morning drinking that stuff when I have visited Liberus."

"So, you have been there?"

"I've been hired a few times as town security or to protect some rich merchant. It has been while since I have been there."

"Well, tonight, we shall have a cup of Ruminn and drink to Liberus. May she always have the best women, the best liquor, and always be free."

The day turned into night and as the wagon was making one of the many turns in Carrann road they came upon an open valley filled with soldiers and tents. Gerabald responded. "Well, what do we have here, an army. I wonder whose army."

Jaedann looked at the army banners. He recognized the sun and double sword sigil instantly. "It is an Anntheian army. Looks like two legions from a rough count. The Accuriann legions to be exact."

"You know your military banners."

"What can I say, I've been around."

Deva was frightened to see the army. She asked. "Why would an Anntheian army be here? We are not in their kingdom are we?""

Jaedann replied. "I do not know, they are further west than they should me. Maybe they are here to quell some barbarian uprising, but they also have four catapults, that only means one thing."

"What?"

"They are going to sack a city or a castle."

Gerabald answered. "Barbarians don't have such things."

Jaedann looked at him. "The only town closest enough that's worth sacking is Liberus."

"Why would they sack Liberus?"

Deva gave him a frightened look, but it was Jaedann who answered. "Tired of the competition with trade since it's the second largest port in Annmar. Maybe they do not want that anymore and to drive most of the trade in Annmar to Anntheian ports."

Gerabald pondered for a moment. "Well, if that is true, then I will miss Liberus, but in the meantime, professional soldiers have money and if they can't pay for women, the next best thing is wine and liquor. I might have the last ever barrels of Ruminn…perhaps I can charge a premium. You don't mind if we venture down there."

Jaedann didn't like the idea, but it was also a good place to blend in. He nodded yes and then told Deva that everything would be okay. He wasn't going to let anything happen to her. Gerabald, turned his wagons down towards the valley and found a Sargenn in the Anntheian army to direct him to the commanding officer. They were allowed to set up camp and sell their goods to the soldier's. Deva was told to stay hidden. Jaedann did not need a bunch of soldiers who had not been with a woman in a while discovering that he was traveling with one. But more importantly, that she was the girl that Anntheia was looking for. Deva put her hair up and wore her hood to make her look like a young monk. Fortunately, she had enough clothes on to cover up the fact that she had breasts, a dead giveaway to anyone suspecting she might be a woman.

20

The Anntheian camp was lively, it felt more like a celebration, but that was how soldiers could be in their downtime. Deva had never seen anything like it before and was curious. She was supposed to be hiding in the back of the wagon as Jaedann helped put up Gerabald's tent, but she kept looking out, trying to see all that she could. Liberus could be lively, however, this was different. More organized it seemed. She noticed that there were women in the camp and asked Jaedann about them. He laughed to himself for in many ways she was like a small child curious about the world around her. He said. "Some are nurses, but most are whores. Big armies will bring whores for the men. Soldiers who are not sexually frustrated fight better."

"Women cannot serve in the army."

"Not in Anntheia. They can only be nurses or whores and they do not take kindly to the women posing as soldiers. That is what happened to Hanniah. She was a nurse and posed as a soldier when the unit she was serving in was short of men. It did not matter how many she killed during a battle, her choice was execution or banishment. You know which one she chose."

Deva shook head in disbelief. Where she was raised, if women could fight, they fought and she had known some fierce women warriors from across the sea. But she was curious about something else. She asked Jaedann. "Are you really from the Kingdom of Belmere? I know you gave fake names, but wondered if there was any truth to it?"

"I really am from Belmere and really have been to Bronnwich. That's why I know about the place. If you are going to give a false name and place of origin, make sure some of the details are true because the truth is the easiest thing to remember."

"What did you do in Belmere, were you always a Ranger?"

"No, I was a soldier at one time, but that was long ago."

"Did you fight in many battles?"

"I fought in my fair share of battles, against Anntheia too. That's another reason I know their banners so well."

Gerabald, finally came back and finished putting the tent up. He was impressed and very thankful because it was hard to put the tent up by himself, the older he got. It was a beast and was better suited for a younger and stronger man. He thanked Jaedann and then said. "I met the Commander and I may have mentioned that you had worked some in Liberus and he was very curious about what you knew about the place. My apologies, I know you want to keep your business your own. But he is very keen to meet you."

Jaedann winced at the notion, He was trying to avoid meeting the Commander just in case a senior officer in the Anntheia army might recognize him from a previous battle, especially as he was killing Anntheia soldiers, which the Commander would certainly not look favorably upon. But it was a risk he had to take because to snub the Commander would be worse. It would draw unwanted attention so he reluctantly agreed. He asked. "Did you sell anything?"

Gerabald got excited. "I did. Two Barrels of Ruminn and a small one to the Commander himself. I told him that you could bring it to him, if you do not mind."

"I do not mind if you will do me a favor. Look after the girl and keep her away from any soldiers. They do not need to know she is here if you know what I mean."

Gerabald nodded as Deva looked a bit confused for she was still too innocent in some ways when it came to the world of men and especially soldiers who would do anything to be with a woman. "I will protect her as if she were my own daughter. " Hopefully it would not come to that, but he did not exactly trust Anntheian soldiers. Jaedann found his way to the Commander's tent with the small barrel of Ruminn. The commander was delighted to see him, he said. "You're the Sellsword and the Ranger that the old man was telling me about."

Jaedann nodded. "I am and I do hire out as those things. And you are?"

The Anntheian officer put forth his hand to greet Jaedann. The former Belmerien knight did not want to take it, he in no way trusted Anntheian soldiers, but took his hand to keep up appearances. " I am Commander Rogier of the Accuriann Legions from Anntheia. I need a scout, somebody who is familiar with that traders town know as Liberus. I understand you may be that man."

Jaedann tried to dissuade him in his reply. "I do not know if I am. I have not had any work there in years. I am sure it has changed from what I remember. "

"Rolannd is it?" Jaedann nodded yes. " You may be surprised. Places like that rarely change and you are the only man that I know that has firsthand knowledge of the place from a military standpoint."

"What is it that you want to know?"

The Commander poured himself a cup Ruminn and then poured Jaedann a cup. " As you can see, we are marching two legions there. We are going to sack the city, but need to know it's weak spots. And where citizens could easily escape. I would rather not march front and center with my soldiers or just use the ballistas to burn the town to the ground. I want to block the roads and box everybody in, but if we know the best places for that then I do not have to stretch my army further than necessary away from a proper frontal attack. Plus, I do not know if my map of Liberus is accurate."

Jaedann saw a map lying on a table. He walked over to the table and took a look. It was surprisingly accurate and looked like a recent map too. "It's a good map. Whoever drew it did a good job. But I am still not your man."

The Commander paused. "That's a shame. We pay very well. At least four times as much as anybody else would for this kind of job."

"It is not about the money. Already have a job that I need to fulfill."

"Which you can continue after you help us and we pay better."

Jaedann laughed. "One job at a time, I complete one job and then do another."

"That is honorable, but I do not have time for honor." The Commander put four bags of Anntheia gold on the table in front of Jaedann. "You should take the gold because we could just conscript you into our service and there is nothing anybody would do about it."

Jaedann gave him a dirty look. "You can put me in chains, but it does not mean I will help you and especially if threatened with torture. I have been tortured before and still did not comply with my captors."

The Commander smiled and replied. "You do seem like a man that does not buckle under pain, but I would not torture you. Your companions, could they withstand torture. You could hear their screams and still not comply. You do not hurt someone to get what you truly want. You hurt what they love the most and from what I here the fair maiden you travel with is quite fetching. I am sure my soldiers would agree after they have used her over and over. Take the gold and do the job I am offering. It is better for you and your companions.

Jaedann was now afraid. How did Commander Rogier know about Deva? It appeared that Gerabald did not have much discretion. The only way to save her from the Army and what they would do to her was to help them. Jaedann pointed on the map to a Northern street. "Right here is the best place to escape Liberus. Put part of your legions here and you will box everybody into the town. If your intention is to sack the city and kill everybody then block this area."

The Commander smiled. "That's exactly what we are going to do, but I still need your help. There is still more scouting you can do. You travel with us in the morning. You and your companions." Jaedann stared at the Commander. He did not say anything, but he was seriously rethinking his plan of blending in especially in plain sight. It was one thing to have regular soldiers see him, he could move in and out without them really noticing, but he talked to the commanding officer, he knew Jaedann's face. There would be no easy way to escape now. He left The Commander's tent and went back to the tent where he and Deva were staying.

Solders had been coming in and out of Gerabald's area buying goods, mostly wine. Deva stayed hidden for the most part. But Gerabald asked for her help with a barrel and the two Anntheian men saw her. They were both enamored with her light reddish blond hair and one of them saw that she was an elf. One of them commented. "Wow, beautiful… she is beautiful. How much is she?"

Gerabald replied. "Oh, she is not one of those girls. She is just a maiden. "

The other soldier said. "Where I come from all maidens are those kinds of girls." Gerabald got nervous and the soldiers crept further in the tent, not taking their eyes off the girl for an instant. He offered them an extra portion of wine. One of the soldiers replied. "I want the girl instead." Deva got frightened when he said that and he came closer. Gerabald said again. "Sorry, she is not for sale." They did not like that answer and the other soldier hit Gerabalf with the butt of his sword, making him bleed and almost knocking him out. The soldier closest to Deva grabbed her and was trying to take her from behind when her fear triggered a defensive response. Her hands started to glow fire again. She put her glowing hands on the soldier's chest to push him away and they burned a hole in it right where the heart was. It killed him instantly. The other soldier came after her and she pushed him back by touching his face and burning it off just like she had done back in Liberus with Lorna. He died instantly too. Deva stood over the bodies, shaking, a mixture of shock and fear. Gerabald on the other hand was woozy from getting hit, but he saw what happened. He did not understand what had just happened, but it made him a little fearful of Deva now.

Jaedann arrived back at the tent to see Deva trying with all of her might to move one of the bodies. "What in the name of the gods just happened."

Deva replied. "I did not mean to, I swear."

Gerabald was still on the ground woozy and trying to get up. Jaedann went over to help him to his feet when he told the Ranger. "The two shittheaps tried to have their way with her. She stopped them with what I assume was fire. I cannot explain it."

Jaedann responded. "None of us can."

"She has done this before?"

"Yes, but if you know any more about her, you your life will be in danger."

Looking at Deva, the old merchant asked. "What was that…some kind of magic?"

She didn't really have an answer. Deva could not say for sure if she really even believed in magic, but she knew that she had powers. The biggest question for her was how did she get these powers. That is what she wanted to know more than anything. Deva responded to his question by shaking her head, no. Jaedann helped Gerabald to a chair and said. "Listen, I hate to do this to you. Whatever you saw, you have to forget about it."

He replied as he looked at Deva. "She has magical abilities…she is special, is she not? There are stories about those who will bring magic back into the world."

"We do not know that for sure and there is no use in conjuring up theories. I have to get her out here and we have to hide these bodies so the Commander of this army does not see them and get suspicious."

"Is Anntheia after her?"

"I will not answer, but you are in danger just knowing us."

"I knew your name was not Rolland, what is your real name?"

"That will get you killed by men from Anntheia and Belmere."

Gerabald stood up. "Sounds like you're wanted in your own country." Jaedann nodded, but did not elaborate. Gerabald continued. "What do you want to do?"

Jaedann looked at the bodies and then one of the wagons. He said. "We put them in one of your wagons and burn it to hide the bodies. Then you can tell them that soldiers did it when you denied them the girl. Maybe it gives us time to escape if they search for the soldiers to punish."

"But my wagon will cost me money."Jaedan handed him three bags of Anntheia gold. "Here, that should take of it."

"Where did you get that?"

"My fee for being their scout when they destroy Liberus. I will not be needing it since I am not helping them. This should cover your losses and then some. Gerabald looked in the bags and smiled. "This will do nicely. Now let me help load the bodies into one of my wagons." They did that while saving the last of the wine that was in the wagon. Jaedannn prepared his horse and then told Gerabald. Once I light the fire, yell out and in the chaos, we will slip out...wait. I need their armor. I have an idea." Deva was curious, but Gerabald understood what he needed it for. Jaedan and Deva put the armor on along with the red undershirts to disguise themselves as Anntheia soldiers. The Armor did not fit Deva, but it was enough to make look like a soldier if f no one looked close enough.

Jaedann lit the fire. it took a few minutes for the fire to really start burning. Jaedann thanked him for his help and Gerabald said, "I am not sure what this is all about, but may the gods keep you safe on your journey."

"Until we meet again." Then they shook hands. Deva kissed him on his cheek. When the fire was high enough, Gerabald yelled out. As the soldiers came running to help put out the fire and stop it from spreading, Jaedan and Deva dressed as Anntheia infantrymen, walked with his horse through the crowd of soldiers with ease. They were too busy to notice them. Finally, they made it out of the camp without any Anntheia soldier saying anything. Jaedann felt relief when they got to the edge of the woods outside of camp, his plan had worked.

21

Commander Rogier was furious as he looked at the burned wagon. How could this kind of fire damage happen in an army camp that was secure and had taken every precaution to make sure they were safe from enemies. He said with an angry tone. "How in five hells could this have happened? Why did it happen." Looking at Geralbald. "You say you were attacked?"

"Gerabald replied. "Yes, Commander, two of your soldiers attacked Rolland's companion."

"Companion?"

"Yes, a young girl."

"He has a young girl with him. I understood that here was two of you, nothing was said about a girl, why is that?" Gerablad was nervous. He said too much. "Just forgot to say anything, that is all."

Commander Rogier found all this to be troubling. Of course it made him suspicious. He looked at one of the officers, get a party together and find these two men, we will hear their story before punishing them." He looked at Gerabald. "Where is Rolland and this girl. I want to talk to them." That's when he saw the sacks of gold he had given to Jaedann. He asked. "He left his gold with you? Why did he leave the gold for you to watch and why is there only three bags when I gave him four?."

Gerabald answered. "He trusts me to watch over it. What else can I say?!"

"But he left three bags, why not leave all of them if he trusts you that much. He paid you something and then took the rest of the gold, did he not? Who is he…who is he really?"

"Just a sellsword with a companion, ghat is all I know."

Commander Rogier pulled out his sword and held the blade to Gerabald's throat, frightening the old man until he nearly pissed his pants "You know more than you are saying, now tell the truth."

"He used to be a Ranger of Liberus and the girl he travels with is an Elf or maybe a Half-Elf, but she said that her business is her own."

The Commander was deeply intrigued now. "An Elf or a Half-Elf, in this part of Annmar with a human. That is a bit out of the ordinary. Part of my orders did say to look out for an Elf in Liberus and either capture it or kill it." He looked at the other officer in the room. "Form a search party, I want men in every direction, until you find the scout I hired and his companion. I think they may be running away."

Gerabald asked. "There must be something dangerous about this Elf," trying to play it off like he didn't know anything. Commander Rogier. "Yes and deadly for you." He sliced the merchant's throat and then chopped off his head. He picked it up with one hand by the hair and stared at the face. "You treacherous shitt, you bring enemies of Anntheia into our camp and then lie about, you deserve nothing less than a traitor's death, but this is the best I can

do. Your friend will get something far worse and now if you
do not mind, I think, I will take my gold back."

Jaedann and Deva had made it far from the camp
through the darkness night. Both of them were exhausted
and the horse was done in from the ride. They needed the
horse to rest. Deva tried to get some sleep in the night, but
the ground was too rocky even when she tried to rest her
head on Jaedann's back. He knew that eventually men from
the camp would come after them so he tried to double back
as much as he could to make it harder to track them. Deva
finally stopped him and said. "I cannot anymore, we have
to stop. We both need rest and this armor is too
uncomfortable." Jaedann did not disagree. He tried to find
a place that was hidden well in the trees. He found a gully
that was hidden. Him and Deva could shield themselves in
along the wall of earth and no one would see them from the
path they had been riding.
    They got settled and Jaedann got some water for them
and the horse. He said as she was taking off the armor.
"Looks like your power came back, you have been trying for
weeks to make it work again. What happened this time?"
    She had a look of dismay. Deva really did not have
any answers to why she could suddenly do it again, but she
did have a theory. "I was afraid…afraid that they were
going to hurt me and I was defending myself. Maybe its fear
that causes me to do it."

"You were afraid when the Crowthornn was trying to have you."

"Yes, but I was tied up, maybe that was the difference."

Jaedann nodded. Maybe, she was right. It could be fear or the natural instinct to defend herself that triggered it, but she could not be restrained either. He said. "I am glad that you can still do it, but control of it is your biggest problem."

Deva softly smiled as she finished getting the last piece of armor off. "I want to, I do not know how to do it. There has to be someone in this land that can teach me."

"I don't know if there are anymore, but if they are out there, I will help you find them." Jaedann left his armor on and suggested that they get some sleep, at least a few hours. They were about 6 or 7 mils from the Anntheian camp. It was still cold outside. The snow may have melted, but it was still cold, so they huddled together to keep warm since they could not build a fire. Jaedann said to her. "I still don't know why you're really here in Annmar. I have to believe you are here or something good. Perhaps to make this shitt world a better place. So Deva Mirarel, I swear to all the gods that I will help you get to where you are going. I do not really believe In prophecies, but I believe you are important somehow and that I will fight for."

It was no surprise that Deva felt safe with Jaedann. What he said filled her up with emotion and tears dripped from her eyes, but they were feelings of good instead of sadness. She replied. "Thank you Jaedann. I am glad that you were the one who found me and I promise not to run off again. I will not leave your side." Jaedann tried to ignore the feelings he had when he was around her, but what she said made him feel good. It gave him a feeling that he had not had since his wife died. He held her close to keep her warm. They were able to get a few hours sleep.

Suddenly, Jaedann woke to screaming. They were from Deva. Where did she go? He was surprised to wake up alone. Jordan grabbed his sword and ran towards the direction of the screams. In a clearing outside of river's shoreline, he saw Deva and four Anntheia soldiers.   A search party had caught up with them. The soldiers were trying to get her to the ground and tie her up. Jaedann did not have his bow, only a sword. He found a rock and threw it, hitting one of the soldiers. Surprised, the leader of the group told them to go find the other one in the wood since the soldiers were looking for two. His plan worked. He was able to separate the four of them, which made it easier to take all of them. Two of them came after Jaedann. One of them swung his sword, Jaedann sliced him with the blade of his own sword right below the abdomen causing his guts to pour out. The other soldier almost got him, but Jaedan parried his swing away and because he was faster, swung his sword back towards the soldier, cutting his throat. Two down. Jaedann grabbed one of the extra swords, walked out of the woods and threw it at the soldier still sitting on his horse. The sword caught him straight in the face. Jaedann could always hit the target dead on when throwing a sword or a dagger. It was just a natural ability that he seemed to have since he first started training as a soldier.

The last soldier standing, grabbed Deva and said. "Get back or I will kill her."

Jaedann laughed it off. "I'm sure your Commander ordered you to bring us back alive. You don't do that, how severe will the punishment be...think about it. Your only way out of this is to take me alive."   The soldier cursed. He knew Jaedann was right, so he threw the dagger at Jaedann and then charged at him. Jaedann swung his sword and knocked the dagger out of the way. Then he ran towards the soldier who swung his sword going for Jaedann's head. The soldier miscalculated as Jaedann rolled underneath the swing to get behind him. He gripped his sword with both hands and swung around to cut the soldier's head clean off when the soldier turned around. Four soldiers came after them, four soldiers were now dead. Jaedann looked at Deva. "What happened, where did you go?"

Frightened, she replied. "I went to get something for us to eat and that's when the soldiers came out of nowhere. I didn't see or hear them. They just came up behind me." Deva had tears in her eyes. Jaedann walked over and held, trying to comfort her. "It's okay. You're okay. They must have been the soldiers the Commander sent after us."

"Will there be more?" She asked.

"Not in this direction. He would have sent soldiers in every direction, looking for us."

"What now?"

Jordan tried to smile and provide some kind of comforting, even beyond just holding her. "We can't stay here. We have to keep moving. Then he looked at the horse that was left behind after he killed the man on top of it. "Can you ride a horse on your own?"

Deva nodded. "I was taught how when I was a little girl. The woman who raised me said it was a useful skill, even for a girl."

Jaedann smiled. "Good, we can cover more ground if we are not on the same horse." He helped her get on the spare horse and they gathered his as well. He also gathered the extra weapons just in case they need them. Food would have to wait. The needed to get away from the area as fast they could. It was too dangerous for them. As the army moved closer to Liberus, there was no telling how many soldiers would be out looking for them when the ones he killed did not return. The Commander would know what direction they were going in by where his men had died. It was only a matter of time before he realized that truth, and Jaedann and Deva had a long way to go to finally be safe from those trying to harm her. A long way to go, indeed!

22

Arunn, Malonn, and Saida were still in Easthavenn, waiting..waiting for their next task. Arunn had sent a a raven with a message back to his father about the Rogues of Hamlinn ships being spotted in Easthavenn. They were waiting on message back from about what to do next. But something was bothering Saida. Everything seemed strange. There were signs and they were pointing to something strange. She wondered if they had been told everything. She asked Arunn that very thing. "Do you think your father would tell you everything?"

He was taken back by the question. He could not remember somebody ever questioning Illrunn Tyriall's motives before. Despite his own disagreements with his father, Arunn still considered him an honorable Elf. He looked at Saida, confounded by the question. "Why would you ask that?"

She answered. "I find all of this strange and there have been strange signs. We do not know what this is all about and if your father does, why does he not tell us everything?"

Malonn responded. "I, too admit that there have been strange things happening. Four ships from the Rogues of

Hamlinn heading in the same direction. A blood moon. An unusual snowfall. I believe there is something greater happening in the land, something that will change our world. What is it?"

Arrun wanted to trust his father. He wanted to have faith in his father as Illrunn did in him, but Elves could be secretive and they were not good at sharing their knowledge with other races. Elves did not even share their secrets with their own kind when it came to the different houses in their own kingdom. The questions that Saida and Malonn asked were not wrong. Arunn felt it too. These were strange times. But all he could say was that his father must know what he was doing. For an Elf did not do anything unless it was for a greater purpose. Saida responded to his friends. "Perhaps we should find out for ourselves what all these things mean."

Arrun replied. "And how would we do that?"

"I hear that there is a seer in Easthavenn, a Druid Elf who can predict signs and see the future."

Malonn thought it was a bit strange. "Why would there be one here. I have never heard of a seer in a port town such as this."

Arrun answered. "Perhaps this is the best place to be. Easy access for those looking to consult a seer and a port for easy travel if the seer would need to leave. I say it does not hurt to talk to one."

After some asking around to the local merchants, the three elves were given directions to this mysterious person. The seer kept to herself, staying hidden for the most part so that she was not easy to find especially from those who deemed what she did as evil and would like nothing better than to kill her. She went by the name Wynnmorla and lived on the edge of the port town in a small building that resembled more of a hut than anything else, but it was out of the way from prying eyes. The Elves knocked on her door only to discover that it was true, Wynnmorla was an elf too. She told them how she became a Druid and practiced the old faith, the faith that magic from the gods had been real and its secrets must be protected. It was this belief that made her leave Dorwinn when she was a young girl and become a Druid. To become someone who protected magical secrets and the power of the gods.

Arunn spoke first. "We are curious about signs of things that may yet come."

Wynnmorla gave Arunn a long look and then replied. "You are far from home, I can see that you are not from here and that you are a Highborn Elf. Maybe the true answers you seek are to the question of why you are really here in Easthavenn."

"My father sent us, but that is not the signs I speak of."

She paused, looking Arunn up and down, again while trying to find the truth of what he was telling. She concluded that he did not know the full reason he was here. He was an Elf left in the dark and an Elf that did not remain in the light either by their choice or someone else's wishes was not a good thing. "You want to know of the blood moon and the snowfall?"

"Yes."

"They are strange things indeed, but they can have different meanings. It is when they are together that the meaning are most powerful."

"How so?"

Wynnmorla paused for a moment. "Snow is the great purifier. It blankets the land in white, washing away her sins as it melts. The longer the thaw, the greater the sin that must be washed away. An orange moon is the sign of things to come, but a blood moon is the sign that something great is already here."

Arunn responded. "Great? You speak of something being great, but what?"

"There is a great change coming to our world, something better for all that reside in Annmar."

"Quit speaking in riddles, what has happened and why did the land need to be purified?"

Wynnmorla turned round and reached for some chicken bones and tea leaves. She put them in a bowl and poured blood from a bird that she has just killed, over everything. "Let us see if there is a clear sign of what has happened." The leaves dissolved quickly, which was a sign in itself. After looking at everything for a moment, Arunn asked. "What do the bones and blood tell you?"

She answered. "It is not what has happened, but who. Tea leaves dissolving fast means it's about a person. Somebody has returned to Annmar."

"That is the great thing that has happened?"

"Perhaps, but I only read the signs. Strangers come and go throughout Annmar, but how many can affect the fate of the future. I believe there is somebody in Annmar that will just do that. The long snowfall is a sign that the land has prepared for a big change to wash away the old and make ready for the new."

The Elves looked bewildered. Wynnmorla did talk in riddles, but seers usually did. She said. "I am a Druid, a priestess of the old faith. We are protectors of the secrets of gods and magic. If someone has returned to Annmar who will affect the world in great ways beyond kings and kingdoms then it can only mean one thing, magic, a power that has not been in the world for 100 years."

Arunn replied. "You think someone has returned with the power of magic?"

"I cannot be for sure, but there is a prophecy about one that will return. One will come from a foreign land with the power of magic."

"It seems that there is always a prophecy telling us of the future, but how many are actually true?"

Wynnmorla. "It is true that prophecies are the wishes for a future that may or may not come to be, but it only takes one coming true that will change our world. Perhaps what you seek is a stranger that will tell you if this one is true or not."

"A stranger, how will we find this person?"

Wynnmorla boiled some water in another cauldron over the burning fire in the fireplace. Then she poured the boiling water into the bowl with blood and chicken ones. The power of water, steam, and blood would create an image, an image of things that were happening far away. Sometimes these images were of the future or the past, or even what was happening at that moment. Wynnmorla looked closely. She saw it and then said. "You will not find your answers in Easthavenn. The stranger you seek is out there now, traveling north by the position of the sun within the steamed image. She travels with a Knight and a Ranger."

"She? This stranger is a girl? And she is traveling with two men."

Wynnmorla sternly looked at Arunn. "No, the Knight and the Ranger are the same man." She closed her eyes and let the blood filled steam from the mixture she created wash over her face. It allowed her to see more images. "He was once a Knight of Belmere and now is a Ranger of Liberus. Find him and you will find her, but there is another that follows them. A mysterious figure clothed in darkness and surrounded by ancient evil."

Saida asked the other two Elves. "Do you know of a former Knight from Belmere that is now a Ranger? I have

not heard of such a person." Malonn shook his head no.
Arunn replied. "I know of whom she speaks of. I am
surprised to know he is still alive, maybe it is no accident
that is in this part of the world."

Wynnmorla said. "Go, if your intentions are good,
which I suspect they are, you must find them. They will
need safe passage." The three Elves left Easthavenn and
headed south to see if they could find the girl and the
Ranger who was once a knight. They hurried for time was
running out. Evil was close behind those they sought.

The snow had finally started to melt in Liberus. For
the first time in weeks, the streets were clear and folks were
able to move around on a regular basis. Not much trade had
been done in Liberus since the huge snowfall. Hanniah and
Rathgar had been left on their own to do patrols, but the
snow had made it almost impossible. However, the snow,
also kept invaders away, it was a natural defense for the city.
Hanniah had taken over Jaedann's duties while he was
away, which included daily meetings with the Magistrate,
although there was not much discussion on the happenings
of Liberus since the snow had shut everybody in. She mostly
just checked on the Magistrate, just to make sure she was
okay.

Vorak had spent most of time reading the journals
they had found and trying to solve the mystery of the girl
who had come to Liberus. The journals were very
informative, providing a lot of detail about Deva's life. The
journals were almost a timeline for her life to help her
understand her history and the reasons why everything

happened. Vorak had been reading them over and over while making his own notes. Hanniah had also been helping him out since his assistant was found dead. Her, Rathgar, and Vorak would often have their evening meals together. Hanniah walked in with sausage and said. "Sausage and Ale, that is what I have for tonight."

Rathgar jokingly said. "Again, is that the only meat we have left in Liberus?"

Hanniah gave him a dirty look and said. "Feel free to go hunt something for us, but the game has been scarce since the snowfall so this is what we have. I am sure in a few hours after your stomach is grumbling, you will not be complaining."

Rathgar gave her a dirty look right back. "Never said I would not eat it and I never turn down ale. But we need to get more meat in Liberus"

"I will leave that to you if you can make time in between the various women you are with every night." Rathgar bashfully shook his head and nodded. Hanniah asked Vorak as she was preparing a plate and a cup of ale for him. "You have been reading those journals for weeks, have you finally learned of the girl's origins?"

Vorak took a sip of ale. "I think so. The person who wrote these is not the most descriptive, almost cryptic in some ways. But I believe the one who wrote these journals, was the woman who took care of Deva."

"Not her mother?"

"No, her mother died in childbirth. It appears that she was a young maiden and farmer's daughter. But I also think that the woman you talked to on the beach and told you to protect the girl before she died, was the one who had taken care of Deva and wrote these journals."

"Who was she?"

"A midwife of some sort." Vorak turned around from sitting at his desca and looked at Hanniah. "The journal jumps around in timeline. Not exactly sure when some stuff happened or how old Deva was when it did, but the journals do have a beginning. The first entry is the night Deva was born and the woman by the name of Searinne was there at that time. She helped deliver a baby, born of Elf and Human blood."

"Do the journals give the mother's name?"

Vorak looked back the notes he had made. "Yes, her name was Morganna."

Both Rathgar and Hanniah were extremely curious about what else Vorak had discovered. The girl had affected so much of their live these past weeks it would be good to know about her and perhaps why she was here. Rathgar asked. "How did the girl come to be born across the Elmsonn sea?"

Vorak looked at some of the notes he had made. "The journal tells of an Elf that came to live with Morganna's people in a place called Kelna. There is no mention of a name, but the Elf is referred to as Lord in the journal. This Elf fell in love and made vows with Morganna."

"This must be the girl's father."

Vorak nodded. "It appears to be true; the journals do not say where the Elf came from."

Hanniah asked. "Kelna, was the girl raised there all of her life?"

Vorak replied. "Yes, there is no mention of any other place except the port town from which they left."

"Do you know of this place?"

"No, I do not. Monks know of some places outside of Annmar, places that have been recorded in the written histories. We know there is a world out there beyond Annmar, but we know very little of it. Now I do know that are sacred places for Elves outside of Annmar. Some across the sea."

"So Kelna could be one of these places?"

Vorak collected his thoughts, trying to think back to all he knew about Elven lore and then said. "It is quite possible and would make sense if an Elf had to leave Annmar, they would most likely go to one of these sacred places."

Hanniah gave him an ominous look wondering if Vorak was still going to suggest that Deva's father was from the House of Mirarel. "You still think her father is a Lord from House Mirarel, but was sent away?"

Vorak replied. "I have no reason to think otherwise and it makes more sense. What if her father was sent away because he showed the same magical abilities as Deva and out of fear the Elves saw that one of their own kind having the power of magic was too dangerous. Perhaps they thought it would bring a war with those who fight to keep magic out of the world and so he had to be sent away in secret."

"Elves have always been secretive and deal greatly in mysticism. It's always one of the reasons they have long life. But why send somebody away even if they had magical abilities?. Would they not be more protected in the Kingdom of Dorwinn?"

"To avoid war. If you believe in the story of the 5 gods, it's a morality tale about how mankind was jealous and couldn't live with someone more powerful than them, so they destroyed those whom they saw as a threat, those who had the power of magic. Ask yourself, has mankind really changed in 100 years?"

Hanniah softly smiled. "I suppose not."

"Elves have also always been good at protecting their own way of life, I feel like all that we truly know of them are from the stories that have been recorded. Any alliances with the Elven kingdom are fragile at best so I can understand why they would have to send a Highborn Elf away to a foreign land, especially if he was part of a prophecy that some would deem too great and would do everything in their power to prevent it from coming true."

Rathgar responded." So, you do believe that she is part of this prophecy, the prophecy of the five who will bring magic into the world. You have no doubt, no other possible explanation?"

Vorak smiled, confident in his beliefs. He had never been a man to blindly believe in anything, but when he was sure of something, he believed it wholeheartedly. "Yes, I do. If nothing else because she is the surviving heir to this Elf so it would stand to reason that she would have the same magical abilities is he did. That it was passed down through his bloodline. And according to the journal he died when she was a baby. No mention of how he died, just that he died suddenly. I think something tragic happened to him."

Hannah asked. "Is this your only reason to believe the girl is part of a prophecy?"

"No" Vorak showed them a page from the journal... it was a drawing of what is referred to as a penntacle, five jagged lines attached to a center with the middle containing a stone. "The girl had a necklace of this drawing. This is an ancient symbol referring to the power of the five gods."

"I've never seen anything like that."

"I wouldn't think so. It's a symbol that has essentially been erased from history ever since the War of the Five Gods. When they died most of their symbols were erased. I have only seen this in a book among the records about the gods at Lenntis."

Rathgar asked in a serious tone. "What does it mean?"

Vorak replied. "It means power. Somebody who wears this symbol has power, the power of the five gods. It is also a symbol for the Penntacle, the five that the prophecy speaks of. This is my other reason for believing she is part of that prophecy and a danger to our world. The real question is, has she come to our world to save it or destroy it."

Hanniah asked. "Why do you say that?"

Vorak paused for a moment, trying to find the right words. "Because those with great power, the kind that can even defeat armies only have two choices for the world in which they live, dominion or defend it. I wonder which one she would even choose or even if she knows."

<h1 style="text-align:center">23</h1>

Jaedenn and Deva had been traveling for three days and they were making good time since they were both on horses and one was not having to carry two people. They did not travel in a straight line. Jaedenn zigzagged and doubled back at least once a day to make it harder to track, something he explained to Deva as she asked what he was doing. Jaedann was still wearing the Anntheian armor just in case they ran into any Barbarian clans who might have been paid by the Anntheian army. It could be the best disguise for the area they were in. Deva did not know where they were. She had no idea what kingdom they were in. She asked Jaedann as their horses were going up a hill where they were.

Jaedann replied. "We are still in Skallvenn, the Barbarian kingdom. And I am not exactly sure, but I think we are close to the Deerhornn Clan. If I am correct, they are further north close to the border."

Deva being curious asked. "Are they like the Crowthornns?"

"All Barbarian clans are for the most part the same. They look for war of some kind and have a healthy appetite for blood and gold. But from what I understand, Deerhornns are easier to deal with. They do not automatically start with cutting your throat."

Deva kind of laughed. "Well, let's hope that does not happen. I would like to see more of Annmar." Jaedann laughed at her wit. She actually had a bit of a sense of humor. He liked that about her. Deva asked another question. "How far are we from that hidden city?"

"I estimate that we have another 4 or 5 days at the most to get there, but we are also going to another place."

"What do you mean? Where?"

"There is a larger bridge built over a deep valley after the Carrann road splits off. It was built specifically for large rolling equipment such as wagons or ballistas to make for easier travel so they did not have to get the equipment over rocky terrain. Especially if the have to travel up and down steep hills. If we can take it out somehow, it will slow down the army and take them longer to get to Liberus."

"But they will still get there eventually and destroy the city."

Jaedann had a serious look when he turned and faced Deva. "True, but I need to buy time so I can figure out a plan on how to defend the town. I won't let her burn to the ground, especially from an Anntheian army. After I find a safe place for you, that is my next task."

Deva was concerned. She may not have known much about military strategy, but even she knew that a small force from Liberus could not defeat the army she saw firsthand. The people defending the city would die. It was not just a possibility, they were surely die. She was going to respond, but then they were caught by surprise. As they came down the hill, they saw a small group of Deerhornn Barbarians.

They were not on horses and Deva said. "We do not have to engage with them, we are on horses and can outrun them."

It would be the smart thing to do, but Jaedan pointed to the left side of the opposite hill. There were three Deerhornns sitting on horses. "We could not outrun them. We could get away from the ones on the ground, but not the ones on horseback. We have gold and extra steel, we may be able to buy our way out of this and avoid bloodshed."

"But you could defeat them, right?"

"Perhaps, but escaping without injury would be difficult. Come on, let us use gold and steel to get out of this." Jaedann and Deva rode to to the Barbarians who were clinging to swords and Ax as if they were ready for a fight. Jaedann was the first to speak. "Hello, are you here to rob travelers."

One of the Deerhornns spoke. He looked like one the leader of the group. "What do you got?"

"Not much…I am just a simple soldier."

The Deerhornn looked at Deva. "She looks like she is worth something."

Deva was disgusted by the comment. Jaedann replied. "She is not one of those girls, but I have some extra swords that you can have."

"We will take those and her. "

"As I said, she is not one of those girls."

The Deerhornn grabbed Deva's leg and tried to feel up here dress. She screamed no, but that did not do anything. Jaedann unsheathed his sword, swung, and chopped off the Barbarian's hand. There were four other Deerhornns and they came after Jaedann. They were able to pull him off his horse, but he swung his sword widely, hoping to hit anything. He chopped off the foot of one of them and then moved out of the way of a falling ax blade. The rest of the barbarians swung their axes, but the weight of the swing made them slow and Jaedann was able to roll away and get back on his feet. Four against one, Jaedann had faced worst odds, but not against Barbarians, some who were almost twice as big as a man. Fortunately for Jaedann, he was faster and was able to dodge their swings. Like a great swordsman, he would duck underneath and slice open their abdomens, letting their guts pour out on the ground for the problem with swinging an ax, is the swing was too wide and slow. Swordsmen could easily duck and cut a man wide open. Jaedann got three of them before the fourth one kicked him to the ground.

The three Deerhornns who were on horses came rushing to where their fallen brothers laid. They surrounded Jaedann. The Deerhornns had him, there was no denying it. Jaedann calculated what he needed to do to survive and hopefully kill the rest. He made hismove, rushed towards the one on the ground, parried the swing of the Deerhornn's ax and then swung back and sliced his throat. Jaedann was good. He was a great swordsman, but none were good enough to stop three warriors who had the high ground. One of them kicked Jaedann towards another of the horseman. Then another Deerhornn was about to swing his sword and deliver a death blow when Deva screamed out. She got everybody's attention with the scream, but it was her glowing hands and the small balls of fire cupped inside her palm that made them afraid. The Deerhornns had never seen anything like that before. Nobody has seen anything like that in 100 years.

Deva yelled at the Barbarians. "Let him go." They backed away in their horses. One of them shouted at her. "Demon!"

Jaedann grabbed the horse's reigns and said. "You may right about her. Now what is your name?"

The Deerhornn paused for a moment, wondering if he should give it. He looked at Deva who nodded at him, subtly letting him know that he should give his name. "Ballguff."

"I assume you are the new leader since I killed the last one." Jaedann grabbed about a third of the gold he had in one of the four pouches he had left. He handed it to Ballguff and said. "You will not speak of what you just saw here today. Now you have a little bit of gold and your lives. Nod to let me know you understand." All three of the Deerhornns nodded and then they rode off. Jaedann looked at Deva, smiling at what she just did. "You are learning to control it, well done."

Deva was taken back, she expected a little more gratitude. "I do not get a thank you for saving you life."

Jaedann thougtht about his response and then factitiously smiled at her. "How many times have I saved your life? About time you start paying me back. "She laughed at his wit. It felt good to laugh, she had not done much of it since running away from Liberus. It was getting dark soon, they needed to find a place to make camp for the night.

They found a place that was secluded about one mil from where they had the run in with the Deehornns. It was heavily wooded and a good place to hide, not easily seen from any open areas or paths. Jaedann built a fire and Deva actually got a rabbit for dinner. She was getting good at finding and catching game just like a Ranger. As they ate, Deva asked. "Why is this land so dangerous? Ever since I got here, people have been trying to kill me or rape me?"

Jaedann softly laughed. "Not every part of Annmar is this rough. You just entered into in roughest part of this world. As for Barbarians, they are simple creatures, blood and gold is what they want the most, followed closely of a woman to warm their bed and their favorite body part. Rape is just natural for them. But not all kingdoms are like that. Not all Barbarians are like that either. Rathgar is not."

"How do you know?"

Jaedann took another bite of his part of the rabbit. "When I first met him, he had just been banished from his clan. He was trying to drink and whore his way through Liberus and looking for any fight he could find. Like I said, Barbarians are always looking for blood. You have to understand, they are warriors, they prove themselves in battle and when they have nothing to fight, it's like death so when you get banished you look for anything you can fight. That is what he was doing until I gave him a purpose. He got a home, something to defend. He got to fight and got money for women and ale. If Barbarians have a purpose that fuels their bloodlust and money to spend on entertainment, then they do not resort to what most of us consider unnatural acts. Plus, it gives them a sense of honor."

Deva smiled. "Well, maybe not all of them are bad."

"No, not everyone is bad. Some just need a purpose, a sense of honor. Then again, somebody who comes to Annmar with power and inspires fear can cause good men to turn bad."

Deva gave Jaedann a dirty look. "You make is sound like I am evil and out to destroy your world."

"I did not say that, nor do I believe it. But all races are the same in one regard, they fear what they have never seen before or what they cannot understand. That also means you will be hunted.

Deva paused for a moment, not liking what Jaedann was saying even though it may be true. Finally, she responded. "My intentions are not evil. I am not here to cause harm. I am just here to find my own purpose."

"I understand, but what is your purpose?"

With a solemn look, Deva replied. "I honestly do not know."

"That is an honest answer. However, I am curious. You said that your destination is Ellisar, why there?"

"The woman who raised me said that is where I needed to go for answers."

"What answers?"

"For who I am and why I have these abilities."

"Do you know anything about Ellisar. I know you were keeping secrets when you first arrived as a precaution, but I would like to think you can finally trust me now after having saved your life more than once."

Deva smiled. "You are right, suppose I can. But truth be told, I do not know anything about Ellisar. The woman who took care of me did not say, perhaps she did not know either. But I think she had a map. We were supposed to meet a guide who would take us."

"Do you know the name of the guide?"

Deva thought about it for a moment. "Naesala, I think. But I do not know where the map is or how to find this guide."

Jaedann nodded and then sofly smiled. "I think I know where they are. The woman who took care of you kept journals. We found them on your ship, they were well hidden. It appears that she had been keeping a journal since you were born."

"Did you read them?"

Jaedann chuckled. "No, did not have a chance to since we were attacked by Crowthornns and then you ran off. "

She laughed at the way he responded, he was playfully scolding her. After all, she did leave abrubtly and it did cause quite a stir. Deva said. "Oh, sorry, I guess I caused a little bit of trouble there."

"It is okay, I have done far worst. The important thing is you are safe now and I will bet you anything, Vorak has read the journals trying to solve the mystery of who you really are."

Deva was a little shocked. It felt ike an invasion of privacy somehow. "I do not know what to say to that. I mean, can I really trust Vorak?"

"Normally I would say, do not trust anyone, but if you had to, then trust a Cleric and Vorak is certainly a good one. Secrets are always safe with him and he can be very helpful."

Deva smiled. "But what if there is not a Liberus to go back to?"

Jaedann paused for a moment. "I am not going to let that happen, somehow, someway, we will find a way to defender her. And even if I am wrong, there has to be more than one way to find the location of Ellisar. I promised that I would get you to where you needed to go and I do not intend to fail my oath to you"

Deva believed him. At least she wanted to, but there were no guarantees in this strange land. However, she felt comforted by Jaedann's words. He had not let her down yet and for now, she was bound to the oath he had made to keep her safe and help get her to Ellisar.

24

Illrunn sat at his great desca in his council chambers where he did most of his work. He was reading the scroll sent to him by raven. He read it more than once taking in every word as if it were the last words he would ever read. The message was from his son Arunn. It was troubling news indeed on more than one account. Illrunn had not decided what to do when his wife walked into the chambers. It was not often that she disturbed him in there and when she did it was always of great importance.

Her name was Ysilda and as she entered the room, Illrunn stood up from his desca. It was proper to do so, but it was also his way of honoring her when she entered a room. Illrunn was a bit surprised to see her and it showed in his tone. "My dear Ysilda, what can I do for you?"

She gave him a stern look, annoyed that he was keeping things from her. "I come to ask of our son. I have not seen him, nor have I heard from him. Even when he is off on an adventure, he will still send me messages by raven. Where is he?"

Illrunn sighed. "I am sorry my love. He is on an errand for me and I asked that he only send messages to me as to keep his location a secret. But I have heard from him, I received a raven today, two to be exact."

Ysilda held out her hand. "May I see the messages?"

"Of course." Ysilda read the messages. She was curious about the one saying that Arunn has seen the ships from the Rogues of Hamlinn at Easthavenn turning south, but it was the other message that surprised her. She asked. "Is this true, the words from the seer in Easthavenn."

Illrunn replied. "Yes, it is true."

"So, the rumors were true."

"Yes."

"And I was not wrong about the signs that have been seen."

Illrunn was surprised to hear her speak of signs. "How do you know these things?"

Ysilda smiled. "My dear husband, you are not the only Highborn elf who can read the signs."

"I was not trying to hide anything from you. I only wanted to be sure of things before I told you the news."

She had a curious look on face."You went to see the Myrenn Guard, I have never known you to visit the Elf Druids and seers unless you had doubts, and it's very unsual for you to have doubts."

"Yes, against my better judgement, I went to see them. As I said, I wanted to be sure."

"And did you find your answers? Did they tell you the identity of this stranger in Annmar."

Illrunn smiled. "This did, she is the girl from Kelna, the daughter of Aiassa Mirarel."

A heartbroken look washed upon Ysilda face, but she was also filled with joy. "My brother's daughter, it is really her?"

"Yes, she has come to Annmar, but I do not know for what purpose."

"We knew one day this would happen ever since we learned of her birth. Did the seers tell you where she is going?"

Illrunn reached for another message on a scroll that was on his desca and handed it to Ysilda. "They could not tell me, but I received a message from Vorak, the Cleric at Liberus. He told me about a Half-Elf who arrived near Liberus and had strange abilities. He sought my council about a prophecy, but this was after a Barbarian clan attacked the city and she ran off. We have no idea where she is."

Ysilda gave her husband another curious look. "Prophecy, are you referring to the Penntacle Prophecy, the same one spoken of about my brother?"

"Yes, the very same, but we both know that Elves are forbidden to talk about it these last eighteen years since Aiassa was sent away. It's also another reason I did not want to tell you until I knew sure."

"Or before you made your decision on whether you violate the wishes of the council and let someone with magic into Dorwinn?"

Illrunn softly laughed. "Yes, that too my love."

"I do not think we have a choice. She must come to Dorwinn."

"We both know it is not that simple."

She gave him a disapproving look, angry at what he was suggesting. "No, it is that simple. We cannot ignore that she exists any longer and now she has come home. Half-Elf or not, she is from House Mirarel, my house."

"This is your house now."

"I am of both House Mirarel and Tyriall, but this girl of my family, she is our son's cousin and do not care what the council thinks, a highborn Elf does not deserve to be shunned in Dorwinn."

Illrunn was frustrated with her insistence that the issue was really that simple for there were other issues to consider. "You really think that the council's true intent is to shun what they do not consider pure enough or enlightened enough for Elves. Like her father, she would be in danger, perhaps no from Elves themselves, but our Kingdom would be."

Ysilda grabbed her husband's hand. "I understand why it was necessary to send my brother away. I understand the danger he posed to our way of life. As much as I might have disagreed with it, I did not go against your vote. I stood by you, but this is different. This is about a child without home and despite the dangers she is of House Mirarel. She should be welcomed here and protected by the Elves. Who better in Annmar to protect someone of magic ability from those who would only destroy it."

Illrunn smiled. "I will not disagree with you on the last part. And I am not afraid of what the council will say or even being an outcast."

"Then what are you afraifd of?"

"War. Whether we like it or not, somebody like her will bring war to our Kingdom. The last time people with magic walked the land of Annmar, the great war happened and the gods were destroyed. That period of enlightenment was over and then darkness came. What happened to our land after the next war when we might have been able to prevent it!"

Ysilda put her hand on Illrunn's face. "You are right to fear those things. Wars will come and go as long as there are those who always want more at the expense of others. But do we not have a duty to protect Elves, even Half-Elves. She is one of us."

Illrunn nodded. "I know. I just wanted to express my concerns before I did what I am about to do." He handed

Ysilda the message he was preparing for the raven he was sending to his son. She read it and was surprised. "You are asking Arunn to find her."

"Yes, but knowing our son and his companions, they are already looking for her after what they learned from the seer in Easthavenn. I am asking him to bring the girl here."

Ysilda kissed him. "You have always been an honorable Elf, it is one of the reasons I fell in love with you. I knew you would do the right thing." He smiled and kissed her back. It was his way of telling her that he had always trusted her and found her council welcoming especially when she was right. A man could have no greater respect for his wife as Illrunn did for Ysilda. It was the same with her towards him and that is what made them perfect for each other considering most Highborn Elven marriages were arranged marriages. The love they had for each other exceeded the borders of Annmar.

It had been another couple of day, but finally Jaedann and Deva arrived at the Bridge. And more important, they were days ahead of the Anntheian army. Deva looked looked at the gully and commented. "Wow, that is deep." Jaedann softly laughed. "Yes, too deep. You fall down or tumble down there then you are dead. Good place for a bridge, do you think?"

Deva laughed. "It is a good for a bridge. How do we destroy it?"

"That is the hard part. The bridge is made of Oak from the Emberwild. The strongest trees in Annmar, they are impenetrable."

"What is the Emberwild?"

"It is the Faerûn Kingdom."

"Faerûn?"

Jaedann smiled again. "Fairies or woodland folk who have wings. The wood in the Emberwild is precious to them, but to sell some of it.   They do not sell much of it and when they do it is at a great profit. Their kingdom has never been destroyed because their trees are soo strong and help to withstand any invasion."

"If the wood is that strong, then there is no way to destroy it, right?"

He smiled confidently. "Well, it is nearly Impenetrable. There is one way to destroy the wood. You do it from the inside out."

"I do not understand."

"If we can cut some grooves in the wood, then lace them with something that will burn, the wood will burn from the inside out and even if does not burn straight through the wood, it will make it weak so that when something heavy moves across it..."

Deva understood what he was saying and finished his sentence. "The weight from something heavy will make the wooden bridge break and what was on it fall into the gully."

"Yes, and hopefully we can destroy some of the ballistas in the process."

"How are you going to cut the wood? It looks pretty thick?"

Jaedann laughed. "Good thing I took an ax from one of the Deerhornns. Should be sharp enough to cut some grooves, but the problem is finding something that easily burns, which we can put in the grooves. Usually, the land is filled with oils that will burn. Let see if we can find some." They searched for about an hour, even traveling as little bit down in the gully, but they finally found a part of the earth that had some kind of mineral oil. It would burn just fine. Deva stared gathering the mineral oil in the extra wine pouches they had acquired on their journey. Jaedann went to work on the bridge, chopping grooves in every other plank and even in the support beams. The wood was very thick and would take a dozen axes and strong men to chop through one the support beams.

Deva brought the pouches and together they soaked the grooves with the oil from the ground. As Jaedann was finishing, he felt a frightful gush of wind blow through his hair. He looked and there it was standing on the bridge in front of him. It was darkness in Elf form, pale with almost white skin, and had dark blood red eyes that seem to stare into his soul. Jaedann had never seen something like this before. It made him nervous and he never got nervous. It gripped Deva with fear. She could feel this thing's dark energy and knew instantly that it had some kind of dark power. Jaedann wrapped his fingers around the grip on his sword.

Ready to draw, he said to the evil standing before him. "Who are you and what do you want?"

Those blood red eyes pierced the serious gaze that both Deva and Jaedann were giving it and then replied. "I only want the girl, if you leave, you will not be harmed."

Jaedann laughed at the thought. "You cannot have the girl, come close and you will leave this bridge without your head."

The thing smirked and replied in kind. "Jaedann Lionnshade, do not be so bold, you cannot win this fight."

"Ah, you know my name, but I do not have the pleasure of yours."

"My name is not important. What I am should make you afraid. For I am a Khronne."

Deva had never heard the name, she did not know what that was. Jaedann had only heard that name in stories, but in all his journeys, had never come across one. He was not even sure that they still existed anymore, but he sternly replied. "I do not care what you are, you still cannot have the girl." The Khronne walked closer and Jaedann moved his hand to the small Anntheian dagger attached to his belt. He threw it at the Khronne, but it was too fast and easily knocked it out of the way. Jaedann drew his sword from the hilt and charged the Khronne. Normally Jaedann would go low and try to cut his enemy in the abdomen while they swung high. The Khronne was fast and unbelievably strong. It saw what Jaedann was doing and knocked him backwards a few feet, even knocking the breath out of the Ranger and causing him to lose his sword. Deva was shocked, who in Annmar really had that kind of strength!

Jaedann got up slowly and gathered his sword. He said. "You think you are the first to knock me down, I am not that easily defeated."

The thing smiled. "And you have never faced someone like me. Lay down your sword and your life will be saved.

Jaedann was mad and charged the Khronne again. It blew somekind of smoke substance from his hand, covering everything around so Jaedann could not see it. He was blind and then all of sudden, he felt a push. It was hard and felt like it was breaking all of his ribs. Jaedann was thrown back about 20 feet, falling hard near Deva. He even fell on part of his sword, slicing open part of his arm. Deva closed her eyes, took a deep breath and spoke something in Elven. Jaedann did not hear what she said, but it seemed calming. Then she clinched her fists and they started to glow. Deva could not control her abilities before, sometimes she could, but not all the time. This time, she focused, thought of what she wanted to do. As she opened her hands, balls of fire floated above her palms. She made fire and it made the Khronne slightly afraid. It had never see something like this before. Not knowing what to do, it took a step back. Deva threw the balls of fire towards the Khronne. It dodged the fire, but Deva made more and kept throwng fire at it. She did not hit the Khronne, but the oil started to burn causing the bridge to catch fire. Her fireballs actually made the bridge burn faster. The Khronne tried to move out of the way and run towards the Deva.

But to no avail, the Khronne did not make it before the bridge gave out and wooden planks fell. The Khronne fell into the gully. Deva went to edge so she could see if the Khronne was dead. She could not see anything, but then she rushed to Jaedann's side who was slow to get up. He wondered if he broke something from all the pain he felt. But he was well enough to say. "I don't know what you did or said to control your abilities, but keep doing it. It seems to work and we need those abilities to get out of here in one piece."

Deva smiled. It was his offand way of paying her a compliment. She asked. "What was that thing?"

Jaedann stood up and looked at his cut. "A Khronne, but then again, it cannot be, they do not exist anymore. They are powerful creatures who have a darker nature, if you know what I mean."

"Whatever it is, it should be dead."

They both got back to their horses. Jaedann replied. "Whether it is dead or not, we should not stay around here to find out" Deva did not argue. They should have stayed and rested since it was almost nighttime, but it was really too dangerous for them now. They would need to ride through the night to get to where they were going way ahead of any other dangers. Jaedann suspected, there was plenty more to come. After all, it was in his nature to be suspicious. He could not say for sure if it was the Belmerien in him or the soldier. Probably, both.

25

The King was angry, more angry than usual. King Lancelynn knocked off the items on his desca when he read the message he just received. A raven has been sent from Commander Rogier. The guards outside his council chambers were startled and rushed to help their troubled king. They were about to go in when Emericc Tabenn walked up. He told the guards to stand down, he would handle the angry king. Emericc walked in and asked what was wrong. King Lancelynn stared him down like he was about to run his word through the spymaster. The King said. "The two legions marching to Liberus have been stalled. He was taking the Soldier's Bridge so they could move the Ballistas and they found it burned down. Now he will have to double back and come in through the south, which will take one to two months if we're lucky."

Emericc was shocked. "The Soldier's Bridge, how did it get burned down. It's made of oak from The Emberwild, it's virtually invincible and cannot be destroyed."

"I do not know, but it is gone. It will take too long to get to Liberus, enough time for them to put an army together to defend the town."

"But how would they know we are coming?"

The King handed Emericc the message. "Commander Rogier reported that there was a Ranger in his camp that came in with a merchant. He had worked in Liberus and the Commander was going to hire him a scout. The Ranger killed two of his men and then escaped alongside a mysterious Elven girl. I think he was a spy or somebody helping this Elf escape Liberus."

"You think the Elven girl is who we are looking for?"

The King thought about it for a moment. "It stands to reason if she is traveling with a Ranger who knows Liberus, perhaps he is really from there. Perhaps he found the one we are looking for and is helping her to escape."

"Then she is not in Liberus anymore."

"It is a possibility, but if we cannot be sure then we cannot take any chances. Liberus has to burn and every one of its inhabitants has to die."

Emericc had a serious look for the King. "I understand that logic, but we should also hunt these two down. It is time to use my assassins. Like you said, we cannot take any chances."

The King nodded. He did not like the idea, but he also understood the necessity for assassins. He preferred straight up fights, battles where you are face to face with your enemy. But this was a secret war only being fought by Anntheia right now. He replied to the spymaster. "Okay, send someone."

"Good, I already have."

King Lancelynn was stunned and perhaps even more angry. "You did what?"

"I already have an assassin trying to find the Ranger and the girl."

"When did this happen?"

Emericc paused, trying to figure out how to explain how he essentially defied a king's command. Although, he seemed to always be doing it by setting things in motion that the king did not know about and would not approve. For that was the job as a spymaster. "I sent a Khronne to accompany Sannson Yondavr. She is an assassin and one of Azrigronn's. I thought it prudent to have one on this mission just in case."

The King was still surprised, but also curious. Even he had to admit it was a smart move. He asked. "Have you heard from this Khronne?"

"Yes, it found them and watched as they stayed in an old Barbarian hut during the snowfall. Then it followed them to Commander Rogier's camp."

"You knew this Ranger and the girl were there?"

Emericc nodded. "Yes,but did not know who they were. I had my suspicions and the Khronne started following them after Sannson was captured and they left Liberus. I hope to get a message from here updating me on where they are."

"Why did you not say anything?"

Emericc smiled. "I am a spymaster, my currency is information. I only tell the King that information when he needs to know so he can focus on the bigger problem and not the inconsequential details."

King Lancelynn smirked at the thought. "I cannot say I like that idea."

"I know, but you have bigger issues to worry about. It's my job to worry about the small details and put into action the things a king does not have time for. Now I am going to send another assassin out to make sure the job gets done and to make sure no one knows that it was done by Anntheia."

The king nodded. He knew that it was pointless to argue. Emericc was making the smart play. There was only one thing to say. "I want them found, both of them. And I want you to bring me their heads." Emericc nodded and said that it would be done, then he walked out and left the King to scheming thoughts.

The rest of their journey took almost a week, Jaedann and Deva made it to their final destination. As they came over the last hill that separated the mountain ranges that connected the Kingdom of Skallvenn and the middle of Annmar, also known as the the neutral lands, the travelers came to the edge of a forest. It was a forest so thick with huge trees that seemed to touch the edge of the blue sky that one could hardly see into the forest. Deva had never seen anything like it before. The look on her face was of pure wonder, which led to Jaedann smiling at her and saying. "Welcome to Foxxwood Forest or simply known as the Foxxwood.

Deva commented. It's huge and looks as if there is no opening.

"It is the thickest forest in Annmar, it will hide anything that goes through it and it is not hard to get lost in The Foxxwood. That is why it is a great place for a hidden city in the trees."

"Is there even a road inside?"

Jaedann laughed. "Yes, but it is more like a small path. You just have to know where to look. The forest is designed to keep out large armies and their weapons. If you think it is hard to navigate the forest, there is also a river that runs right down the middle with no bridges and only certain parts of it that are easy to cross on foot or horseback. The forest is a perfect defense for anybody trying to invade the northwest region of Annmar"

"What is on the other side of the forest?"

"The great Elven Kingdom of Dorwinn and the Faerûn Kingdom known as the The Emberwild. To the southwest is the Halfling Kingdom of Yorynn. Nobody who has ever tried to invade these kingdoms from the south has ever been successful. "

Deva stared at the forest and marveled at its beauty as well as the enormity of it. She asked. "How do we find the entrance to this hidden city?"

"There are four entrances. Two on either side of the Valstonn River. The city itself spreads out in the trees over the river.   There should be an entrance to the south not too far from where we enter the forest. It's hidden, but there are signs, which are not too hard to find." Jaedann and Deva rode to the edge of The Foxxwood. The Ranger, good at finding things, even the smallest things of great important in nature, found a narrow path. It was so narrow that horses could not travel side by side so he went first. And then he found the signs to the entrance of the hidden city with ease. They were Elven, Faerûn, and Gnome symbols They were symbols of the three races that occupied Cohnnwood, the hidden city in the forest. After about three mils into the forest, Jaedann found the southern entrance. Deva was confused for she could not see it. However, she did see the Elven symbol on the tree, the symbol for the Elven tree of life.

Deva looked up and could not see a city in the trees. The branches were too thick, she could hear sounds though. Was is people talking, was it music, she could not tell as the sounds seemed muffled. She asked. "How do we get up there?"

Jaedann unwrapped the thick rope that circled the big tree. It was covered in ivy to disguise the fact that it was a rope. "We pull this and someone from the city will come down on a lift and then bring us up."

She looked around, the place did not appear to have any defenses. "How do they defend the place. I do not see any guards or weapons."

"Believe me, they are up there watching us."
"Really?"

Jaedann took a bow and attached an arrow. He shot it into the trees towards the edge of the city and then motioned for Deva and the horses to move out the way. An arrow, that was not his came flying down from the tree, hitting the ground near them and startling Deva. Then a second arrow followed right behind. Jaedann said. "See, they know exactly where we are."

Frightened, Deva replied. "They could have killed us."

"That was just warning shots, but they can easily kill us. The archers in this place are exceptionally skilled."

Deva nodded. "I see, I guess we should not make them angry."

Jaedann laughed. "No, let's not do that. Now, humans are not allowed up there so I am going to disguise myself in a cloak. You have to do the talking. You have to take the lead here."

"What do I say?"

"Just tell them that you are being hunted and need refuge. That is all you should have to say. And when describing me, just say I am an Elf who was deformed in battle, that is why I wear the cloak. They should buy that explanation because Elves go to great lengths to hide their deformities." Jaedann handed her what they had left in Anntheian gold. "Here, you will need this. You will have to pay a couple of gold pieces for us to enter the city."

Deva was a bit nervous. "Anything else?"

"Do not be afraid. You are strong and confident, remember that. You can do this." Deva nodded in agreement. She did not know if she truly believed his words, but she felt better when he said them. He had a way of comforting her. Jaedann pulled the ivy rope a few times and slowly a wooden lift covered in foliage, mostly ivy immerged from the thick branches. There were two Elves, fierce looking and far from elegance that Deva had been led to believe all Elves possessed. They also had weapons that Deva had never seen before. They were called crossbows. The guards pointed them at Deva and asked her why she wanted entry into the city. She told them exactly what Jaedann had told her to say. The guards did not even ask her who was hunting her. The fact that an Elf or Half-Elf was being hunted was good enough for them. It actually cost her a total of six gold pieces for both her and Jaedann. They were told to leave the horses, somebody would gather them and take them to the Stables that were hidden in the forest for horses were not allowed in Cohnnwood.

As they were getting on the lift, Jaedann received a funny look by one of the Elven guards. He asked. "How are you deformed? You don't look bad to me." Jaedann replied. "Part of my face is burned. It is too ugly even to roguish Elves such as yourselves. It would make you sick to your stomach so you don't want to see it." The guard was slightly curious, but also did not like the look of disgusting things so he left it alone and said no more about the matter. After a few minutes, they reached the edge of the city. It was 120 meters in the air. It was a long way up to be sure, but the fall from such a height would definitely kill someone. Cohnnwood was well camouflaged. Jaedann and Deva did not even see the lights until they were about 50 meters up. There was a bottom layer of branches that kept everything well hidden due to how thick they were. If you were to look up from the ground, you would never know that there was a city in the trees.

Finally, they reached the top. Both of them were amazed at how the city was constructed. Well lit and full of life just like any other city, it had anything one could ask for. Pathways or roads were constructed much like a bridge with the heavy oak from the Foxxwood, the same strong wood found in the Emberwild, and built all around the large trees which were used as braces. It looked as if the trees grew right in the middle of the city and it was hard to imagine that the city was 100 meters off the ground. Buildings were constructed on the heavy wooded paths in Cohnnwood, there were no huts, but actual wood buildings, some even two stories. The wood was so strong that it was like building a city on the ground itself. Deva smiled when she saw it since it was filled with amusements that she had only dreamed of and the best part, the place was filled with, Elves, Half-Elves, Halflings, and Faerûn, also known as Fairies in the common tongue. She had never seen a Fairy before with their large luminescent wings. Deva asked when they got to the top. "What now?"

One of the guards replied. "You will have to register. The high council knows of everybody that stays in Cohnnwood. If you get a room, you can register at the Inn and your names will be given to the High Council along with where you are staying."

"Where is the best place to go?"

"If you are looking for a place that usually has some rooms, check out the Applewhisk Tavern. Peonni Plumgloss will set you up. She owns the place."

Deva thanked the guard then she and Jaedann made their way to the Applewhisk Tavern. They went by numerous merchants and places to eat and drink. The Applewhisk was to the east of the city, near the edge. It was two stories and did not look as if it had a whole lot of people. That was good for Deva and Jaedann, he thought. They did not need to be around people as they were trying to hide. When they walked in, Peonni Plumgloss was behind the bar serving ale to some Elves. She was Fae. She was tall with dark, glistening eyes, and the most beautiful porcelain skin that Deva had ever seen. Even Jaedann was amazed at her beauty. Deva took the lead and went up to the bar to get registered. Peonni was naturally suspicious of everyone who came into her tavern until she got to know them and she remembered every face who passed through. The Fae had exceptional memory for they remembered every detail as if they had lived it themselves. She looked at the two strangers and said. "What is your business at the Applewhisk?"

Deva tried to smile. "We need a room."

"Rooms we have. For how long?"

Deva looked at Jaedann, she did not know the answer
to that, but Jaedann showed her three fingers. Deva
understood. "At least three nights."

Peonni nodded. "4 silver pieces or 2 gold pieces for
each night." Deva counted out 6 pieces of gold from the bag
that Jaedann gave her. Peonni asked as she was handed the
gold. "What is your business here?" Deva, remembering
what Jaedann has said to the traveling merchant, weeks
before, replied. "Our business is our own."

Peonni smiled. "It is wise of you to keep your
business to yourself. You should know who to trust before
giving details out like that." She got out the registration
book and asked Deva to put her and her companion's name
down. Deva was smart enough to give fake names. She put
Serna down for herself and put Lorgoras down for Jaedann.
It sounded like an Elf name at least. After the names were
written down, Peonni showed the two travelers to their
room on the second floor. It was nice and even had a
window, but Deva never thought to ask about the bed. There
was only one. She liked Jaedann, but not enough to sleep in
the same bed with him. She was going to say something to
Peonni about it, but Jaedann stopped her by shaking his
head no. When the owner left, Jaedann simply said that he
would sleep on the floor, trying to make Deva feel as
comfortable as possible. He knew being in the same bed
could be a bit awkward. Deva then asked. "Now what"

Jaedann smiled and said. "Now we get cleaned up,
separately of course, and we wait."

26

Jaedann and Deva had been in the hidden city for the better part of a day now. They kept pretty much to themselves, only coming out of the room to get meals at the bar. Peonni Plumgloss did not pry when she saw Deva, although she was suspicious of the two travelers. Not knowing what to make of them, they seemed an odd pair, and she had never seen Jaedann's face either, which would have caused even more suspicion. Peonni did not know he was a human, but she concluded that the two must have been lovers the way they never left the room and socialized in the tavern. Although, it was not true. Deva mostly slept in the bed for it had been ages ago since she slept in one or that is the way is seemed. Jaedann just let her sleep. He wanted to explore Cohnnwood since he had never been or would even be let into the city. This is where being a Ranger came in handy for he could move virtually unseen even in a city like this, even being a human. Most folks never gave a second thought to someone hidden under a cloak since everybody was seemed to be hiding from something in Cohnnwood.

Jaedann left the room and quietly moved through the tavern without being seen. Peonni noticed him, but with her heightened senses noticed everything around her. Fairies were like that. She did not say anything and did not try to make conversation. Jaedann just wandered into the streets. It was mostly filled with street merchants and taverns. There was even a brothel, where one could spend some time with an Elf or Fairy. In parts of Annmar that would be considered a luxury and one would have to pay top dollar for something like that. Jaedann could buy jewels from the Elven Kingdom of Dorwinn or from the Emberwild. He could buy musical instruments from Yorynn, which was known to make the finest mandolins, flutes, drums, and harps in all of Annmar. They also made this instrument called a guitar, which was like a mandolin, but twice as big and made a deeper harmonix sound. The two instruments sounded great when put together especially with a drum. Jaedann could also buy weapons. There was no shortage of Elven steel, which was the strongest in the land. Belmere blacksmiths used the same techniques, but the secrets in the Elven steel were known only to the Elves. Where they got minerals to make steel was still a big mystery in Annmar. Some think it was from across the sea. Elven swords were very valuable in Annmar.

Jaedann stopped by one of the merchant shops. He did not need a sword for he still carried his Belmerien Knight's sword. He was allowed to take that when he was banished. But Jaedann fancied a smallsword, commonly known as a parrying dagger. To have one made of Elven steel would be great. He found one he liked from the Halfling shopkeeper. It only cost him 10 gold pieces and they still had plenty left. As he was making his purchase, Jaedann slightly peered over his left shoulder. He felt like he was being watched. There was a mysterious figure that seemed to be following him. They were wearing a cloak too. Jaedann could not tell what race he or she was, probably Elf or Half-Elf. He also did not know if they were some kind of guard of Cohnnwood just checking him out or something worse. Jaedann did nothing to bring attention to himself, he would just see how far this mystery figure would follow. Jaedann circled back around and made it back to the Applewhisk tavern with the mysterious figure still following him, but that is as far as it went. Once Jaedann went back inside the tavern, the mysterious figure disappeared.

Deva was awake and a bit frantic when she could not find Jaedann. When he walked inside the room, she threw is arms around him, thinking that he had just left her now that they had arrived at the hidden city in the trees. Jaedann calmed her down and said. "I am not going anywhere. I would not leave without saying goodbye."

She smiled. "You will have to excuse me, I was afraid that you would just leave or even worse, something happened to you."

"No, just did a bit of exploring. I have never seen this place. It is quite impressive."

"Well, do not go anywhere without telling me. I cannot lose you too."

Jaedann smiled back at her, comforting her at the same time and letting her know that he would always make sure she was safe…always. "Let's have our dinner in the courtyard next to the fire."

"Okay, that sounds great."

Jaedann took off his heavy cloak. "It is starting to get cold, so wear my heavy cloak. I will wear the lighter one." Deva nodded and Jaedann put the heavy cloak on her including the hood to help shield her face. His other cloak, which was his backup cloak and he kept with his bedroll would be just fine. He could still stay hidden. Good Rangers usually had two cloaks for such occasions. Both of them got stew and some wine, and then sat in the courtyard. Nobody was out there so they had the small area to themselves. Deva commented that it was beautiful out on the courtyard among the large oak trees of The Foxxwood.   Both of them quickly finished their cup of wine and so, Jaedann left to get some more, leaving Deva alone, but that was actually the plan. There were two entrances into the courtyard. Jaedann snuck through the back entrance as not to be seen. Deva was sitting next to the fire and had her back to the main entrance into the courtyard when all of a sudden somebody came up behind her, holding a blade to her throat, and said. "It's not good to keep your guard down, Ranger."

Deva almost screamed, but the blade at her throat kept her from doing that, but the mysterious stranger could feel her trembling. He was about to say something else when he suddenly the blade of an Elven smallsword touched his throat and he could feel someone behind him. It was Jaedann and he courteously replied. "That is good advice Elf, glad I did not do such a thing, but you on the other hand should not be following someone who could easily kill you. I am assuming, it was you following me earlier." The Elf did not reply, but he was hardly alone too. One of his friends came up behind Jaedann and put her dagger underneath Jaedann's manhood, saying. "You should heed your own advice, Ranger. And I was the one following you."

Jaedann started to laugh. The Elves were clearly warriors and matched in his skill to sneak upon unsuspecting strangers. He said. "Well then, we have ourselves a bit of a standoff. Might I suggest we have a cup of wine or ale, sit around the fire, and work out our differences or we can just kill each other now. I guarantee if die here today, I will take both of you with me."

The Elf who had a blade to Deva's throat said. "I have no doubt you could Jaedann of House Barrenn or is it Lionnshade now?"

Jaedann was surprised. No one called him that anymore. It was a name he had not used in a long time, a name he could never use again. "You know me and you knew me years before I became a Ranger."

The Elf puts his blade down from Deva's throat, turned around, smiled and replied. "And you know me, knight.

Jaedann was shocked, this time in a good way. He did the know the Elf. He had fought side by side with the Elf more than once, long ago. He said, "I do know you, Arunn Tyriall and it has been a very long time."

"Too long, my friend. I have been looking for you and had a feeling I would find you in this hidden city. We have much to discuss." He looked at Saida. "It is okay, put the blade down. We are not here to kill him, especially after I clearly fell for his trap." Arunn looked back at Jaedann and said. "You have not lost your skill at misdirection and laying traps for those who are after you."

He smiled at his old friend and the compliment he received. "It made me a good Knight, but even better Ranger. Now, what are you doing here?"

"Looking for you and a mysterious stranger who is being hunted and might need our help." Arunn looked at Deva. "I suppose you are that stranger, my Elven friends and I are at your service." Deva was confused. She was not quite afraid, but more or less confused because she did not know who these Elves were. She did not know if she could trust her own kind. She responded. "Thank You, but how do you know I am that stranger you speak of."

Arunn confidently replied to the girl, showing her that he knew more than she realized. "You are here in a hidden city within the trees and with a Ranger who is not supposed to be here. It is an odd pairing unless there is a purpose to your journey such as being a stranger in Annmar and trying to find the sacred place for magic users you are supposed to go to."

The part about magic stunned Deva. How could he possibly know about her and what she could do. Or was he just guessing. No, he had to know. Elves were very keen individuals. Jaedann replied to Arunn. "You say you are here to help, but how did you know where we would be?"

"We knew you were traveling north and I suspected that you if you were traveling with an Elf or Half-Elf, you would try to find Cohnnwood. It was the logical thing to do."

Jaedann nodded. "Yes, it was." Arunn introduced his two companions. They all shook hands, even Deva who was still a little weary of those she had not met, but she trusted Jaedann, if he trusted these Elves then she would too. Jaedann asked as they all sat down around the fire and Malonn kept his eyes on the two entrances to the courtyard to make sure they would not be disturbed. "How did you know about us?"

Arunn softly smiled. "My father, the Lord of House Tyriall. He sent me on a mission, but also spoke of a mysterious stranger who had returned to Annmar. Someone with magical abilities who could very well fulfill a prophecy. "Deva was stunned to hear such a thing, did the Elves know about her? Arunn continued. "My father did not elaborate on those details. But there have also been signs, the orange moon, then a blood moon, an unusually heavy snowfall in this part of the world, and Barbarians raiding close to coast, traveling further than they usually do as if they are looking for something."

Jaedann was a bit spooked, not because there were signs, but that others might have seen them and come looking for the girl when there were already too many enemies looking for her. "I agree that the signs have been odd, maybe even disturbing, but for me that is not why I help the girl."

"We also saw a Druid in Easthavenn who is a seer. She saw you traveling north together."

Jaedann was taken back, those with the gift of foresight could be a dangerous thing, especially with the kind of folks who chose to believe in what they saw. Jaedann was more practical, he only believed in what he could see in front, like an enemy he was about to kill. He said. "That would explain your knowledge of such things. But I would urge caution with what is seen from this foresight when it comes, not all is what it seems."

"I think the important question is, who is she?" Arunn was looking at Deva when he said that. It was chilling for Deva and she did not know how to respond. Jaedann looked at her and said. "It's up to you if you want to tell them."

Deva replied. "Do you trust them with this?"

"I trust Arunn and I do not trust most folks, but it is whether you should trust them or not."

Deva looked at the Elves and then looked back at Jaedann. She was hesitant to say anything. To be honest, she only trusted one person in Annimar, maybe two, but she did respond. "If you trust them, then I will too." Giving

Arunn a confidant but serious look, Deva said. "My name is Deva Mirarel. I was born in a place across the sea called Kelna."

All three Elves were shocked. Of course, they recognized the name, House Mirarel, one of the oldest and most powerful houses in the Elven Kingdom of Dorwinn. Arunn's mother was from House Mirarel, he wondered if his parents knew her father. The Elves even recognized the city name of Kelna, an ancient and secret place for Elves. Nobody said a thing for a moment, but then Arunn asked. "Who is your father?"

Deva sighed, for she was a bit heartbroken with her answer. "I do not know."

Saida finally asked. "Do you have magical abilities?"

Deva replied to her. "I do not know what you would call it, but I can do some things that are not natural." That is all she said for she did not want to show them as to arouse suspicions in Cohnnwood.

Arunn asked Jaedann. "Is this true?"

Deva was annoyed by his question, and asked Arunn. "You do not believe me, do you?"

"I do not know you well enough, but I trust him."

Jaedann responded. "It is true. During the Crowthornn attack on Liberus, fire shot from her hands and she killed three of them."

Arunn replied. Well then, it appears that you are the one we are looking for."

Deva said. "I do not know about any prophecy. I am just trying to find who I really am and why I have these abilities."

Arunn looked at both Jaedann and Deva, curious about what would happen next. He asked them. "What is your plan?"

Jaedann replied. "What do you mean?"

"You both ended up here together. Jaedann you are clearly helping her, what is your plan beyond this night."

Jaedann tried to think of a good answer. He had none. "Truthfully, I only wanted to get her out of Liberus and someplace safe." Jaedann told the Elves what had happened with the council at Liberus and then he continued. "I did not have a plan beyond getting Deva to Cohnnwood." Deva was going to say something, but they were interrupted by Peonni Plumgloss. She came into the courtyard to warn Jaedann and Deva. "It is not my business, we all keep to ourselves here, but those in charge of this place are interested in you because you paid with Anntheia gold. I will not turn you over as all who eat, drink, and stay at my place are protected, but you should not stay here anymore. It is not safe. I will not be able to stop them if they search my place." She looked at Jaedann. "And you, Ranger, you are not even supposed to be here being human and all."

Jaedann pulled back his hood. "How did you know?"

"You forget that Fae have heightened senses and I also saw your brown eyes, you cannot be an Elf."

He slid his hand over the pommel of his sword and then firmly wrapped his fingers on the grip. "Are you going to turn me in?"

"Keep your sword sheathed, Ranger. Your business is your own and I figure if a Ranger is escorting an Elf to a safe-haven, it must be important and no danger to us. You are okay with me until you are not, If you get my meaning."

Jaedann nodded. He understood perfectly. "Thank You."

"Now you must get out of here, quickly."

Deva became afraid again. Was there no place she could hide? Deva thanked her. The Elves knew of a place they could go that would be well hidden within Cohnnwood. They all left separately, but Arunn helped escort Jaedann and Deva out of the Applewhisk Tavern without being seen. It was easy for Elves to blend in a place like this unlike other parts of Annmar for it made it much easier to escape the danger that was waiting for them.

27

It was evident those in charge were looking for someone…someone who was not supposed to be in Cohnnwodd. The Elves along with Jaedann and Deva made it to a safe location in Cohnnwood since the two of them were the ones being hunted. Each major house in Dorwinn had a livng space in Cohnnwood. It was their safe haven within this hidden city. These living spaces were used as a place to hide out if necessary, a place where they could stay if they were traveling in secret and there was no better place for that kind of secrecy than in Cohnnwood, a place left to survive on their own and hide from the rest of the world. Arunn took them to the living space for House Tyriall. It was the safest place for them because even the authorities in Cohnnwodd would not ask questions if a Lord from House Tyriall and his guests were staying there for a while. Arunn, Saida, and Malonn had already been staying there a day or so.

The living space had a balcony and while Deva talked with Saida and Malonn, learning about Dorwinn, Arunn and Jaedann had a chance to talk on the balcony. Arunn asked him. "How did you find her?"

"Me and the other Rangers of Liberus while on patrol, came upon their ship as it was being raided by Crowthornns. She was the only left alive. The Crowthornns were paid in gold from someone hired by the King of Anntheia. It was sheer luck we found her."

Arunn thought for a moment. "How did the King know she had come to Annmar."

"That is what I have been trying to figure out. I do not remember any signs that a magic user was coming to Annmar… the signs you spoke of earlier did not happen until she arrived."

"Perhaps a seer saw this happening, but I have not known the King and the royal houses Anntheia to believe in that stuff. Seerers are not usually found in Anntheia unless it is of a dark nature."

"However, they knew and whether she is part of this prophecy or not, the girl is here now, but after I get her some place safe, I have bigger problems. Two Anntheian Legions are marching to Liberus with the intent of burning it to the ground and killing everybody there. I have to figure out how to stop it."

Arunn put his hand on his friend's shoulder, trying to reassure him. "You cannot do that alone. You will need help. But there is something else that you need to worry about. We were sent to Easthavenn to see which direction ships from the Rogues of Hamlinn would turn. Four ships turned southwest."

"Four ships, together? The Rogues of Hamlinn do not travel with that many ships all at once. Pirate strategy is to sail one by one as to not have the entire fleet captured or sunk in battle."

"What reason would they have to send four ships together, maybe they are smuggling something large that requires four ships?"

Jaedann thought for a moment. "No, they would pick-up separately and sail separately so they would not lose the entire cargo. Four ships sailing together, going to the same location, means only one thing, blockade."

Arunn was stunned at the notion, he replied. "What would be of such great importance to the southwest that would be worth blockading."

Jaedann sighed. "Liberus. Anntheia is making sure no one escapes by ship, they are going to sink it and everything, and make Liberus a graveyard." Jaedann looked out over the balcony. "How do I stop it with a few Rangers and archers."

"You get help."

"It's not like I can ask for help from anybody in Belmere. I'm banished, remember."

"No, seek help from the Elves. Seek help from my father. Come to Dorwinn with me."

Jaedann looked over at Deva. "She would be safer in Dorwinn, but I do not see the Elves helping a trading town not governed by any kingdom or fighting Anntheia that could potentially start a war."

Arunn smiled. "You may be surprised. But you will not know for sure unless you ask for his help. And the girl may find out who she really is in Dorwinn."

"It is not a bad idea, but I need to send a raven to Vorak, the Cleric in Liberus. They need to know what's coming."

"We can send one out now if you like."

"Yes, let's do that. One more thing, while I agree that going to Dorwinn is a good idea, whether we go or not is up to Deva." And so Jaedann asked her. Deva was a little apprehensive about leaving for another place when they were already in a hidden city, but she was also very curious about the Elven Kingdom. It was obvious that her father came from there. This was her chance to find out about her Elven family. She agreed. Deva needed to see the place her father came from and learn more about Elvish culture since she did not really receive a formal education. She barely even knew the Elvish language. They would leave at first light when it would be easier to sneak out.

It was later in the night and Deva managed to sneak out of the building they were staying at. Everybody else was sleeping except Arunn, but he did not notice she left. Deva could be very quiet when she needed to be and sneaking about. When she was a child she used to play a hiding game with other children and won nearly every time. For her to sneak past an Elf meant that she was really good at sneaking away undetected, a skill that would serve her well in the future. Before they left Cohnnwood, Deva had something important to do. She went back to the Applewisk Tavern. She wore her cloak so no one could recognize her. Peonni was behind the bar and when Deva went up and asked for her, she was surprised to see Deva. Peonni commented. "What are you doing here, you should not be back with those in charge looking for you.

Deva softly replied. "I know, but since you did not turn us in, I feel like I can trust you. You protect those that come to your place and I bet you also keep their secrets."

Peonni smiled at the compliment. "That's why people trust me, and this place. I sense you are about to ask me to do something."

"Yes, because of one small simple gesture of kindness, you can be trusted. Can you keep something for me?

Peonni was immensely curious. She had hidden stuff for folks before, but usually it was smuggled goods like weapons or sometimes money. Deva did not seem like the type who had something of much value, but it was obvious whatever she had was important. She replied. "I can hide something for you, but it depends on how big it is and if I will have to use one of my storage rooms."

Smiling, Deva replied. "No, it's nothing like that." Deva handed her a box. "It's small, you can put it away somewhere and forget about it."

Peonni still curious, even more so for Fae, asked. "What is it?"

"Something I cannot keep with me; it would be too dangerous. But I will be back for it. It is not worth anything for those who might want to steal it, but it has some value for me."

"Sounds like a family heirloom. When something of no value has value only to one person, it is usually an heirloom."

Deva laughed. "Something like that." Then Deva handed her a few gold pieces and said. "For your trouble, can I count on you?"

Peonni nodded and her fairy wings glistened in the light, which always let those around now that she was telling the truth. "I have a chest in the back that stays locked. That is where I keep important things hidden, you and your secrets will always be protected at the Applewisk. "

"Thank You, my friend."

"Safe travels whatever your real name is."

Deva laughed. "I guess it's no surprise, you knew our names were not real."

"Most people who come here have a false name. Cohnnwood is a place for those to escape to and hide, mostly from their past. Real names are unusual. But my name is really Peonni."

She paused and wondered if she should tell Peonni the truth. She finally said. "My name is Deva Mirarel. Remember that name when I come back this way again."

"Safe travels Deva Mirarel."

Deva left the Applewisk Tavern and snuck back to where her, Jaedann, and the Elves were staying. Peonni went to the back room and put the box in the chest she kept locked. But the box made Peonni curious, more curious than she should have been. She opened the box and saw a necklace, a strange necklace with five jagged points in the circle with a sapphire in the middle. Peonni had never seen anything like it before. Was it Elven? It was not Faerûn, that much she knew. The sapphire was worth something, but she had a feeling the necklace itself was worth a whole lot more. It was a symbol of great importance, or so she thought. Peonni was sure that someday Deva would be back for the necklace. She had a feeling it would bring great change to Annmar.

It was first light, although there was not much light in the heavily dense forest known as The Foxxwood. The three Elves along with Jaedann and Deva were lowered to the ground from Cohnnwood. A group of foxes looking for food scattered when their horses were brought to them form the hidden stables on the ground. They were curious about what was going on. Saida who always had a fondness for animals threw them some leftover bacon that she had tucked away in her pouch. Arunn looked at Jaedann and said. "If we take the Easternn road, we will save a day or two."

Jaedann smiled. "We will follow your direction." Arunn knew best how to get to where they were going and Jaedann liked they were saving a day or two since time was not their friend. But as the travelers started out a mysterious stranger stood in their way. Although, it was not that mysterious to Deva and Jaedann. Arunn was the first to see it. Deva froze as fear gripped her once again. She asked. "What is that thing? Why is it not dead?"

Jaedann told Arunn about their encounter with it on The Soldier's Bridge. Arunn responded to the both of them. "It's a Khronne, sometimes referred as a Dark Elf, but a mixture of elf, human, and Barbarian. They should not exist anymore."

Jaedann replied. "I think nature has different intentions and this thing should be dead."

Arunn said. "Then let us send it to the afterlife." The Khronne who had unnatural strength, picked up a log. The log was thrown towards the horses, not hitting them, but scattering them and even knocking Jaedann and Arunn off theirs. Malonn and Saida both drew their bows and fired arrows at the Khronne, which knocked them out of the way with its sword.   The two Elves kept trying to fire arrows, but not one them hit their intended target. Deva was trying to create fire, but could only manage an orange glow in her hands. Arunn said to Jaedann as they gathered themselves. "If this thing is after you and the girl then you need to get out of here and let us deal with the Khronne. Get the girl and take the north path."

Jaedann did not argue. If they could not kill the Khronne before then they might not be able to do so now.

Deva's safety was more important. He got his horse and got to Deva, grabbed her reigns and said. "Let the Elves handle this, we have to get out of here." She agreed and they snuck around through the trees where the Khronne was standing. The Elves were able to keep it distracted as Jaedann and Deva moved through the trees, but then the Khronne saw them and threw some smaller logs at them. They barely missed, but the Khronne took an arrow to the leg from one of the Elves. Jaedann and Deva were able to get away, but dealing with the Khronne was another matter. The Elves circled the Khronne and continued to fire even putting three more arrows into it, but the Khronne was strong and it did not seem to faze it. Could it be killed? Arunn was beginning to wonder. The Khronne threw a rock and hit Malonn, breaking his bow hand. Saida put one more arrow in the Khronne, but knowing that the girl had gotten away, it ran back into the woods, disappearing into The Foxxwood as fast as it has appeared out of nowhere.

28

Vorak was tinkering at his workbench and trying to train a new assistant. Jaedann was gone and nobody knew for sure if he would return. Perhaps he and the girl would find a place together and hide. Most in Liberus thought that, mostly because the Magistrate was telling people that he had helped her escape so it was easy to assume that he was hiding with her and would never come back. After all he was a banished prince of Belmere and not beholding to Liberus. It was just a place that most people who had nowhere to go, ended up there. But Vorak was hoping that was not the case. He hoped that he would see his friend again or at least hear from him once more. He was sitting at his bench when the raven with a message arrived. Most of the ravens that came to Liberus came to the Cleric's building. Most of the messages were for other people, but this one as not. It was from Jaedann. Vorak was delighted to read the message, but shocked when he finished the final words. He looked at his new assistant and said. "Find

Hanniah and Rathgar and have them meet me at the Magistrate's office …it is important."

Minutes later they all were with the Magistrate. Thorsha was curious to why she had to be interrupted for this, but when she heard it had something to do with Jaedann, she stopped what she was doing immediately. Vorak said to the three of them. "Jaedann sent a message and the news is not good."

Thorsha asked. "Is he with the girl?"

"Yes."

"I knew it. He did help her escape."

Vorak gave her a dirty look. "That is not true, but it is not the most pressing matter right now. There is an Anntheian army on the way to level the city. Two legions to be exact with ballistas."

Hanniah said. "Fuk the gods, you cannot be serious!"

"Jaedann scouted them after the snow melted and somehow ended up in their camp."

Thorsha asked. "How do we know this is true and not some ruse by that traitor."

Hanniah rolled her eyes at the notion that Jaedann could be a traitor. He was too honorable to be one. "Thorsha, why would he lie about an army coming here when we cannot possibly defend the place. A traitor does not do that. You may not like what he did, but he is clearly warning us."

Thorsha asked. "Can this be verified?"

Vorak looked the message. "Jaedann says they will be coming from the southern route because he destroyed The Soldier's Bridge." He looked at Rathgar. "You could ride out that way and scout their position."

Rathgar nodded. "I can do that, but it may take me a week depending on where they are at."

Thorsha agreed. She needed more information before she made any kind of decision. Vorak replied. "That will be good. We need to know how long it will be before they are here."

Hanniah asked the obvious question. "This is all well and good, but what are we to do about this army marching towards Liberus? We do not have enough men and women to defend this place and barely got out alive when the Crowthornns attacked."

Vorak looked back at the message. "Jaedann did say in his message, his next desitnation."

Thorsha was very curious to know where Jaedann was going. Vorak could see it in her eyes and did not trust it to be mere curiosity. Would she be so bold as to hire an assassain to kill who she thought was a traitor? But despite his suspicions of the Magistrate, he answered. "He and the girl are going to Dorwinn to seek help from the Elves."

"Or that is where he is going to hide the girl."

"Thorsha, I do not think that is his intention. I think he is going there to ask for help, to get an Elven army."

"Why?"

"Who else could he ask for help, certainly no one in Belmere. And it's a smart move."

Thorsha was not satisfied with his answer. She did not like hearing about Elven armies as she was not very fond of Elves. Her dealings with them had been murky at best. "I do not like the idea of an army of Elves coming here to defend this place. Certainly, we can find allies elsewhere."

"What does it matter where we get help. Is it not better to be alive than debate where we get the help." Thorsha did not say anything after that. But Hanniah asked. "So, what do we do now?"

Vorak said. "We wait. Jaedann said to wait for his instructions." That was all they could do for now except try and prepare for the war that was coming to Liberus.

It had been a long journey from Cohnnwood, but the Elves along with Jaedann and Deva, finally arrived in the Kingdom of Dorwinn. Deva was amazed at how beautiful the land was. She had never seen so much green. It was filled with endless meadows and rollings fields along with majestic mountains and waterfalls. It was a perfect dream, if there was such a thing. Dorwinn was a large kingdom with many of the great houses to the north, but House Tyriall sat close to the border of the kingdom. The group made their way to a city in the mountains, high above some of the largest waterfalls in Dorwinn. It was the seat of power for House Tyriall. Horns were blown by Elven Archers to announce the arrival of its citizens coming home and that of visitors. As they made their way up the mountain road, Deva asked Jaedann. "Where exactly are we going?" They turned the corner and the stone archway and entrance to the city. Jaedann replied. "Welcome to Elnnaril, the seat of power for House Tyriall."

"We are not in the capital city?"

"No, that would be Taranonn. The great Elven capital is further north in the very center of Dorwinn. This is the home of Lord Illrunn Tyriall, Arunn's father."

"Ah, I see. This place looks as if it would be a capital city.

Jaedann smiled. "Most Elven cities could pass for a capital city, they are the most beautiful cities in Annmar."

Illrunn and his wife Ysilda were standing on the steps of the Great Hall of Elnnaril waiting to greet their son and his companions when they arrived. Arunn was happy to be home. He was happy to see his father. That was not always the case in the past when he had returned from an adventure as he and his father did not always see eye to eye. But this was different. Illrun was glad to see his son return. Even though he would never say it, he always worried about his son when he left Dorwinn, probably more so than his mother. Arunn got off his horse and walked up to him and said. "Father, it is good to be home."

"It is good to have you home son, your mother and I were worried." Illrunn replied.

"There is much to tell you."

"I suppose there is. Malonn looks to be injured.

"We encounted something strange in The Foxxwood that we need to tell you about it, but for now Malonn needs Elven medicine." Illrunn motioned for two Elves to help Malonn to their infirmary. Jaedann had gotten off hif horse as well along with Deva and then they walked up the steps. Illrunn looked at the Belmerien Knight and said. "Jaedann of House Barrenn, it has been a long time." Deva heard the name Barrenn, again, and thought it strange, but did not ask about it. Jaedann replied to Illrunn. "Lord Tyriall, it has been a long time. It is good to see you again."

"And you. I should like to hear how you ended up in Liberus and how you came to be involved in all this."

Jaedann smiled. "It is an interesting story for sure, probably better told over Ale."

Illrunn smiled back. "That we can certainly provide."

"Lord and Lady Tyriall, this is Deva." The girl nodded and greeted them both. Ysilda smiled at her. She felt an overwhelming sense of compassion and joy all at the same time when gazing upon her kin. Ysilda said to Illrunn. "She looks like my brother. There is no doubt."

Deva overheard and was taken back by the comment. She never knew much about her father, mostly just the name and that he was born in Annmar, so it was natural for her to be very curious about how Lady Tyriall knew this. Deva asked. "I am sorry Lady Tyriall, how do you know that? Do you know who I am?"

"Yes, my child. You are Deva Mirarel." Deva was shocked that she knew that. How could she if she was not using the name anymore. Ysilda said. "Your father was my brother. I was of House Mirarel before I married Illrunn." Everybody standing round Deva heard what Lady Tyriall said and were stunned by the words she spoke. Jaedann did not know this of Lady Tyriall, he did not even know that she was born into House Mirarel. Arunn was shocked more than anyone, all sorts of questions ran through is mind when hearing the news that he and the girl were cousins. Deva asked. "But how do you know of me?"

Ysilda held her hands with a loving touch and said. "We have known about you for a long time, but that is a story for another time, which Illrunn and I are happy to tell. But now is the time for rest and refreshment after such a long journey."

That is what the travelers did. Afterall, they desperately needed it. Hours later they had dinner on the terrace of Lord Tyriall's home. Jaedann began to tell them of their journey starting with the attack by the Crowthornns, what they found out from Sansonn Yvandr to when Deva ran off. They talked of the signs from the blood moon to the snowfall. Jaedann told them about their encounter with the Anntheian army. Then he told them about the encounter with the strange being with abnormal strength and speed.

Arunn told of his encounter with the being and how they did not know what it was. Illrunn did, however, know what it was. He said to them. "You encountered a Khronne from what you are describing."

Deva asked. "What is a Khronne?"

Illrunn gave her a serious look. "It is an ancient evil, something that is not supposed to exist anymore and was born from dark magic."

Jaedann commented. "They are dark Elves, are they not?"

"Yes," Ilrunn reluctantly said. "They were born of darkness. Legend has it that they were created in the battle between the gods Anion and Cimis, a battle of dark magic versus Elven magic and when they were created, they had the power to use both. It was Khronnes who helped mankind defeat the gods and when there were no more gods they ceased to exist or so people thought. I have never heard of anyone seeing a Khronne in 100 years."

Jaedann asked. "But no one knows for sure they ceased to exist?"

Illrunn sighed. "No, no one knows for sure, but like many things regarding the nature of magic they could have been in hiding until the time was right."

Arunn asked his father. "What do you mean by when the time is right?"

"When magic returns to the Annmar, son." Illrunn looked Deva at that moment. She was now certain that the Elves knew her secret as she had been wondering ever since they entered the city of Elnnaril. There was no use in hiding the fact that she had at least some magical abilities. Illrunn continued. "I know one thing, if a Khronne has been seen its purpose is to stop the return of magic, but it is also not alone. I believe it is another sign of things to come."

Jaedann asked. "You say that it is not alone, what makes you think that?"

"Khronnes are often not alone, meaning there is always more than one in existence. Also, the Oracles of Erinnity."

"That name sounds familiar. I seem to remember hearing that name in a story when I was a child."

Arunn commented. "It sounds familiar to me as well."

Illrunn looked at his son and then at Jaedann. "It is an ancient society formed for one purpose, to stop the power of the gods or magic. Nobody knows who started it or even created it, but Legend has it that Anion in his war with the other gods simply whispered into man's ear and a few of them formed the Oracles of Erinnity. Then when Khronnes were born, they were brought into the society and used for that purpose of destroying Magic. This secret society was believed to have disappeared, I don't think they ever went away. I think they have always been in hiding, ready to destroy magic again if it were to ever come back into the world."

Jaedann replied to Illrunn. "Any you think that this who is really behind it all?"

"I do, but who leads this group now is the bigger question. At the height its power there would be an equal number of men and Khronnes. If that is true to today, then there will be a Khronne that leads the other Khronnes.

"Do you have a theory on who might lead his group again?"

"No, I do not, the only thing I am sure of, it will be someone with power. But this matter should be taken before the Elven Council. We will need to discuss how this will affect the Elves especially if war is coming as this will affect all races in Annmar."

Arunn was going to say something, but Jaedann interrupted. While they were enjoying a nice meal and feeling rested, there were more important matters to discuss and Jaedann had to ask a great favor. He said. "Lord Tyriall, there is something I must ask of you."

"Jaedann of House Barrenn, you want to ask for the help of the Elves in defeating the Anntheian army that marches towards Liberus."

Jaedan softly smiled at Illrunn. "You are perceptive as always. Yes, that is what I have come to ask."

"And I cannot give you help. It is true that we have our alliances with other kingdoms, but Elves cannot interfere with the affairs of men and places who reside outside those kingdoms. It is unfortunate what will happen, but Liberus have been destroyed before and rebuilt. I believe we will see her rise again one day."

"But what of the innocent people who will die there, do their lives mean nothing?"

"All lives are worth something, Jaedann, but they are not worth more than the Elves who would die if we were to help. And I have a duty to the Kingdom of Dorwinn to protect Elven blood from being shed especially at the expense of others. This is not our fight."

A sad and angry look washed over of Jaedann's face. "Words I did not expect to hear. My father always said you could trust the Elves when most would not. Perhaps he was wrong."

"It is easy to think that at this moment. But Elves do not have an alliance with Liberus as we do with Belmere. And I owe you no other explanation. However, just because I cannot offer help does not mean there is not somebody who can." Illrunn motioned to the Elves standing at the chamber doors to let someone in. A man came through the doors that was only recognized to one other sitting at the

table. Jaedann knew him instantly, even though he had not
seen this man in eight years. His name was Degorenn
Annsier and they served together in the Lionnshade Brigade
as Knights of Belmere. He was a welcomed sight for the
man who had just been refused help from the Elves. A
welcomed sight indeed.

29

Jaedan had not seen a a Belemerien Knight in over eight years. It felt good to see a familiar face. He missed his homeland even though he did not let on that he did, but it was only natural. Liberus may have been his home. He may have been a man without a homeland, but in his heart, would always be from Belmere. Jaedann would be a Belemerien Knight more than he was ever a prince. Jaedann got up and greeted Degorenn. He said. "Majorenn Annsier, it has been a long time, but it brings joy to my heart to see you again."

Degorenn smiled as they shook hands. "Jaedann Barrenn, somehow I knew you would not be dead. It is good to see you too sir. But it is Genneral now. I have been in command of the Lionnshade Brigade for two years now."

Jaedann smiled. "And you are a good fit for command. You were trained well."

"You should know, you trained me."

"And that's how I know you're a good fit for command." Both men laughed as if they were brothers again in the army. Jaedann asked, "I am curious, this was the last place I expected to see you, if I was ever to see you again."

"I am here because we have been tracking the Rogues of Hamlinn, multiple ships to be exact. Because of our alliance with Dorwinn, we were sent a raven about the four ships that sailed together. We are here for supplies and to rest for a night or two before we go south to investigate what they are doing and put a stop to it. You know Belmere is the only Kingdom willing to end to that rogue nation of thieves."

Jaedann replied. "I think I know where those ships are going. Arunn spotted them in Easthavenn turning to the south."

"I suspect they are going to Liberus and then across the Elmsonn Sea for a smuggling operation."

"No, I think they intend to blockade Liberus."

Degorenn was shocked to hear that. It was hard to believe, but he had never known Jaedann to be a liar or to not know the true nature of things. He asked. "What for? What is so important that they would send four ships to blockade the port?"

"The same reason there are two Anntheian Legions marching towards Liberus to burn the city and kill every soul there." Jaedann pointed at Deva. "They want to kill her and prevent anyone from escaping the city."

Degorenn looked at Deva, a bit confused why a young girl would be such a threat, but also curious. "Why her? What is so special about her?" Deva saw that Jaedann had pointed at her and then overhead part of the conversation. She walked over as Jaedann was saying to Degorenn. "It is not my place to say. It is her secret."

Deva said. "That is true, but I do not think it will remain a secret for too long. Hello, I am Deva Mirarel, the daughter of Aiassa Mirarel or so I have been told."

Degorenn replied. "Of House Mirarel here in Dorwinn. Your Lord Aiassa Mirarel's daughter, but you are a…"

"Yes, I am a Half Elf and I know that must seem strange, but that is not the strangest thing about me." Deva looked at Jaedann for reassurance. He said to her. "It is up to you, but you can trust him with your secret. He is a brother of Belmere." Degorenn smiled at Jaedann's confidence and so Deva responded. "I have abilities. I guess you would call it magic." She held out her hands and while she did not create fire per say, her hands glowed a burning orange. Degorenn stepped back almost losing his balance because he was so shocked. He had never seen something like that before. Powers like that only resided in children's stories about gods and warriors. Deva said. "It is okay, I will not hurt you, just wanted to show you so you would believe."

Degorenn looked at his old friend and asked. "Jaedann Barrenn, how could this be? How are you involved?"

Jaedann shook his head. It was still hard for him to believe it too. "I was the one who found her. And I am the one protecting her as she travels to the place where she is supposed to go."

"You may not be a Knight anymore, but I guess that would never stop you from finding a cause or protecting someone."

"No, once a Knight, always a Knight."

Deva finally had to ask for she had heard the name more than once now. "Jaedann, why do they call you Barrenn. Your surname is Lionnshade?"

Degorenn laughed at the surname Jaedann had given himself, but it was appropriate if he could not use his birth name anymore that he would use Lionnshade. He asked. "Does she not know who you really are?"

"No."

Deva curiously asked. "Who are you if Jaedann Lionnshade is not your real name?"

Jaedann was reluctant to tell her. His past did not matter anymore, but he also knew that she would not look at him the same way anymore as he had begun to care for her, deeply, and more than he probably should care. He could not explain why. Perhaps, it was the oath he swore to protect her. Perhaps it was because she needed saving and protection from those trying to kill her. Whatever it was he cared for her and did not want her to see him differently, but he could not lie to her anymore. "My name is Jaedann of House Barrenn in the Kingdom of Belmere. The second son of King Jagorenn and the brother of the current King of Belmere, Jornnus Barrenn."

Deva was stunned. "You are a Prince of Belmere?"

"Yes, and a Knight. And I was once in command of the Lionnshade brigade." Deva was angry. He had lied to her and while she was told not to really trust anybody in Annmar by the woman who took care of her, she began to trust Jaedann. Deva had trusted him with her life and now all she felt was betrayal. Was he going to eventually kill her? Was that his plan all along? Deva looked at him with a deathly stare, penetrating the armor he had around his heart. It hurt to see her look at him that way and then she stormed off, finding a place to be alone. Jaedann tried to say something, but Deva would not hear it.

Degorenn commented. "Godsdamn, I have not seen a woman get that mad since…

"I know, she has been gone eight years and I can see still hear her tone when she was mad at me. She was always a handful, but that's what made her beautiful too."

"You should go talk to her, make things right."

Jaedann nodded. "I will talk with you later."

Deva was alone when Jaedann found her sitting in part of the hallway filled with statues. She was siting on a bench in the shadows, saddened and trying to hide from everyone. When she was sad, she always preferred to be alone. Jaedann almost did not see her when he walked by. He did not know what to say except, "I am sorry that I did not tell you my real name."

Deva looked at him while a tear fell down her face. "Why did you not tell me? We spent all that time together. Told stories to each other. I told you more about me. I trusted you."

"I know. But I did not tell you for the same reason you were not truthful about your name when you arrived in Annmar. For me outside of Belmere, it is not wise to use my real name, especially with no title anymore. My family has too many enemies. Some would kill me just for the name. Some would try and ransom me to my brother only to be disappointed when he refused and then they would most likely kill me. I have a dangerous name outside of Belmere."

Deva nodded. She understood his reasons and responded. "But why could you not tell me? I thought we had a bond and could trust each other?"

"I feel like we do have a bond now, but that is also my past. The man you know is not the same who was banished from his homeland. And I want you to know me for who I am now, not some idea you have me of me because of a name."

"You have never lied to me at least that I know of and this feels like you have been lying to me the whole time."

Jaedann tried to give her a comforting look. "I have not been lying, I just did not tell you everything, there is a difference."

"I do not see it that way."

Jaedann softly smiled. "My wife used to say the same thing. But from now on, I will not lie to you. You can ask anything you want and I will tell you the truth. I swear on my oath to protect you, I will tell you the truth.

Deva stood up and looked at him for the longest time. Jaedann felt that he should say something else, but his words would be based off her questions to him. Deva finally asked. "What happned? Why have you been banished?."

Jaedann sat down and said. "It is a long story and what you have to understand is Belmere likes to think of itself as one big Kingdom. In some ways it is, but in most ways it's really just a land of small kingdoms ruled by the different royal houses. Part of the rule of law means that a house can challenge for the crown. My father and my grandfather were both Kings, that is how house Barrenn came to rule because my grandfather challenged and had enough support to take the crown when there was not a clear heir with the previous house. There are some who do not consider House Barrenn the rightful house to rule Belmere. There was a rumor that my mother was unfaithful because my father was always unfaithful to her and that me and my brother are not rightful heirs. So there was a war. Three of the houses rebelled when my father died and challenged my brother for the crown. It started a war. At the time I was a Knight and in command of the Lionnshade Brigade. We were posted at one of the port cities in the North and our job was to disrupt supply lines. Against my better judgement my wife was there and she had our son during that time. My brother was never that smart when it came to military strategy, I was always the better soldier in our family. The newly crowned King showed his stupidity when he ordered my Brigade to fight with one of our main armies leaving the port city undefended. Another small Brigade was supposed to arrive and defend the city, but never arrived. I don't know if it just did not arrive in time or were ordered somewhere else, but when the enemy came through the port, they killed everybody in the city including my wife and newborn son.

Deva had a look of shock. "Fuk the gods. I am sorry".

Jaedann nodded, acknowledging her sincerity. He continued. "You can imagine how angry I was when I founded out it was my brother who ordered our Brigade away from the city. Well short end of the story is I tried to kill him. I walked into the throne room where he was sitting and I tried to kill my own brother. Almost did. I took out most of the Kingsguard, didn't get them all, but left a scar on my brother's face. For my crime in trying to kill our King I should have been put to death, but my mother intervened along with some of the nobles and my life was spared. My punishment was banishment. I gave up my name and my title and left Belmere for good."

Deva sat next to him. "Who can blame you! Your wife and child were killed because of your brother's stupidity. I think I would have done the same if I were in your place."

"Most would, but it is treason to try and kill the King even if it is your own brother. That may be the worst crime and nevermind if he deserved it. I swore to protect my king and broke that oath."

"Then make up for it by staying true to your oath to me."

Jaedann smiled. "I can do that. I swore to protect you and even though I may not have the title of knight anymore, I still have the heart of the knight and I will go to my grave living up to the oath I made to you."

Deva kissed him. Jaedann was caught by surprise and she was surprised that she did it. It was a small kiss, not passionate, but meaningful,

nonetheless. Jaedann also did not stop her. He had to admit he was taken with her as much as she was taken with him. Deva commented. "I cannot really see you as a prince."

Jaedann laughed. "I never really thought of myself as one. I was too much of a soldier, still am I suppose. "

Deva smiled. "I can certainly see you as a Knight… an honorable Knight, protecting those who cannot defend themselves. A Knight of Annmar!" They smiled at each other, taking comfort in the simple truths about each other and as they looked to the future whatever that may be.

30

Degorenn was reading in the great library of Elnnaril when Jaedann found him. They did not get to finish their conversation. Jaedann commented. "Illrunn told me you were in here." Degorenn smiled. "You caught me. I always try to take advantage of their magnificent libraries when I come to Dorwinn. I am always amazed at the abundance of the written word the Elves have." Jaedann nodded. He agreed with the observation, although he was not much of a reader. He said. "That is the one thing about Elves, they are meticulous record keepers and are second only to Lenntis when it comes to books. I used to think Belmere had huge libraries until I came here for the first time."

Degorenn laughed. "Looking at all these books, it makes you realize that Belmere does not care for written records as much as other Kingdoms. Our knowledge is in our experience."

"And our history is in the stories and the legends we tell."

"Quite right and I for one would not change that. Although, I would not be opposed to more books I can get my hands on."

Jaedann changed the subject. "I need to ask you something, a favor of sorts."

Degorenn gave him a serious look. "Illrunn said you would need to ask me for one, but I do not think I can give you what you ask for."

"Do you know what I am going to ask?"

Degorenn stood up. "You need our help to fight the Anntheian army that is marching towards Liberus."

"I guess what I have to ask is not that big of a secret."

"Not in a place like this my friend and not when it comes to war."

Jordan laughed at his statement since he was not wrong, especially that of war. Secrets were always hard to keep in war and those involved rarely took secrets to the grave. He asked. "So, can I count on your help, one Belmerien Knight to another?"

Degorenn had only a serious look on his face when he replied. "No and it is not because I do not want to, but Belmere cannot be involved in this fight."

"Even if the enemy is Anntheia?"

"Especially because it is Anntheia. Tensions with them always run hot, but we do what we can to avoid ending up in a full scale war with them. Minor skirmishes along our border or in the Endless March are one thing, but meeting them on a different battlefield is a prelude to a full scale war and the Lionnshade brigade cannot do that. My mandate is to find and hunt down the Rogues of Hamlinn who cause harm to Belmere and that is what I am doing."

Jaedann shook his head in disbelief. "I was told to come here because I could find help and everywhere I turn, there is none. It is as if no one cares what happens to Liberus."

"Most Lords and Kings do not. Liberus lives outside the laws of Kingdoms and is merely tolerated because most people need something that comes through the city. Most will let the place be destroyed and do business with another port city."

"I know that, but if we let Anntheia march outside their borders and just destroy a city without defense or retribution, where do they go next? They will be able to get away with anything."

Degorenn softly smiled. "I do not disagree, but I am following a King's command and cannot deviate from that."

Jaedann was not happy. Hearing no from a fellow Knight of Belmere was disappointing because they always stood by each other's side, especially in battle or the threat of one. "I understand, but excuse me if I think my brother is getting soft when it comes our enemies."

"You are not the only one who thinks that and one of those men is a big critic of your brother's reign. He is someone who also might help you. Someone who would want Belmere to stop an Anntheian Army."

Hearing that surprised Jaedann and it made him very curious. "Who?" He asked.

"Tibautt Fensenn."

Jaedann was shocked to hear the name. "You cannot be serious."

"I am."

"The man who rebelled against my house, my family and challenged for the throne. The man whose war caused the death of my wife and child."

Degorenn nodded. "That would be the one."

"You do know I tried to kill him once."

"I remember."

"Why would he help me?"

Degorenn smiled. "Because the only thing he hates worse than your brother are Anntheian soldiers. I think he would be happy to defy your brother just to kill them and despite your history with the man, I think he would help you just to make King Jornnus angry."

"I did not think of that. But I have to ask…how can I trust him?"

"You do not have to trust him to get him to fight for your cause. Besides, he may not trust you, but you can still fight for the same thing. Send him a message, explain what is happening, and ask for his help. You may be surprised by the answer."

Jaedann shook his head. "Unbelievable. I cannot believe this is my last resort."

Degorenn laughed. "The help we usually need can come from the strangest places, but if you truly value Liberus and her people then you seek help from anywhere you can find it."

"It seems like I told you something like that before."

"You did when no one wanted the help of Barbarians to defend the town of Rockwhich from Anntheia and you wanted to have better numbers to fight the legion that was sent to sack that town. And you know what…you were right, we needed them to win the day."

Jaedann nodded. There was nothing more to teach Degorenn if he was applying the same he had been taught by Jaedann to the current predicament. How could he argue with such sound logic? He said. "Well, at this point I have nothing left to lose except a town that I have grown to love if I do not find help defending her."

"That is a good way of looking at it. And it is not like we cannot help at least a little bit. If those four ships are really set on blockading Liberus, the Lionnshade brigade can stop them as it fits within our mandate. Perhaps give people a chance to escape Liberus before the place is burned to the ground." Jaedann thanked his old friend. It was not a perfect plan, but the start of one. He was thankful for that at least. But now he had to send a message to the man he swore if he ever saw again, he would kill. Help can come from the strangest of places indeed.

Deva wanted to explore all she could of Dorwinn. She may have been just a Half-Elf, but part of her family from was from Dorwinn. And more importantly, she had family, she was not just some orphaned Half-Elf from across the sea. Deva walked around after talking with Jaedann and found the great hall outside the main library in Elnnaril. It was filled with Statues of Elves and Elven Relics, but what caught her attention was the huge skylight that gave a perfect view of the moon and the stars. Deva had never seen them so clear, but of course Dorwinn was known to have the best view of the sky because of its location in the western part of Annmar.

Illrunn and Ysilda walked into the great hall and found Deva. She looked that them and said. "I hope you do not mind, I was curious about this place."

Ysilda replied. "We do not mind. In fact, we were looking for you. You must have lots of questions."

Deva's smile. "I do. I want to know everything."

Softly laughing, Illrunn answered. "Everything will take a very long time. For now, let us start with the most important things that you want to know."

"Fair enough. You speak of my abilities as magic. I do not know what that is and had not heard of the word before I came to Annmar."

Illrunn stepped closer to her and pointed to a statue of the god Cimis. "Do you see that statue?" Deva answered yes. Illrunn said. "That is Cimis, the god of Wisdom, one of the five gods who created the world, not only Annmar, but everything around it. The gods had great power. They were more powerful than all the races in Annmar. You have the power of the gods and we call that power magic."

Deva did not know what to think. She had never heard of these things before, not even stories about the gods. She replied. "I do not know of any gods."

"No one ever told you the story of the five gods?"

Deva shook her head no. "I was not told how the world was created."

Ysilda responded. "Then my child, it is time you be told the story of creation as we know it. I know you have a journey ahead of you and that is why you have come to Annmar. The first step in knowing where you are going is to know where you come from." Deva nodded, acknowledging that she understood Ysilda's meaning.

Illrunn continued. The first thing you should know is that there was a war 100 years ago where man rose up and killed the five gods. They did it out of jealousy and fear. And for their power and perceived dominion over all the races. Dominion that was never true, for all races lived in harmony among the gods. The five gods watched over the world and never sought dominion. They created a world where all could live in peace with one another and even though that did not always happen, for of course, there was conflict, but despite that, all could live in peace with the gods. The world prospered. It expanded and civilization reached to the very edge of the whole world. But one god in particular was jealous of the other gods and started a rebellion. It was Anion, the god of war and the preferred god of humans. He whispered into man's ears that the other gods wanted to control them and by the killing the other gods, man could become more powerful. They were tempted by a serpent's tongue. They were tempted by their own greed and made to believe in false promises. Anion catered to their desires and so a handful them formed armies and one by one, killed the gods as Anion himself fought each god so he could be the one true god. Some say that Anion along with his first followers in this rebellion formed the Oracles of Erinnity and it was they who started the war with the gods. It was at the end of this war that the power of the gods or magic as we call it disappeared from the world. Man's greed for power consumed them so much that they even killed the god who started the rebellion."

Deva curiously asked. "Where did the gods come from? How did everything begin?"

"That is a long story." Ysilda interrupted. "You should hear that story too." So Illrunn told Deva the story of the five gods. She listened intently, taking in every word. Deva was fascinated because she had never heard a creation story before. It was no surprise that Deva would be curious about how the world was created, but like most people she just accepted that the world accidently came into existence and that was that. When Illrunn finished the story, Deva asked. "How come I have never head of the gods, do people still believe in them?"

Illrunn was amused by her comment. "Some do, others believe that it is just a myth and never happened. And that magic never existed. After 100 years and very little recorded history, the story might as well just be a myth, but you prove that it is not. Unfortunately, that makes you dangerous."

Deva sighed. "People keep saying that. Why should people fear me? Just because I have what you call magical abilities, doesn't mean I seek to control anyone or cause harm."

"That may be true, but you have a power that most would kill for in order to possess. And there are those who would do anything to keep magic from coming back into the world unless they could control it."

Deva started to cry. "I only came to Annmar to find out who I am and to find my place in the world."

Ysilda replied to the girl. "That is all any of us truly seek. Knowing who we are and what our place is in the world is part our own journey. You are the daughter of Aiassa Mirarel, my brother. You are a Highborn Elf even if you are just a Half-Elf.

"Does that mean this is my home?"

"If I have anything to say about it, yes."

It pleased Deva to hear that, but she still felt uncertain and it showed in her tone. "It's nice to hear, but I do not know you and I do not know anything about my father. Was he like me?"

Ysilda softly smiled. "If you are asking if he had magical abilities too, yes. He could do strange things when we were children. He could move things without touching them. He could start a fire with his hands. But he could not always control it. Our father kept him sheltered and away from other Elves out of fear that he would harm someone. And then a tragedy happened twenty years ago when we were both grown. I was already married to Illrunn. Your father became dangerous."

Curiosity showered over Deva as she wanted to know every detail of what happened. "What did he do that was so tragic?"

"Someone made him angry and then they fought. Because he couldn't control his abilities, when he touched the other Elf's face, he burned him so severely the other Elf died. Fortunately, no one was around to see it, but our father found my brother in tears standing over the body.

Our father knew that Aaissa would never be safe and that he could destroy the Elven Kingdom without any self-control. He knew that his own son was a danger so he sent him away."

Illrunn spoke up. "You should know that he did go before the Elven council and explained what had happened. He told the council about Aiassa's abilities and they voted to banish him. One member even wanted him dead. It was the council's decision that led to Aiassa being sent away."

Deva asked. "Why did he say anything at all to the council?"

"This was not something that could be hidden from them and their decision was not an easy one. Only under the most extreme of circumstances could an Elf be banished and usually when they committed a heinous crime."

"If I have the same abilities that would make me a danger to them. I still do not understand why I should b considered a danger. I do not wish anybody harm for I have a good heart, can't you see that?"

Illrunn softly smiled and in a comforting tone replied to Deva. "Of course we can, it is not hard to see that your heart is pure. But the greatest fear of any race is living with those who are more powerful and may seek dominion over them. There are those who will never accept you, who only fear your abilities and cannot see that you have a good heart. One war was already fought to rid the world of your kind and wars will be fought again to stop those like you, thus making you dangerous. It is not your fault. However, some will embrace you and your abilities, and as you can see, protect you."

Deva tried to smile and then responded. "But would Elves accept me?"

"Some maybe, but you are still dangerous to the Elves as well."

"Then that would make me an outcast as well. Elves would not accept me, will they?"

Ysilda replied. "Times have changed. There are Elves who do not fear magic as they once did."

Illrunn offered another thought. "That may be true. Elves may have become more tolerant towards the offspring of one of their own who has magic, but that does mean the council would allow it. They will still have to decide on whether you could stay or not. And we cannot simply just hide you here in Dorwinn."

Deva looked away, trying to hide the sad look on her face as she replied. "I understand. It just feels that nobody wants me, not even my own kind. I am sure none of you have ever been orphaned by those that are supposed to love you the most. I never knew my mother and barely remember my father. I do not doubt that I was loved. The woman who watched over me, showed me great kindness, but I still felt alone without the ones who brought me into this world."

Ysilda was brought to tears. She felt sympathy for the girl, even though she could not truly understand where Deva was coming from. Ysilda had always had family and had always lived with her own kind. She said to the girl. "You are not alone in this world. We cannot make the decision for you to stay, it is up to the council. But House Tyriall can offer you protection. We will stand by your side for whatever journey you have to make." Deva smiled.

Illrunn did not always like when Ysilda spoke for House Tyriall since he was the Lord Manor of the Royal House, but he rarely disagreed with her when she was the voice of their house. This was would not be one of the times he disagreed. He spoke up. "She is right, we may not be able to decide on whether you can stay or not, but we can offer you protection. House Tyriall will be bound to your fate, whatever that may be." Deva began to cry, not because she was sad. They were tears of joy. For what she wanted most was to be a part of a family, a community, or a kingdom. Illrunn said. "We will still have to speak to the council and I will do that on your behalf." That was all Deva could hope for her, but she also knew that Dorwinn was not the final destination in her journey. It was only one place along her journey and now their fates were intertwined.

31

The city of Bannburgh was the seat of House Fensenn in the Kingdom of Belmere. It was the city most westerly in the Kingdom and nestled within the mountain ranges that connected Belmere to Anntheia and Guirinn. House Fensenn was known to have the fiercest warriors in Belmere, but it was their Lord that struck the most fear among the other royal houses in Belmere and of course, the enemies of Belmere. Tibautt Fensenn was a prickly sort, he was rarely pleasant, but had a strong sense of honor and justice. Perhaps more so than any other man in Belmere. He never did anything for his own selfish desires, his actions were based on what he believed to be truly right even when it meant starting a rebellion against his king and challenged for the throne. Jaedann did not know if sending a message and asking for help was the right thing to do, but he knew that having knights from   House Fensenn would certainly even the odds. A knight of House Fensenn was worth more than four Anntheian soldiers. Jaedann felt strange sending Tibautt Fensenn a message asking for help, but Tibautt would think it was even more strange to be receiving the message from a man who had threatened to kill him.

Tibautt Fensenn sat in his chair at the Lord's table in the great hall of Bannburgh reading the message over and over. Was this a sick joke? Was is some kind of trap? Had House Barrenn finally come to kill him for his treachery. His second oldest son walked in after being summoned. He was next in line to be Lord of House Fensenn after his older brother was killed in the rebellion eight years before. His father handed him the note and said. "Thamonn, read that and tell me what you make it."

His son read it and was shocked. Thamonn replied. "This cannot be true. It has to be a trap."

"That is what I thought too, but why would King Jornnus not just summon me to the capital himself and then have his assassins kill me. Why use his banished brother?"

Thamonn thought about it for a moment. "To make us believe this has to be true. To make us believe that Jaedann is our friend and ally."

"You think the King would use his own brother who he banished to kill us?"

"Why not? We would trust him now, would we not?"

Tibautt shook his head. It was all too hard to believe. "I know that Jaedann Barrenn would have no problem taking our heads, he threatened to do so if he ever saw me again, but I do not buy that King Jornnus would use his brother to do so. He hates Jaedann more than we ever could."

Thamonn replied. "You think this message is true. That Jaedann Barrenn is really asking for our help."

"It strange enough to actually be true. But there is only one way to find out."

"Are you seriously considering this?"

Tibautt stood up. He did not say anything for a moment. "Cannot say for sure that this is not some kind of trap, but if I am to die for my past transgressions, then I will die on the battlefield, not taken by a coward with a knife in the dark or to the back. If I am to die, I will face my enemy, look into his eyes and show him that I am not afraid and then try to kill him in the process. I will meet Jaedann at the Pike's Ridge. But if what he says is true, then it will give me great pleasure to kill Anntheian soldiers as well."

Thamonn did not agree with his father's plan, but he did not dare argue. He simply asked. "How many men do you want me to assemble?"

His father put his hand on Thamonn's shoulder. "You will stay here in my stead. You will be the Lord of House Fensenn while I take 350 men and ride to meet Jaedann Barrenn. If this is a trap and I should die then as the Lord of House Fensenn, you will do everything in your power to kill all in House Barrenn and erase their identity from this world." Thamonn was a bit stunned by those words, but also understood. It would be a matter of honor to avenge his father's death if that came to be at the hands of House Barrenn. Tibautt walked out of the Great Hall to prepare for the long ride.

Illrunn Tyriall had called for a special assembly of the Elven Council in Dorwinn's capital city of Taranonn. Rarely did this happen unless it was under the most dire of circumstances. He could not remember the last time this was done, but he knew that it had only been done twice in the last 18 years. One of them was the time the council made the decision to send Deva's father away. It was unusual and certainly made the rest of the council curious. Lady Nuala

Rhistall of House Rhistall was the first to speak. Lord Tyiall, you have asked this to council to convene outside of our normal time. What matter is so important that we need to meet?"

Illrunn spoke as he looked at each of the council members, "I called this council to tell you of Deva Mirarel. "They were all surprised by the name, but none more than Sontar Mirarel, the brother of Neremynn. Illrunn continued. "She is the daughter of Aiassa Mirarel and has come to Annmar."

Sontar asked the question that was on the council's mind. "How do you know she is the daughter of my brother and not some imposter?"

"Because she looks like him and has the same abilities he had."

Lord Rathal Anfalenn of House Anfalenn asked. "What abilities do you refer to?"

"Lord Anfalenn, I think you know what I am referring too."

"If you refer to magic, we all agreed to not speak of it when Aiassa Mirarel was sent away."

"That is true, but it must be talked about again for it has returned through the bloodline of Mirarel."

Sontar replied in anger. He would not have his family name insulted with lies. "Do not spread your falsehoods regarding the name Mirarel. It was under tragic circumstances that my nephew had to be sent away, but to claim some stranger is his offspring and her defects are somehow because of our bloodline shows that you have no honor."

Illrunn gave Sontar a strange look. He could not believe what he was hearing and that his honor would be questioned. He said. "I have no reason to lie and if you do not want to believe what I am saying to be true, that is your choice, but it does not make what I have to say less true. Nor can we pretend that what Aiassa Mirarel had was not magic."

Lady Kaylessa Volwinn of House Volwinn responded. "How did you come to know of this girl?"

Illrunn replied to her. "She is in Elnnaril." The members of the council were shocked, no one expected to have someone with magic ability in their kingdom again. It was disturbing to say the least. Kaylessa nervously asked. "Why was she brought to Dorwinn without our knowledge or consent."

"My apologies for that, but she was being escorted by a Ranger and former prince of Belmere. My son found them and brought them to Dorwinn for their safety. But my wife Ysilda and I have known of her existence since she was a baby. Ysilda stayed informed with what happened to her brother."

Nuala replied. "I cannot say that I am surprised. It would be hard to forget about a loved one that was sent away or banished. But while the news of the girl being in Dorwinn is cause for concern, I must ask, what are your intentions?"

Illrunn was serious with his look towards Nuala. "I want to keep her safe, I want her to stay in Dorwinn and that is why I have brought this matter before the council. I would not dare keep her a secret from this council."

Sontar was the first to speak toward his request. "Out of the question. If she has the same defects as my brother, then she must be sent away as she poses a threat."

Nuala responded. "Sontar is not wrong in his view of the matter."

Illrunn shook his head, hoping that the council would be more open regarding one with magic abilities compared to 18 years ago, but perhaps not. He said. "It is interesting,

Sontar that you talk about magical abilities as if they are a defect. I do not believe so, I believe that magic will reign again in Annmar one day. There is even a prophecy about the return of magic."

Rathal replied. "You are referring to the prophecy about the five who will bring magic back into the world?"

"Yes, and there have been signs confirming that this may be coming true."

"And you think this girl may be one of the five?"

Illrunn paused for a moment, trying to find the right words. "This prophecy was spoken about 18 years ago when we decided to send Aiassa Mirarel away. I cannot say for sure if he was one of the five, but if Aiassa might have been then it is conceivable that his daughter would be since he has passed. Regardless of what you believe, I think we have to consider this a possibility."

Nuala said. "Okay, let's say it is true. She will pose the greatest threat to Dorwinn because of those who will do anything to stop the return of magic and I am not talking about Humans, Dwarves, or Barbarians, but dark forces that were created out of hate for the gods and their power. We will see the return of these dark warriors who will destroy everything in their way just to stop the return of magic."

"They are already here, out of the shadows, and hunting for the girl."

"How do you know this?"

"My son Arunn encountered one when he, the girl, and the Ranger left the Emberwild. I do not think there is any use in denying the fact that magic has returned and those dark forces you speak of are upon us."

Kaylessa responded. "If that is true, then the girl cannot stay here."

"On the contrary, who better to protect her than Elves. Who better than Elves to foster and protect those with magic in Annmar especially when one is of Elven blood."

Nuala replied with a compassionate tone. "You make a good and logical argument Illrunn, but you invite war to our borders and that is why she cannot stay."

"Does the entire council feel this way?" Illrunn looked at each of the other's faces as they all said yes. He knew what the answer would be, but was disappointed nonetheless. Nuala said to Illrunn. "You may be right about her and the prophecy, but she should remain in hiding until the day comes that all of the five are found. Right now, it is too dangerous."

Illrunn looked at Nuala and paused for a moment, trying not to say something out of anger. Finally, he mustered the words. "I do not agree with this decision, but I will follow the decision of this council." Nuala nodded towards him in agreement. Illrunn continued. "However, I have pledged the protection of my house to Deva Mirarel, which is my right to do. She will not remain in our borders, but she will be protected by House Tyriall." The rest of the council did not like this, especially Sontar Mirarel who seemed intent not to acknowledge the girl and her bloodline, but they could not argue. It was his right to offer protection as Lord of House Tyriall to anyone he so chose. But this did not come without a grave warning from the council that it was a mistake and the girl would bring ruin to his house. Illrunn ignored the warning and considered it ignorant and intolerant, something unbecoming from Elves.

While Illrunn had been away to the capital city in Dorwinn, Jaedann and Deva stayed behind, eagerly awaiting the council's decision about Deva. She was nervous, but understood what was at stake. She understood the danger she brought to the Elven Kingdom. Both of them sat in the library of Elnnaril. It was one of the largest libraries in Annmar. Deva had never seen so many books in her life and yearned to read each one of them, to learn more of the Elven Kingdom and even Annmar itself. It was peaceful as the two of them read books, but it only lasted so long before they were interrupted by Degorenn. He has a message for Jaedann.

"There you are," he said. "Jaedann I received a message for you...from Tibautt Fensenn."

Jaedann was surprised. He was almost sure that it was a fool's errand to ask the man for help but never thought he would get a reply. At least Lord Fensenn was courteous enough to tell him no in a message. He said. "You must be joking, he sent a reply back."

"Yes, he did." Degorenn handed the message to him. "He will meet you at Pike's Ridge with 350 men to hear you what you have to say. It is not exactly a yes, but he is willing to listen to you."

"Well, that's something. and he has 350 men...if he's just meeting me so we can talk, why all the men."

Degorenn smiled. "Probably wants to make sure you do not kill him."

Jaedann laughed. "That is fair. But then again, he could be making sure that he actually kills me this time."

"That may be true and only one way to find out."

Jaedann closed his book. "Pike's Ridge is a few days away from here. We should leave immediately if he is already on his way. I know Tibautt Fensenn does not like to be kept waiting."

"I think that is the least of your worries. He could still decide to kill you."

"That's true and I would not blame him."

Deva stood up from her chair and asked. "You are leaving. Let me come with you."

Jaedann smiled. "Not this time. You are safer here in Dorwinn and this is something I need to do without having to worry about you."

"I can take care of myself."

"I know, but there are those in Belmere that would not welcome your existence. Lord Fensenn may be one of them."

Deva gave him a strange look. "Then why would you trust him to fight with us?"

"It's not about trusting him with my life or yours, I only trust that our purpose is the same when defeating an Anntheian army."

"But there is a chance he could kill you?"

"Yes, and It's a risk I have to take to get help in defeating the army marching towards Liberus."

"So, I may never see you again."

Jaedann tried to smile. "That is always a possibility when one goes on a journey, but in your heart, do really believe that?"

Deva smiled. "No."

"Then we will see each other again." Jaedann and Deva embraced. She held onto him a little bit longer than normal and then finally he walked out of the library with Degorenn. The two of them rode out together as Deva sadly watched them leave, truly fearing that Jaedann may never return. Degorenn and Jaedann rode hard, hoping to get to Pike's Ridge in less than two days. They did, making better time than most people would on a journey like this. It was night when they finally arrived.

As they came up the steep hill leading to Pike's Ridge, they saw the fires from the encampment of House Fensenn's soldiers. Jaedan would be lying to himself if he did not feel a little bit nervous. Degorenn and Jaedann entered camp. They were escorted to Tibautt Fensenn's tent. His guards took Jaedann's sword. He didn't complain for he understood why. Jaedann was the first to speak as the guard handed the sword to Tibautt. "Making sure I don't kill you or making sure it's easier to kill me?"

Tibautt Fensenn laughed. "Both. Besides you can never be too careful."

"That we can agree on. We are off to a good start."

"I must confess, I thought you were dead."

"No, just banished."

"I was surprised that your brother let you live."

Jaedann softly laughed. "He did not want to. But our mother and some of the other Lords convinced him not to kill me."

"There's something I have always wanted to tell you."

"What is that?"

"I was very sorry to hear about your wife and child. You should know that was not done on my orders and House Fensenn does not condone the killing of women and children. You may blame me for it, but I wanted you to know that it was not done on my orders."

"No, you only started the rebellion against my house that led to their death."

"And if you want to kill me for it someday, I understand."

Jaedann smiled. "Maybe one day, but I appreciate your words. Now I am here because I need your help." Jaedann proceeded to tell him about the Anntheian army and what he encountered. He laid out the numbers and a little bit of his strategy.

Tibautt paused for a moment, taking it all in. He said. "I would say you do not have enough men, but the Knights of House Fensenn are worth four of every Anntheian soldier so the numbers would be a little more even."

"That's why I am asking for your help. You still have the fiercest warriors in Belmere, there is no denying that."

"Damn straight we do and you know why, because we don't coddle our children. They are raised from when they can walk to be warriors and that also includes the women. Women are not just for birthing future soldiers. That is something that the rest of the houses in Belmere do not understand including yours."

Jaedann shook his dead, not completely agreeing with his assessment. He replied. "You are not wrong except for my house. My father believed the same and that is why my sister was trained as a soldier too."

Tibautt smiled. "Perhaps your father was not as much of an idiot as I took him for."

"No, and perhaps you are not as much of a horse's ass I took you for."

Tibautt laughed. He was a horse's ass and he knew it, but he always did right by his people and that made him a better man than most. He replied. "I am one, but I am okay with that. Now, you have the beginnings of a good plan, but what I really want to know is, why should we give two shitts about Liberus? What does it matter if Anntheia destroys it? It is just a smuggler's town."

Jaedann stepped closer to the edge of Tibautt's desca. "It's more than that. Whether people want to admit it, Annmar relies on it as an alternative to shipping goods through Anntheia and paying double the taxes."

"They could do that through Belmere. Besides if Liberus is destroyed, it can be rebuilt again."

"All of that is true, but there is more." Jaedann debated on whether to tell him truth, but the only way to build the trust they needed to fight in the the same battle was to tell the man the truth. Jaedann continued. "There is a girl that King Lancelynn of Anntheia wants dead, that's why he is destroying the city."

Tibautt thought it was strange. "All that for one girl. I do not know of any girl that is worth destroying a city over."

"This one has special abilities that are worth killing for."

"Special abilities…you mean like magic?"

"Yes."

"So, it is true."

Jaedann seemed confused by his words. "What is true?"

"That a magic user has returned to Annmar?"

"How do you know about that?"

Tibautt softly smiled. "My wife speaks to oracles. She pays attention to signs and likes to know the future of things. I have never really believed in signs, but she said to me weeks ago that everything was about to change. Magic had returned and prophecy would be fulfilled. Is it this girl?"

Jaedann paused looking for the right words. "I do not know for sure, all I know is she is special and the King of Anntheia wants her dead. That's enough for me to know she needs to be protected at all costs."

Tibautt handed Jaedann back his sword. "That is good enough for me too. I would gladly march across the world to send thousands of Anntheian soldiers to the afterlife. I hate them worst than I hate your brother."

Jaedann laughed at the comment. "These days, I cannot say I disagree with you."

"The let us drink and forget old grievances. Let us go spill some Anntheian blood."

Jaedann reached out his hand. Tibautt gladly accepted it and shook his hand. Once again, they were allies. Tibautt remarked. "I also have to say, I am surprised that you kept your Belmerien Knight's sword."

Jaedann softly smiled. "They can banish me from my homeland. They can strip me of my title, but they cannot unmake me a knight. I was raised to be a Knight of Belmere. I have the heart of a Knight and that will never be taken away. This sword is my reminder of that and the only way they can take it is when I am dead."

"Spoken like a true knight of Belmere, but do you know why you should never lose your Belmerien Sword?"

Jaedann confidently smiled. "Because they are the best swords made in Annmar. Nobody in Annmar matches the skill of a swordsmith in Belmere.

"True on both accounts. My father once told me that it had to do with the minerals and ore found in the northern mountains of Belmere. No other region could lay claim to finer minerals that would make a great sword. It was not only the craftsmanship, but what they were made of and that is what made the steel lighter and sharper."

"There is no finer steel than Bellmorann Steel. You may not know this, but when Knights of the Lionnshade brigade are sent to the Bellmora Mountains to train, we are also taught to mine the ore necessary to make a sword since it lives deep in those mountains and then craft weapons from it because you never know when you might be alone and have to make your own weapons. I made my old dagger. Use to be attached to my belt, but now resides on my boot or in it depending on whose company I am in."

Tibautt gave him a strange look, realizing that his guards probably missed the dagger in his boot when they searched him, but then smiled. "A skill all true men of Belmere should know. And I like that you kept the lion's head for your pummel."

Jaedann looked at Tibautt and then to Degorenn. "I may not wear the tunic or command them anymore, but I will always be a part of the Lionnshade Brigade. They cannot stop me staying to true to my vows. The Lionnshade is a part of me."

"I can respect that and I forget, what do you call your sword?"

Jaedann smiled. "Vindicator!"

Tibautt let out a boisterous laugh. "That is a fine name, a very fine name for a sword." Then the two men shared a drink together and forgot their old grudges. They raised their mugs and both said, "By the blood of the old gods, we defend what is ours and fight for those who cannot!" Tonight, they were on the same side.

32

It had been six days since Jaedann and Degorenn left for Pike's Ridge, but they finally returned to Elnnaril and with help. Deva was very happy to see Jaedan, a part of her still feared that he would not return. When she saw him walk up the main stairs to the great hall, she ran towards him and embraced him. Jaedann had to admit, he was happy to see her too. She said to him. "You are alive."

Jaedann smiled. "I am and I brought help."

"Enough to save Liberus?"

"There are no guarantees I can save the city, but the people will be better defended now." Illrunn was back from the capital and greeted Jaedann. He had not told him or Deva about the council's decision about her staying in Dorwinn. Truth be told, he did not want to disappoint her. Illrunn greeted Jaedann and said. "It is good to have you back, I am sure there is much to discuss."

"Yes," Jaedann replied, "a battle plan of sorts. As you can see, I brought help."

"I see that." Illrunn greeted Tibet Fensenn. "Lord Fennsen, It is a pleasure to see you again."

Tibautt and Illrunn had only met once before, but Lord Fensenn could never forget someone like Lord Illrunn Tyriall. Even as an Elf, he made quite an impression. He replied to Illrunn's greeting. "Lord Tyriall, it is a pleasure to see you again and thank you for your hospitality."

Illrunn nodded. "I am glad that you could aid Jaedann in his quest. I am happy to offer you shelter, food, and whatever supplies you and your men need."

Tibautt nodded back. "Thank You Lord Tyriall."

"Illrunn looked at Jaedann and Deva. "I need to speak to the both of you in private." So, they went to Ilrunn's private library. Jaedann could tell by the look on his face that it was not good news. Illrunn spoke. "The council has decided that Deva cannot stay in Dorwinn." Deva was devastated to hear the news, but Jaedann had a feeling that it would be the outcome. Jaedann asked. "What was their reason?"

Illrunn looked at Deva because the answer concerned her. "They you fear you pose a threat because of who is hunting you."

With a sad look on her face and trying to hold back the tears, she replied back. "Because it might cause a war with Anntheia."

"That is part of it, but mostly because of the ancient evil that is hunting you, which I spoke of when you first came here. You are a threat if that comes to Dorwinn."

"I did not ask for this, why should I be blamed for it?"

"It is not about blame; their decision is out of fear and they have good reason to be afraid even if you yourself are not a threat to this Kingdom."

Tears filled Deva's eyes. "What can I do? I feel like I just found a home, like I found my family and now I am being shunned just like my father. My name is just that, a name and it does not mean anything."

Illrunn put his hands on the girl's shoulders, trying to comfort her. "You are not being shunned by all Elves. You are not an outcast and while you may not be able to stay in this Kingdom, you will not be abandoned."

"Then what am I supposed to do?"

Illrunn looked at both Jaedann and Deva. "You will have to go into hiding. It is the only way to keep you safe. But remember, you will have the protection of my house. I will send Elves that I completely trust to keep you safe along with Jaedann"

Deva replied. "All I wanted was to find my place in this world, to find my family and where I truly belong. It is not fair."

"No, it is not fair, this world rarely is fair. But you have those who will keep you safe and help on your journey. That is also a rare thing." There was nothing more to say. Deva's destiny was not in Dorwinn. The three of them returned to Illrunn's council room with the long marble table. Jaedann had battle plans to discuss. They found Tibautt, Degorenn, and Arunn sitting at the table with a makeshift map of Liberus. Tibautt was the first to speak. "So, tell us how you plan to defend Liberus and kill the Anntheia Army, while being outnumbered."

Jaedann replied. "Well, first off, the people must be saved. They cannot be sacrificed, not even one person if it may help us."

"That will make things more difficult."

"Yes, but not impossible. If the Lionnshade brigade cannot fight with us and their only mandate is to stop the Rogues of Hamlinn ships, then that will work to our advantage."

Degorenn asked. "How so?"

"Instead of sinking their ships, you sneak aboard, kill them all, and take over the ships. Then we get the people of Liberus onto the ships."

Degorenn softly smiled, he knew where he was going with the plan. "You want the Anntheian army to think people are still in the city when they try to burn it down."

"Yes, but they will safely be on the ships. The buildings can be sacrificed because they can be rebuilt, but not the people that make Liberus. Once the Anntheians feel like they have bombarded the city with enough fireballs from their ballistas, the army will walk into the city and kill what's left, but that is where we draw them into a trap."

Tibautt Fensenn asked. "You mean that is where we will be waiting for them or at least on the other side of the fire and then we kill them?"

"Not exactly, I want to use their own ballistas on them. We come from behind, take over the ballistas, fire on the city and take out most their soldiers. Then we march in and kill the rest. We need to get their numbers down before we engage their army."

"That is a good plan, but when I fight Anntheian soldiers, I face them before I kill them and I do not care about the odds."

Jaedann rolled his eyes. "I am not trying to wound your pride, but we are outnumbered and this is best way to even the odds."

"Fuk the odds, a Belmerien Knight always faces his enemy before he kills them, we do not sneak up behind them like wolves, or have you forgotten that in your banishment?"

"If all you want to do is die in battle so the bards will sing songs about you then go find another battle because in this one, it's about saving as many people as we can including you and your men. I will not waste the blood of any man because of your pride."

Tibautt slammed the table. "A true fight is man versus man, knight versus knight, you asked for my help then let's face our enemy the right way and if we die, then we die, but it will be a glorious death. If we cannot fight the Belmerien way, then my men and I will go home."

Jaedann was furious. He understood the honor of fighting face to face, but battles and wars were won with the best strategy. The difference between a true soldier and a Lord with foolish notions of honor is the one who understood the value of strategy in a war. Jaedann may have been a prince at one time, but he was always a true soldier at heart. With an angry tone, he replied. "Insult me all you want, I have not forgotten how a Knight of Belmere fights, but the smart soldier finds the best strategy that saves the most lives."

"And sometimes you have to sacrifice them for the greater good, even innocent lives. Some may have to be sacrificed along with the city."

"Not if I can help it and my strategy is also about protecting something of great value, even more valuable than gold." That got everybody's attention, they were extremely curious by what Jaedann meant. Tibautt asked. "What is so great in value that it would be more valuable than gold."

Jaedann looked at everybody in the room and then turned his attention to Deva and said. "Two journals that belong to you. They were found on the ship you came in. The one who cared for you wrote the details of your life in them."

Deva, shocked at what she was hearing, asked. "Why didn't you tell me?"

"We wanted to give them to you when all of this was over."

"Who is we?"

"Vorak and I. He has them now and is keeping them safe."

Tibautt did not care about such things, he did not see what this had to do with the battle and angrily replied. "Bounded pages are not worth any more than the paper I use to wipe ass, why give a shitt about them. Let them burn with the rest of the city."

Jaedann responded with a touch of anger of his own. "We can't let them burn those secrets. They have great value, such as how to find Ellisar, a place that part of the prophecy. And whether any if us truly believe in the prophecy, at the very least Ellisar is an important place for her so we cannot let the journals burn."

Tibautt still did not care about the journals, but Deva suddenly valued nothing greater than the journals that now belonged to her. She said. "If what you say is true, they must have answers I need, which does makes them important. They must be kept safe, no matter what and we are still outnumbered."

Jaedann replied. "Yes, that is true, but I wanted you to stay here where it was safe. I cannot have you going into the lion's den where you could die."

Deva was insistent. "I go where those journals are and I do not need your permission." Before Jaedann could respond, she looked at Illrunn and said. "You promised to protect me since I cannot stay in Dorwinn, I ask for your protection. I am going to Liberus, please send Elven warriors to help me."

Illrunn shook his head, not wanting to go against his own duty to his city's defenses by sending soldiers that needed to remain here. He said. "I cannot send an army to Liberus, this is not the fight of Elves."

Deva did not like his answer. "Then send them to protect me, even if it's just a small army. I am going to Liberus regardless, I ask that you do not break your word when it comes to protecting me."

"I too, wanted you to stay here in order to remain safe, but I cannot stop you from going either. I will not send an army, but I will send a few hundred Elves to protect you and help in the battle to come."

Deva nodded. "Thank You."

Jaedann responded. "Okay, that changes things. Tibautt, you get your wish. Your army will stand at the back of the city and greet the Anntheians as they walk through Liberus. You can face them when you kill them."

Tibautt nodded. "Gladly and when those who are left, retreat, you and the Elves can kill the last of them, but trust me there will be not that many."

Jaedann smiled. "That I believe. Now it appears we have a plan. We will force the Anntheians into a position where we surround them once the people are safely out of the city and on those ships. Degorenn you will have to get there at least a day before us and take over those ships."

Degorenn smiled at the idea of finally killing these rogues who lived outside of any law and taking their ships. He did not like Rogues of Hamlinn very much like most n Belmere. "My men and I can do that. We will leave tonight."

"Okay, the only thing left to figure out is the fastest way to Liberus before that army arrives or all of this is for nothing." Illrunn spoke up. "I can help you with that, I know the fastest way south. Elves are the masters of speed and I promise that you will get there before Anntheia does." Jaedann nodded. This was one of the reasons Elves made the best allies and the worst enemy. He was glad that he never had to experience the latter.

It was time to finally leave Dorwinn for the battle that would soon come. The fastest way to Liberus was not on foot, but by sea. They would go to the beginning of the Marasonn River, to an Elven port where some of their largest ships were located. The river, which lead through Dorwinn and the edge of the Kingdom of Yorynn came out into the Gleaming Gulf which surrounded Dorwinn, Skallvenn, and the land outside Liberus. They would come to a secret port that only smugglers knew about, it was called the Dragonnfly port and only two days ride to Liberus from there. If all went right, Jaedann, Tibuatt Fensenn, and the small Elven army would arrive days before the Anntheian army did. After all, Elven ships were to known to be the fastest ships in Annmar.

Before everybody left,Illrunn spoke to his son in private, Arunn. He had something great and important to tell him. Ilrunn started off by saying. "Son, I know you and I have not always been in agreement and I have looked down upon some of your choices, but there is only one person, I trust for what I am about to ask."

Arunn was curious, but also felt a sense of pride that his father was coming to him even though he did not know what he was about to ask. "What is it father?"

"You know that I have pledged our house to protect Deva, well, I cannot think of no one better to protect her. I want you to go with her and Jaedann."

Arunn was a bit stunned. His father was asking a great deal. "I am honored."

"I know son, but what I ask is no small task so you should hear it all before you decide what to do. You do have the right to refuse what I ask, it is not a command."

"I understand."

Illrunn stepped closer. "This is not about one battle or even the journey she must take. I have-not doubt that her journey to Ellisar will be perilous. She will need good people on her side. But it is more than that. War is coming."

Hearing his father talk about war, gave Illrunn an uneasy feeling. He had to ask. "What makes you think that?"

"If someone with magic has returned to Annmar, it will bring war from those who try to stop the return of magic. I do not know when it will come or who we will be fighting, but war is inevitable. And that is when she will need our protection the most. Deva must be allowed to fulfill her destiny. No matter what."

"Are you referring to the prophecy and whether she is one of the five?"

"Whether she is or not, I do believe she has a part to play in the shaping of our world, which includes the return of magic. You will stay with her and help guide her until she has fulfilled her destiny."

"I will do what you ask of me, not just for you, but for our family, and for the honor of the Elves. I will not refuse my duty when it comes to that."

Illrunn smiled. "I did not think you would refuse, but I wanted to give you the choice because the choice is yours and cannot be based on my own wishes."

"I understand father and I will protect her until my last breath."

Illrunn put his hands on his son's shoulders. "I do not know when I will see you again."

"It may be a while, but I will send messages to let you know where I am and what is going on."

Illrunn who had been speaking the common language up to this point for the sake of his guests, finally spoke in the Elven tongue. "Biodhh fàbharr aigg narr diathann airr dohh thurrass."

Arunn smiled. "May the gods find favor in your journey as well, father."

The two men walked out to the main stairs at the entrance of Elnnaril, where the rest of the party was waiting to leave. Deva walked up to Ysilda and hugged her as a tear ran down her face. She was sad to leave just as she found her true family, or at the least the one that wanted her. It was because of that, that Deva felt a kinship with Ysilda. She was the like the mother she never knew. Ysilda said to her. "Do not cry my child. We will see each other again."

"I hope so," Deva replied. "I would like that very much."

"To finally meet my brother's child has brought great joy to my heart. And for the rest of House Mirarel, they should be ashamed for not wanting to see how special you are, but you will always have a home among us despite what the Elven council might say."

Deva cried tears of joy. "Thank You for saying that. Until we see each other again." Ysilda spoke Elven. "Síocháinn leatt inn éineachtt leatt arr dohh thurass." Deva had a curious look, for she did not know the Elven tongue. Ysilda said. "May you find peace on your journey." Deva smiled and said goodbye to Ysilda and Illrunn.

Finally, Jaedann said goodbye to Illrunn and thanked him for his hospitality. Illrunn replied. "Until we see each other again Jaedann Barrenn, I wish you good fortune on your journey." Jaedann nodded and the party rode off for the port at the Marasonn River. As they were riding through the lush green fields outside Elnnaril, Deva looked back and stared for a moment. Jaedann asked what was wrong. Deva said. "I wonder if I will see this place again, just wanted to take one last look if I do not." Jaedann replied. "I have no doubt, you have a long life ahead of you and will live long enough to see this place again."

33

It was darker than usual on this particular night. There was no moon, thus making it perfect for Degorenn and the Lionnshade brigade to quietly sneak out into the sea surrounding Liberus towards the four ships blockading the port. The Rogues of Hamlinn had arrived a week earlier to blockade the ports of Liberus and nobody had been hurt so far, but no ships from Liberus had been able to leave or enter the port. They were hurting business, that much was for sure. Degorenn had about 70 men divided into four small boats. Each one slowly rowed towards each large ship occupied by the Rogues. None of them were detected and one by one, they used grappling devices with ropes tied to the end to hook on the railings and slowly climb aboard. Doing this in the middle of the night meant they had a better chance that everybody was sleeping or were passed out drunk. The only men they had to contend with were the three watchers on the deck and the watcher at the top of the main sail. A good archer could take the man out at the top of the sail. But the real trick was taking everybody out the same time, so no one rang the alarm bells. If even one of them went off, the other ships could hear the bells and the full crew would be woken up.

The Lionnshade brigade was heavily outnumbered and while they may have been able to kill the crews, they would surely lose half of the brigade. Degorenn did not want to lose even a single man. The brigade was trained well and precision was the key. Degorenn led a few men up the rope to the ship he was about to take over. They had not been seen. When he gave the signal, he pulled his Belmerien dagger out of its sheath as well as two other men, the archer who climbed aboard aimed an arrow towards the watcher at the top of the main sail. One…two…three, they all moved at the same time, Degorenn and the two other men threw their daggers at the watchmen on the deck and killed them. The Archer shot his arrow and hit the man on the sail tower. He fell overboard into the water. Now all they had to do was make sure that no one else came up from below.

One of the many weapons that the brigade used was an herbal substance that when when sprinkled on something and then when lit on fire, the fumes would cause people who smelled it to faint. The plant that it derived from was called Chlorfornnium. It could be quite deadly if used right such as knocking someone out and then killing them in their sleep. Degorenn had four big balls of twigs and vines rolled up into a ball. The men covered their mouth and nose with cloth, they lit the balls of twigs and vines. The fumes were intense, which was the idea. They threw them down below where the Rogues men ate and slept. It only took a few minutes before the sound of men rolling out of their hammocks fell to the floor, passed out. The only person left was the captain. Chances were, he would not be passed out as he had his own cabin shielded with two large doors. Degorenn and his men waited a little bit for the fumes to subside, but still kept their mouths and noses covered just to be on the safe side when they walked down below to the captain's quarters. He had not been knocked out. Degorenn could hear him snoring so he banged on the door and said. "Captain of the ship, my name if Degorenn of the Lionnshade brigade from Belmere, we are taking over your ship. All of your men have been knocked out, so do not try and resist. Will you give your ship up peacefully?"

The captain was trying to be brave so he opened the door, but the Belmerien was not there. Degorenn pulled out his sword and cautiously walked into the captain's quarters. The captain was hiding behind the door and wildly swung his sword trying to hit anyone he could. It was a fool's errand, but he was a fighting captain and would go down with his ship before giving her up. Degorenn ducked and came underneath with his sword slicing the captain's stomach and letting his intestines fall out. Then he said to the captain. "You could not make this easy, could you! We had already captured your ship and was not trying to bluff you out."

"May the god's fuk you dead."

Degorenn shook his head in disbelief and replied. "You first." Then he cut the captain's head off. Looking at his men. "Every time we do this, these godsdamn fools have to try and be brave when they know we have taken over. One of these days, one of them will be smart and just give us their ship."

One of the men replied. "If they are not from Belmere, I do not trust them to be that smart." They all laughed because for them it was a simple truth. Each ship went pretty much the same way. It was easy to take out the crew and the Captains were killed for trying to fight back. The Lionnshade brigade was known to be merciful. They did the dirty work when it came to war so others could make honorable choices. When each ship was taken over, someone would send a signal. They shot a fire arrow into the sky.

Jaedann and Tibautt stood on a hilltop watching for the signal. When they saw the fire arrows, Jaedann commented. "Great, looks like part one of our plan has succeeded. We have the ships."

Tibautt replied. "I will not be happy until I know they have killed all the crew, there is no room for mercy in this battle."

"Of course, they will, I even told them to do so."

"Really, I thought you would have shown mercy."

Jaedann laughed. "No, not this time. War is a dirty business and we do not have time to be merciful…those crews have to die for us to accomplish our objective.

Tibautt smiled. "Good, I am glad you understand that."

"Do not worry Lord Fensenn, I am not as soft as you think I am."

Tibautt laughed at his comment. "Do you miss being a part of the brigade and doing stuff like that?"

"Yes, but I still do not like killing unarmed people even if its necessary."

"I understand that. Kill some Anntheian soldiers later, that will make you feel better, it always does for me." Both men laughed. There was simple truth in that statement that always made sense…no matter the circumstances and it was something that both men could agree on.

It had been months since Jaedann had stepped foot in Liberus. The place felt different, even though for the most part it was the same. The place rarely changed and there was a certain comfort in knowing that. Jaedann was still a wanted man so he wore a cloak to keep himself from being seen. As a Ranger, he could make himself not be seen if needed without the use of magic. He needed to find Vorak and his fellow Rangers. The sun was barely peaking over the ridge when he come into town from the northwest. Since it was still early morning, most people were just getting up and starting their day or still passed out drunk since the nightlife in Liberus was always exciting. He imagined Rathgar in a bed with at least two tavern wenches. Jaedann knew that Vorak would be up…he started his day earlier than most so that is where he went first.

He was right, Vorak was sturring about as the girl he found to keep his bed warm was still asleep. Jaedann quietly snuck into his building and nearly scared Vorak to death. Vorak shouted, waking the girl in his bed. "Fuk the gods. Jaedann what are you doing here? When did you get in?"

Smiling, Jaedann replied. "Good morning to you too. Been here since late last night. Me and the small army that came with me who are camped one mil outside the city on those top ridges to the northwest."

Vorak was surprised. "I knew it, you did bring help. How many?"

"Not enough, but then again enough to keep us in the fight if all goes according to plan."

"What does that mean?"

"Lord Tibautt Fensenn brought a small army from his House in Belmere."

Vorak was shocked to hear that. "I thought you hated him because he started a rebellion years ago and challenged your family for the throne."

"He did and I do hate him as much as he hates me. But he hates Anntheia more and knowing what they want with Deva, he offered his help. "What can I say, it's a strange world that we live in!"

Vorak laughed. "That's one way to put it."

"We also have a small brigade of Elves from House Tyriall in Dorwinn. Lord Tyriall offered his protection to Deva. They came to protect her and help us fight."

There was another look of surprise on Vorak's face when he heard that Deva was among them. "You brought her back here?"

"I did not…she came on her own to get her, her journals and the Elven council would not let her stay in Dorwinn."

"Why not?"

"Fear! Fear for what may come looking for her and they do not want to risk the security of Dorwinn or be dragged into a war over a girl with magic."

Vorak shook his head. "I suppose I can understand that. But about her journals, I have been reading through them. They are, well, I guess interesting would be the right word. But they are filled with lots of mysteries that not even I can begin to comprehend. I have lots of questions."

"That will have to be for another time, we have a battle to prepare for. The journals, are they safe?"

"Yes, Jaedann. I have even kept them out of the way of prying eyes."

Jaedann softly laughed. He knew what that meant. "So that means Thorsha does not know about them."

"Yes, only myself, Hanniah, Rathgar, and you know of their existence"

"Good. We need to get them out of the city and we need to speak to Thorsha."

Vorak gave him another look of shock, not really knowing what he was getting at with this plan. He said. "Are you playing the fool now? She still wants you dead for helping Deva escape or at least what she thinks you did."

"I know, but I cannot worry about that now. We need to get the people out of Liberus before the that Anntheian army arrives."

"I do not know if we can convince her of that, she still thinks the message you sent about the army was false. Besides, she is too busy trying to contend with the Blockade."

Jaedann laughed. "She does not have to worry about that anymore…we took care of it last night."

"What do you mean?"

"The Lionnshade Brigade from Belmere snuck aboard and took over the ships."

Another surprise hit   Vorak. "Your old unit, how did you manage to enlist their help?"

"Long story, but for another time. Let's get Hanniah and Rathgar and then take me to see Thorsha." Vorak took Jaedann to find Rathgar. They had to wake him up from his slumber with two lovely large breasted tavern wenches. Rathgar was overjoyed to see Jaedann. He quickly gathered his clothes and weapons, and then they went to the main building to find the magistrate. Hanniah was out on patrol. Thorsha was not happy to see Jaedann and immediately called out for her guards when seeing his face. Barack tried to stop her, but to no avail. One of the guards came from behind and tried to cut Jaedann down with his sword, but Jaedann was too fast and too smart to let the simple guard take him down. Jaedann ducked underneath his swing, pulled out a dagger, and stabbed it into the guard's face. The he took the guards sword and with two swings knocked the other guard's sword out of his hands and then sliced open his throat.

Jaedann was furious and let Thorsha know it. "These men are dead because of you and they did not have to die. Stop trying to kill me."

Thorsha was angry. All she had was blood lust for Jaedann and it kept her from thinking objectively. She replied. "You went against our council's wishes. Went against our rule of law just to help that girl and that means you owe me a debt. I take death as A payment."

"Fine, you think I owe you a debt, I can repay that debt by saving this city. I did not come back for your backwards ass justice, especially when I did not do the thing you accuse me of. The girl ran off on her own because you betrayed what Liberus stands for when it comes to protecting its citizens, even strangers like her."

Thorsha was still mad and everyone could hear it in her tone. "Save my city, you mean from the mysterious Anntheian army you made up."

"Believe me or not, but it will not stop the fact that they are on their way and will burn this city to the ground. Why would I make something like that up anyway?"

Thorsha gave him a dirty look. "Perhaps you wanted to cause such a frenzy just to have us abandon the city and then claim it for yourself and that girl. Or maybe you are still a Belmerien knight and a spy, trying to claim this city for Belmere."

Jaedann laughed. "What ridiculous fantasies you have, I hope I can have the same when I reach old age." Thorsha threw him another dirty look for the comment about her age. Jaedann continued. "We have no time for this. While we squabble over false accusations, that army is almost here and we are not prepared to defend this place. It will not be like defending it against a hundred Barbarians.

We cannot win against two legions of Anntheian soldiers, but I have a plan."

Thorsha stared at him for a moment. She still did not want to believe him. "Why should I do anything based on what you say?"

Hanniah walked into the main building, back from her patrol. She responded to Thorsha's statement. "Because Jaedann is right and I have seen this army." She walked up to the group and looked at Jaedann. "Glad you are finally back. I would say that I miss you, but I have been too busy doing your job to miss you." Jaedann laughed at her comment. Hanniah looked at Thorsha and said. "He was not lying, there is an Anntheian army about 18 mils from here with four ballistas. They will be here here by nightfall."

Thorsha was shocked. She never doubted anything that Hanniah had to say. The two had grown somewhat close since Jaedann left. Thorsha asked. "Okay, I may not believe you, but I believe her, what do we do?"

Jaedann replied to Thorsha. "As I was saying, I have a plan and I brought help. The first thing we need to do is get people out of the city." Jaedann explained the rest of his plan and told them in great detail about everybody he brought to help. Even though the odds were against them, it was a good plan, or at least the best plan under their current circumstances. But unfortunately, they had little time to make it work.

34

Commander Tolbernn Rogier walked out of his tent and was greeted by the Magerus who was his second in command. Rogier asked him. "Is everybody in position." The Magerus replied. "Yes Commander, all four ballistas are where they are supposed to be. The men are waiting on your order!"

The Commander smiled confidently as if he had already won the battle. Over confidence always seemed to be an Anntheian army's undoing. He said to his Magerus. "Good, let's begin, sound the horns."

The Magerus paused. It was his job as second in command to provide alternatives, the same as it was for Commander Rogier to do for his Genneral. He responded with that alternative. "Commander, we should wait until early morning when the men have had a chance to rest after the long march. The city is not going anywhere and our men will be better fighters with a little rest and food."

Rogier seemed to get angry. "Magerus, we do this now. This is a city with no standing army, this will be quick and the men should have no problem killing defenseless people. We should be done in an hour and then they can rest or celebrate throught the night after the city is sacked."

The Magerus nodded and gave the command to the men with the long, curved horns made out of animal tusks that could amplify sound upwards of one mil away. The ballistas were in four centralized positions that would allow them to bombard each direction of the city equally. One horn would be blown as a signal to the next closest one and then that horn would be blown to signal the closet one to it until all four horns had been blown as one big signal that they all acknowledge the command and could start catapulting fireballs into the city. All four horns would blow again to signal the ballista operators that they could stop the bombardment. Rogier was at the southern position. One Legion of soldiers were with him and would enter the city from the south and one legion of soldiers was to the north of the city and would enter it from that direction. All four horns blew and the battle had begun.

Jaedann and Hanniah were helping some of the last people into small boats that would take them to the large ships when they heard the horns sound. Not everybody was out of the city yet. Most were. The Magistrate was one of the last to leave on a boat to the one of the four big ships in the bay. Mostly it was some of the shop keepers and their families who were still in the city, they had stayed behind to try and save as much of their goods as they could, knowing the city was about to burn. Jaedann, shocked to hear the horns because he thought they had more time, or at least hoped they would, said. "Damn, now it begins."

"What do we do with the rest of these people? We have not time to get them out of here?"

Jaedann looked around. "Not much we can do now, get whoever you can behind the line."

"What line?"

"Behind Tibautt Fensenn's men, get them near the water and over by that cove at the edge of the beach. That is the safest place for them now. "Then Jaedann looked up and saw a fire arrow shoot in the sky. It was a signal from one of his towermen. Fireballs were coming and all they could do was hope everybody was out the city for nothing could be done about them now if they were not. Jaedann walked over to Tibautt and gave one last command. "Lord Fensenn, let the soldiers come to you when they enter the city."

Tibautt, stubborn as always, replied. "As soon as see them we charge hard and fast and will kill every last one of them."

Jaedann rolled his eyes at what he thought was a stupid strategy. "For the love of the gods, wait so we don't kill you and your men when we fire their own fireballs on them after we take over the the ballistas. I'm trying to save you and your men."

"Fine, have it your way, but do not make me wait too long before I can spill Anntheian blood on this god's forsaken beach. "

Jaedann laughed at his Belmerien sentiment. "I will try not to make you wait too long. I will meet you in the middle of the city."

Tibautt Fensenn nodded and then Jadann jumped on his horse and rode off towards the northern beach rode. He had to get around the enemy lines and meet up with Arunn and the rest of the Elves to begin the second part of his plan. As he rode north fast and hard, he could see the fireballs reigning down on the city. They were big, as big as five men put together and would cause a tremendous amount of damage. He made it to the woods and as he was about to turn east, he saw the second legion sitting there, waiting to engage. He was spotted by some of the archers who thought he was citizen trying to escape. Two of them strung their bows and fired arrows at him as he rode by. Jaedann had his bow as well and quickly shot them both as they were trying to reload. He did not have time to engage the rest of them so he rode around the army as they tried to shoot him off his horse. They missed and he safely got away.

Deva had stayed behind the enemy lines with the Arunn and the Elves. They were trying to keep her as far from danger as possible. The Elves were located on a ridge hidden in the woods as the tall trees went up the hill. They were in a good position to see the fireballs be lauched into the city. It was frightening to watch and it made Deva nervous. She knew that Jaedann and the others were not actually in the city, but it scared her nonetheless. Being nervous, she looked at Arunn and said. "Okay, enough, take out the the ballistas." Arunn replied. "No, it's not time yet."

"They have fired. We have waited long enough."

Arunn gave her a stern look. "No, not until we hear their horns sound and the army marching into the city. We have to time this right."

Deve did not like the answer. She just wanted to get this over with. There was too much damage, too many chanceS that those fighting for her could get killed. Deva was young and it showed as she was prone to rush into things. She finally turned around so she did not have to see the fireballs coming down on the city. After a few minutes and about four rounds of fireballs, they heard the Anntheian horns sound again. They were done with the bombardment and both sets of legions started to advance. Arunn could see the Anntheian commander start to advance with the southern legion. Liberus was devoured in flames. It looked as if a dragon had flown over, breathing fire and laying waste to the city. The light from the fire could be seen for mils including ships sailing outside the bay in the Elmsonn sea. Most of Liberus's citizens had never seen fires so big. It was hard to watch, but sacrificing the buildings of the city instead of her people just to lay a trap for the enemy had been the right move.

When the legions were far enough away and closer to the city, Arunn shot a fire arrow into the sky, signaling the small groups of Elven archers waiting outside the treelines near the ballistas, it was time to strike. One arrow to strike, two arrows to use the ballista to fire on the city on top of the Anntheian soldiers were the signals. The elves were excellent shots with a bow. They came out of nowhere and stealthly killed the Anntheians operating the ballistas and then they sounded their Elven horns to let Arunn know they had captured the ballistas. Three hornes sounded, but not a fourth. Something was wrong, it was not like Elves to be defeated by a few measly ballista operators, but Arunn could not worry about that right now. They had three ballistas and they needed to have them fire into Liberus onto of the Anntheian soldiers. Arunn used an Elven spyglass and could see that the legions were in the city, they were right where the Jaedann and the Elves needed them to be. Arunn shot two fire arrows in the sky to signal the Elves to catapult fireballs. Deva could see three fireballs shoot towards the city. She was happy to see that and know that their plan was working, but she had to ask. "Which ballista position did not blow their horn?"

Arunn thought for a moment. "I believe it was the one to the far north." Fear grabbed hold of Deva. She said. "That's the one Jaedann is going to. He's in danger, we have to help." Deva found a horse, climbed on, and rode off in that direction. Arunn shouted. "Deva, no. Jaedann can take care of himself. She would not hear it and continued to ride. He had no choice, but to chase after her. Deva rode full steam ahead past the other ballistas until she came the far north position. That's when she saw it. The Khronne who had been hunting her down was still alive and found them. The Khronne had killed the Elven archers. Jaedann came riding onto the position as well, but from the opposite side. Deva was mad and her hands started to glow. Jaedann yelled out. "Deva, no, I have this." He rode towards the Khronne and fired two arrows at it. The Khronne knocked them out of the way with the Elven bow it had picked up. Then it picked up a log nearby, throwing at Jaedann and knocking him off his horse. He fell hard to the ground and cracked a rib.

Deva had, had a enough. She charged the Khronne and out of anger shot fireballs from her hands towards it. The Khronne was fast, but not fast enough to escape the barrage of fireballs coming from Deva's hands. The Khronne caught on fire, but it did not stop it, it threw a log towards Deva knocking her to the ground, but it was enough to distract the Khronne as Arunn came up from behind Deva, firing four arrows simultaneously and hitting the Khronne twice. The arrows stunned it, but it had enough strength to throw another log at full speed, this time towards Arunn. By this time Jaedann had finally gotten up and was running towards the Khronne. It heard Jaedann and grabbed another log, intending to swing and knock Jaedann into the trees with a deadly blow. As a Ranger and former Knight, Jaedann was too smart to fall for that. As Jaedann come close, he tucked low and rolled underneath the swing cutting the Khronne's abdomen open. The Khronne tried to grab Jaedann and throw him with its super strength, but Deva had gotten up and shot two fireballs at the Khronne. It was enough of a distraction that the Khronne could not grab Jaedann and give him enough time to make two swings with his sword, one downwards cutting open the Khronnes chest open, letting it's blood spill and then the final blow. Jaedann swung back around and cut the Khronnes head off.

Deva and Arunn walked up to Jaedann as he stood over the Khronnes body without a head. "He said, staring at the lifeless head, by itself. "If that does not fuking kill it, then I will quit being a Ranger and go into hiding."

Arunn commented. "If that thing is not dead by now then we might as well all quit, there will be no way to defeat something like that." He looked at Deva and said. "Do not run off like that, it was stupid. We have to protect you."

Deva shot her cousin a dirty look. "If it were not for me distracting this thing with fireballs you would not have been able to kill it so what I did was not that stupid."

Jaedann shook his head. "Maybe not stupid, but foolish. You cannot keep putting yourself in danger like that, but thank you. You were a big help." Deva smiled. He had never really complimented her before, at least for saving his life. He looked around. The Khronne destroyed all the oil to help light these fireballs, there is no way they could light them with fire and shoot them. They needed to shoot at least a few. Deva looked at the big balls and said. "Perhaps I can help. After all I can create fire with my hands." Jaedann and Arunn both laughed. She was not wrong.

Jaedann loaded a ball in the cup of the ballista. Deva stood by it, closed her eyes and thought of fire. She was able to control it and then touched the ball in the cup. It worked, it caught on fire. Jaedann pulled the trigger and a fireball went flying through the air. They loaded another ball into the cup and Deva did the same thing as before. The ball caught on fire and Jaedann launched it towards Liberus with the Anntheian soldiers in the streets looking for people to kill. The part of their plan was working, now it was time to meet in the middle of Liberus and destroy the rest of the army.

35

Anntheian soldiers were scattererd throughout a burning Liberus looking for the the leftover citizens who had not been killed by the huge fireballs. They could not find any except for a few people who had not been able to escape. It was men without weapons and women too. The soldiers killed what they could find. One of the sargenns said to Commander Rogier. "Commander, there appears to be no one here, only some women and old men. We cannot even find burnt bodies from our fireballs."

Commander Rogier was confused. It was strange they could not find anybody as the city was abandoned. He looked around. "As strange as this is, the citizens have to be here. There is usually upwards of two thousand or more people in this city at any given time, and it is not like they knew we were coming." Then the Commander paused after his last statement. It got him thinking. "Perhaps they were warned somehow and there are numerous hiding places in this city. Tell your men to search everything, including under the buidlings and built-in cellars. Also search the area and see if there are caves around here. If they are hiding anywhere, we will just burn them out with torches." As soon as he gave the command, Rogier heard something whizzing though the air. He looked up and saw three fireballs flying towards the city. He yelled. "Scatter now! Fireballs are coming!"

The rest of the soldiers in both legions saw the fireballs flying through the air and started running out of the direction of where they they thought the fireballs would hit. When they did hit, the fireballs killed many soldiers instantly and many others caught on fire. As soon as Commander Rogier thought he was safe, four more fireballs came flying into the city killing even more soldiers. The commander realized that they were trapped. He ordered the horns to be blown, giving the signal for his army to retreat. Then he yelled orders to the legion as he was with to run towards the beach outside of the city. It would get them out of range of the fireballs. As they were running another wave of fireballs came flying into the city. They were doing their job and killing most of the Anntheian soldiers. Commander Rogier looked around and saw most of his men being burnt alive. He led what men he could find that were still alive to the beach and that's where he saw what was waiting for them.

Four rounds of fireballs from their own ballistas has been launched into the city of Liberus. The ballistas were positioned perfectly, which made the Anntheian soldiers perfect targets when they entered the city. Two-thirds of his men were killed during the bombardment and it split the two legions into small groups of men. Commander Rogier thought to himself, how could he had been so stupid, he walked into a trap without really scouting the area like he was supposed to. But that did not not matter now as he saw the Belmerien army waiting for them. It was a small army, but enough to inflict serious damage to the rest of the Anntheians. His men were scattered. He tried to get them in some kind of formation so they could fight better. He even had some archers with him and commanded them to fire at the Belmeriens.

Lord Fensenn gave the command to start walking towards the Anntheians. He did not charge them as instructed by Jaedann, but was merely trying to get them to charge his army. The Belmerien archers fired one round of arrows in the sky. They hit some of their targets, but not all. That's when Commander Rogier made another blunder. To get out of the way of the falling arrows, he told his men to charge the Belmeriens since most of his men did not have their shields, which were lost when they scattered from the fireballs and could protect them. Lord Fensenn saw them charge and ordered his men to stop. He said. "Hold the line here, let them come to us." When the Anntheias were close enough, he ordered the front line who had long spears to take a knee and point the spears up as he stepped in front. Tibuatt pulled a hatchet from his belt and when the first Anntheian soldier got within six feet of him, he threw the hatchet from the handle and put the blade into the soldier's face, making him fall backwards. Then he stepped back behind the line until the Anntheians reached them and got caught by the spears. Tibautt yelled one more command. "Kill them all!"

Anntheian soldiers were scattering down from the city onto the northside of the beach near the cave that Hanniah and some citizens of Liberus were hiding. Some of them saw her and rushed over to try to kill whomever they could. Hanniah was an excellent swordsman and cut down the first two soldiers who came after her before she got knocked down. One of the men she was protecting, hit the soldier with his walking staff. It distracted the soldier enough so Hanniah could get back up and slice open his backside with her sword, but there more soldiers coming, too many and she did not know of she could get them all. She was always prepared to die. She embraced death as inevitable as getting up in the morning and patrolling Liberus. Hanniah knew death could claim her on any day. She put her sword up and waited for it with the bravery of a true warrior as the Anntheian soldiers ran towards her.

Out of nowhere, Jaedann appeared on horseback, sword in hand and started cutting down the soldiers that were running towards Hanniah with his sword. Arunn was right behind him and shooting what he could with his arrows. The two of them got them all except the first two running towards Hanniah. She quickly cut open the first one by coming underneath his sword swing. Arunn shot the second one in the back the head with an arrow. Jaedann and Arunn killed about twenty soldiers in total. Hanniah looked at Jaedann and said. "Your timing is impeccable as usual."

He smiled. "Ah, you did not really need me, did you?"

Laughing, she replied. "I'm sure I would have killed most of them, but thanks for the help." Jaedann asked Arunn to stay on tha part of the beach and kill any stragglers who came out the city. Jaedann rode off to join his fellow Belmeriens in the main fight.

The last of the fireballs from the catapults were shot into Liberus four rounds of fireballs in total. Each postion blew their Elven horns to signal to the others that they were done. Arunn who was on the far north position blew his horn twice to signal the Elven advancement; the small Elven army was a mixture of swordsmen and archers. They started marching from the top ridge through the Anntheian encampment, killing any soldier or stewards they could find until there was nothing left but tents, barrels of wine, and bags of Anntheian gold. Rathgar remained with Elves and came in from behind. He was accompanied by his fellow Ravennbeaks who as it turned out, stayed in Liberus spending the gold that they stole from the dead Crowthornn corpses. They had been having quite a good time the past few months, so of course they stayed and fought with Rathgar and the chance to claim more gold.

Finally, Rathgar, the Ravennbeaks, and the Elves marched through the burning city. Rathgar was getting plenty of blood on his axes, which is what he preferred. So were the other Ravennbeaks. There was not much resistance from soldiers in the city. Most were dead from the fireballs, some were burning, and the ones that were still alive, tried to put up a fight, but were easily cut down. The Magerus who was second in command was still in the city, hiding, and trying to find a way out of it. He did not want to fight against such insurmountable odds. The Magerus knew this battle was over. He was just trying to get back to the Anntheian camp and perhaps escape, when he saw Rathgar swinging away and killing everything he could. Somehow, he mustered a little courage and charged the Barbarians. Rathgar did not see him coming and paid the price. His arm got cut open, but he was not dead. He shouted. "Fuk the gods, what shitt did this to me?" Then he saw the Magerus come at him again. This time he parried the Anntheian's swing and swung his ax around catching the soldier in the back. The Magerus fell to the ground, screaming in agony. He said. "Anntheian coward, you even scream like a little girl who just lost her doll."

One of the other Ravennbeaks came up to Rathgar and asked what happened. Rathgar explained how this soldier hid like a coward and then rushed him. The Magerus was still alive when the other Ravennbeak took his ax and chopped his head off. He said to Rathgar. "That is how cowards die, on the ground with no head." Rathgar laughed and did not disagree. They continued to walk through Liberus as she burned with the Elven army and kill what Anntheian soldier's they could find. There were not many left, but enough to add plenty of blood to Rathgar's axes and that gave him great pleasure. Some of the soldiers put up a fight, but in all the confusion and in trying not be burned by the huge flames that engulfed the city, the Anntheian soldiers were not really a match for the Elves and the Barbarians. Between the Elven arrows and the Barbarians blades, they were taken down pretty easy. Finally, the Elves and the Barbarians reached the western part of the city to the beach line where Lord Fensenn's men were engaged in battle with the only organized part of the legions that were left. Commander Rogier, finally, put what men he had left into a defensive formation with shields so they could defend themselves against the Belmeriens. The line was holding for now.

Tibautt Fensenn and the rest of Belmeriens were doing pretty well against the Anntheian formation. There were true to their warrior legends and even though they were outnumbered nearly three to one, the Belmeriens were killing the Anntheians at a rapid pace. Finally, they broke through the Anntheian line. Tibet, a big man of stature who towered over most of his enemies, killed pretty much everything in his path. Swords were crossed by Belmeriens and Anntheians every split second and that part of the beach was nearly soaked in blood. Tibautt had lost a few men, but there were more Anntheians dead, which was the idea. Commander Rogier stood in the middle and behind the formation surrounded by a back line of soldiers, he barked orders for his men to hold their ground, but he did not anticipate what was behind them.

All of sudden there were arrows flying towards them, nearly killing every man on the back line. He ordered the rest of his soldiers to form a defensive circle. Yes, they were surrounded, but it was the only way they could properly defend themselves. Belmeriens with their long spears, poked and pushed the Anntheians until they could not move anymore and then one by one, they killed the last of the Anntheian soldiers. Elves fired arrows into the faces of Anntheian soldiers and like dominoes, the soldiers fell until only Commander Rogier was standing with two other soldiers. Tibuatt pushed his way to the front of the Belmerien line. Rathgar did the same through the Elven line on the backside. Tibuatt killed one of the last two soldiers and Rathgar killed the other. Only Commander Rogier was left. He kept swinging his sword wildly trying to defend himself, but no one killed him yet since he was the commanding officer and by rule of war, the commanding officer was allowed to surrender.

Jaedann reached the front of the line and stood in front of Commander Rogier. He calmly asked. "Do you surrender?"

Rogier was confused. How did this happen? How could he have been defeated? He had the greater numbers. With anger, He replied. "It's you, the man I hired to be a scout and then ran off with my gold. How can this be? How do you have an army?"

Jaedann confidently smiled. "Because I put one together and knew how to defeat the likes of you. Do you surrender or should we just kill you?"

"I see Belmeriens and Elves…you know what this means? Involving two other kingdoms means there will be war in Annmar. You just started a war."

"And the unprevoked attack on a free city is not an act of war. Anntheia crossed borders and sent legions to sack a city that had done nothing to Anntheia. That in itself is an act of war…a war you just started."

"Just because you defeated me does not mean you can stop what is coming."

Jaedann rolled his eyes at the defeated commander. "So, you are declaring war. Good, because there are plenty of kingdoms that will rise up against you. Now do you surrender?"

Commander Rogier swung his sword at Jaedann and he parried it away from the Anntheian commander. Tibautt swung his sword and cut Rogier on the back of the leg, making him kneel to the ground. He grumbled. "Right where an Anntheian soldier belongs, on his knees."

Jaedann looked at Commander Rogier and then replied to Tibuatt. "I could not agree more." He asked the commander one final time. "Do you surrender or do want to die here?"

Commander Rogier shot him an angry look and cursed at the man who defeated him. "Fuk your surrender and fuk your Belmerien and Elven army. I will never surrender to someone like you."

Jaedann smiled. "Okay then…death it is." He looked up at Rathgar and told him. "Take his head."

Rathgar smiled back at his friend and replied. "Gladly." He swung his ax that was already dripping with blood and cut Commander Rogier's head off. The crowd of soldiers cheered. The Jaedann picked up the head, held it up so everybody could see and said. "We have defeated the Anntheian army. We have sent thousands of them to the afterlife. They thought they could easily defeat this city, but we showed them that they were wrong. Now the streets and this beach are covered in Anntheian blood. This victory is yours. Take pride in what you have done. " The crowd of soldiers and Barbarians raised their swords to the sky and cheered. Even the Elves who fought cheered even though they were more of a reserved people. Elves showed joy in their own way, but still knew how to celebrate with others when the time called for it. This was one of those times. Jaedann looked off in the distance and saw Deva standing with Hanniah and Arunn. He winked and smiled at her, letting her know that she had nothing to fear this day. They had won. They had defeated the army and the Khronne who come to kill her. Tears filled her eyes as she smiled back. Ever since she had stepped foot in Annmar, there had been this deep fear that harm would come to her, that she would never find out who she really was and worst yet, die soon.

Today that fear had disappeared. Today she felt protected and more importantly, loved.

36

Liberus was in ruins, nearly burnt to the ground and the smoke could be seen for mils. The people were being escorted from the ships and the cave back to the city to find what they had left from all the damage. Men were already moving the dead bodies out of the city and putting them in mass graves as well as finding what shields and swords they could. What was left would be stored for the city's new armory and the army that would have to be created if citizens of Liberus were going to defend her properly. The cleanup would take a while and the rebuilding would take even longer, but not before there was a celebration the next day. Jaedann ended up in the Great Hall, which miraculously was still standing and only had one wall burnt halfway down. Thorsha, the Magistrate got back on shore from one of the ships and made her way back to the Great Hall as well, finding Jaedann waiting for her.

Thorsha was the first to speak. "You allowed the city to be destroyed, was it worth it?"

Jaedann shook his head at her idiotic question, but responded in kind. "Look at the people returning, you tell me because as far as I am concerned, yes. Those people are alive, buildings being burned down is not worth more than their lives."

"I never thought I would see this city be burned to the ground by another kingdom. Then again, I never thought we would be able to defeat a standing army."

Jaedann smiled. "That is because my strategy in getting help and using the burning city as a trap was the right strategy."

"I suppose it was. And I suppose you do not think I should have you killed."

"I figure it's the least you can do since I just saved your life."

Thorsha did not like the fact that he did. The look on her face said as much. "I will not have you killed today and you can even be a Ranger of Liberus again if you so choose, but do you really think this is the last we have seen of Anntheia? King Lancelynn will not stop until he gets what he wants."

Jaedann nodded. "I agree, but he will stop coming after the girl if he thinks she is dead."

This made Thorsha curious. "What do you mean?"

"Deva will have to go into hiding, she will be hunted. The Elves will not let her stay in Dorwinn. So, the best place to hide is in plain sight under a disguise while the world thinks she is dead. We will give the Anntheian king their dead girl."

"So, your plan is to use a dead body and fake her death."

"Yes, we give them what they want and we found a dead girl that will serve as a decoy."

"And where will the girl hide?"

"Right here."

"You have gone mad, that cannot possibly work."

Jaedann confidently smiled. "Yes, we will hide the fact that she is a Half-Elf. We will hide her ears, darken her hair, and train her to be a Ranger. I will make her look like a Barbarian woman."

Thorsha shook her head in disbelief. "You know I could just send a message to the King and say that she is still here for a handsome reward."

"You could, but then you will die with any Anntheian that comes looking for her. I do not care if it makes me a wanted man…make no mistake, I will kill you and all you love for that betrayal"

Thorsha could see in his eyes that he was telling the truth. She replied. "Fine, I will keep your secret, but in return, I ask a favor. "

"What is that?"

"My son will be under your protection. I know you do not like him."

"Because he is an idiot and his stupidity causes harm to others."

"Be that as it may, I want him protected and that is the price you pay for me keeping your secret."

Jaedann did not say anything for a moment, carefully thinking it over. It was a steep price that he did not like, but Deva was worth it. He agreed to her terms even though he knew that somehow it would come back to haunt him.

The citizens of Liberus celebrated that night along with the Belmerien soldiers from House Fensenn. They celebrated in burnt out buildings, but there was food with plenty of ale or Ruminn that had not been destroyed by the fires. Some merchants were able to hide the stock well enough so that nothing would not be destroyed. It was quite the celebration. Jaedann had a pint of ale with Tibautt and Degorenn, remembering what it was like to drink with fellow Belmerien soldiers, he missed it. It was hard not to miss it for his heart still belonged in Belmere. He still felt like a Knight of Belmere. Jaedann said to Tibautt as he downed another ale. "I want to thank you for helping me. You did not have to."

Tibautt smiled. "It was the least I could to do put the past behind us. And I have not had that much pleasure in killing someone for quite sometime." All three men laughed. Jaedann responded. "Well, there is also some bounty. We found seven chests of gold in the Commander's tent, one of them is yours. And Degorenn, you take one too."

Tibuatt replied. "I do not need the gold. But my men and I can hit every brothel along the way home and enjoy ourselves courtesy of the King of Anntheia." Degorenn said. "We might do the same in the ports we visit when we sail our new ships home." Tibautt smiled at Degorenn. "And it's not really for us as we are married men, but for our men."

Degorenn laughed. "Sure, let that be truth we tell, it is for our men."

Jaedann smiled. "Well then, it is well deserved…for your men as you say." Jaedann was being a bit humorous in his statement, then he stood up and said his final words to the men. "It was a pleasure fighting with you, I hope to stand beside you on the field of battle once again someday."

Tibuatt stood up, took a sip of ale and replied. "All you have to do is ask. I would be honored to share the field of battle with you again." With those the words, the past was the past. Amends had been made and at least for Jaedann, there was no more ill will towards House Fensenn.

Jaedann excused himself and went to Voraks place where Deva, Arunn, Hanniah, and Rathgar were waiting. Voraks place had taken some serious damage, but it was liveable and his worktable was still intact. When Jaedann arrived, he presented Deva with the Journals that were meant to be given to her. Vorak had waited for Jaedann before giving them to her. He said to the girl. "Deva, these belong to you. We have kept them safe until you returned."

Deva took the two large bound books and asked. "Have you read through the books?"

"I have. It is mostly details about your life from the time you, written by the woman who took care of you. But there is also information about Ellisar. I believe she gave you a guide on how to find the place, but it is not exactly clear. It seems as if it written in mystery speak?"

"Do you know how to read it?"

"Some, but a great deal will have to be deciphered. Between the Ancient Elven language and the symbols, she made it hard for anybody to understand it and I think she did it on purpose, because Ellisar is meant to be a secret place, hidden from the outside world so its truths can only be known to those with magic."

Deva did not know what to say to that. All of this was still a big mystery to her. There were still more questions than answers regarding her abilities and her destiny. She asked. "How can we decipher what is in these books."

Vorak smiled. "There is a way, there are people that I know who can help. And we will all help you." Jaedann spoke up. "Deva, wherever Elissar is, he speaks the truth, we will help you get there. Whether you are part of a prophecy or not, you have destiny as someone with magic. There is no denying that you will shape the world of Annmar and I believe for the good of all who live here. It will take time, but we will help you on your journey."

Vorak began to speak again. "You should take some time and read through the journals, learn more about who you are and why you are."

Deva replied. "Thank you, all of you. But I have to ask. If I am to be in hiding what is next for me? Where am I supposed to go?"

Jaedann answered. "You are not going anywhere. Hiding in plain sight is better, but you will need a different look. One that will go with the Ranger that we will train you to be."

Deva was curious. "A Ranger? Me, a Ranger!"

"Yes, you are stronger than you look when you are not using magic. And the best thing to do is to hide the fact that you are a Half-Elf and make you a Ranger of Liberus. No one will think anything of it or question your existence."

Deva did know if she could change her appearance so drastically. She loved the way she looked. She loved her long strawberry blondish hair and had never considered what she could look like if it were darker. Would she still be pretty? Despite those misgivings, she agreed and Hanniah brought out of bowl of herbs and other things that would be used to die Deva's hair after they cut it. She would not have to change her name since only a few people knew her real name was Deva and her true orgin. Tomorrow, she would look like a whole new person, tomorrow she would be the mystery she was supposed to be.

The next day Jaedann still had unfinished business. He still had to what was commonly known as settle up with the true commander of the Anntheian legions that had been sent to destroy Liberus. Jaedann had sent a messenger boy to Genneral Rulf Orwaynn with a mesaage that said, he could collect what was left of the legions he had sent to destroy Liberus. Genneral Orwaynn was a bit stunned by the message. It was true that he had not received a raven from Commander Rogier, but there was nothing to worry about since it should have been an easy victory for his second in command. But the Genneral was curious by the message and it came under a banner of truce. He also took a small detachment and rode to the location that was given in the message.

He met Jaedann in an open field about halfway between the Anntheian camp and Liberus. It was the perfect place to meet in order to avoid an ambush. Jaedann had with him Arunn, Rathgar and their new Ranger. Deva had her new look. Her hair was short but propped up by a headband that also covered her Elf ears. She had paint around her eyes just like Barbarian women, and her hair was dark. She was unrecognizable, which was the point. The Genneral rode to Jaedann's horse but stopped about six feet away. He said as he looked at Jaedann. "I know you, I am sure of that. We have met on the field of battle, have we not."

Jaedann replied. "Yes, a long time ago."

"You are from Belmere?"

"I was born there, yes, and I used to be a Knight."

Genneral Orwaynn nodded. "You asked me out here, what do you have for me? Or more importantly, what happened to my army?"

Jaedann threw a sack with Commander Rogier's head in it. "They are all dead and you can have your commander's head as a parting gift."

The Genneral was shocked. This could not be true. He was sure this was a lie, but then one of men looked in the bag and pulled the commander's head out. It was true. The Genneral replied. "You defeated my army and did not give this man the courtesy of surrender."

"We did, he chose death instead and he was not very brave about it. But we at least gave you the head so you can honor him in whatever may be your custom."

"I do not believe anybody from Liberus could defeat two Anntheian legions, unless you are telling me that Belmere helped in some way. "

Jaedann laughed. "No, but we could call on plenty of people that take great pleasure in killing Anntheian soldiers. We formed a small army and your commander was stupid enough to fall for our trap. Your legions were not that hard to defeat."

This enraged Genneral Orwyann. "But it is your defeat that is coming. Those two legions are but a small taste of the wrath that I will bring to Liberus."

Jordan laughed at the useless threat. "Genneral, there is no need. You were sent by your king to kill an Elf girl who supposedly had some kind of power as confirmed by the broker used to hire the Crowthornns that almost burned the city to the ground. We killed the girl for you, we do not want her kind in Liberus. So, tell your King there is no need to destroy the city for just one small girl." Jaedann through two sacks towards the ground. Another Anntheian soldier pulled the heads out the sacks. "We cut her ears off, her eyes out, and then cut her head off as a warning that we do not welcome her kind. And the other head of the despicable being that was sent to kill her too as if Anntheian legions would not be enough. Tell whoever sent this thing, their kind is not welcome in Liberus either. All this should be payment enough for Anntheia to leave Liberus alone. "

Genneral Orwaynn was even more angry now, it showed in his tone. "I cannot promise that this is over. Our King will want justice for the killing of his soldiers."

"Then he should have not sent them in the first place."

The Genneral finally realized how he knew Jaedann's face, he remembered his true identity. "I do know…you are Prince Jaedann Barrenn. Second in line to the Throne of Belmere and a Knight from the Lionnbshade Brigade. So Belmere is truely behind the death of my army."

"I am not those things anymore. I was banished years ago. I am just a Ranger of Liberus."

"Is that so?"

Jaedann smiled. "Yes Genneral, you should know that before your King is stupid enough to declare war with Belmere. Also, tell your King, in Belmere, a King who declares that people must die, swings the sword himself. He does not cower in an ivory tower and send his lackey to a King's job." Jaedann did not wait for a response by Genneral Orwaynn, although he knew what he said would anger him. He essentially called the King of Anntheia a coward and he knew of no king that would ever let that stand. Part of him was challenging King Lancelynn just to see if he would actually meet him on the field of battle. But mostly he made the comment as a Belmerien taking a chance to insult an enemy king. Deva asked as they were riding away. "Did that make you feel better to insult their king?"

Jaedann smiled. "Yes, very much so."

"What if he comes with an army to destroy Liberus."

King Lancelynn would never dare do that himself. Cowards never do. But enough of all that. It's time to start the next part of your journey." The four of them rode off towards the sun as itr was in full view over the peak behind them. They went back to Liberus to find out what lay next for the Rangers of Liberus.

King Lancelynn was furious as he stared at the two heads, one of the girl with magic and the other of the Khronne who was sent to kill her. He should have been happy, but a Belmerien called him a coward after defeating two of his legions. This was not the outcome he had hoped for. Azrigronn examined the heads and tried to give him some words of comfort, but they were more of logic than comfort as Khronnes did not feel sympathy. It said. "Do not worry about insults from a banished prince, you are victorious more than you know."

The King, still angry, was also curious by her choice of words. "What do you mean?" They gave us the head of the Elf with magic. Her blood is powerful, the kind of power that created my kind. I can use it create something more powerful."

"You want to use some kind of sorcery to defeat magic."

"No, to control its use for the right people. We cannot ignore magic and the power of the gods, but only a select few should have use of that power. Only the right Kings should have use of that power. You have been chosen to be one."

The king was a bit confused. "So, what you are telling me is that you can use the blood from this head to create something like you that I can use?"

Azigronn smiled. "I can do much more that. The blood of magic can create magic for others to wield it. You can become the most powerful king in Annmar."

King Lancelynn smiled. "I would like that more than anything."

"But now it is time for you to complete part of your destiny. It is time for the Oracles of Erinnity to come out of hiding. It is time to control the fate of the world. You must make new alliances to reform the Oracles of Erinnity for it has to be more than just Khronnes living in the shadows."

"I do not know where to begin in making these alliances."

Azigronn smiled again. "For even you and your enemies now have a common enemy. Sometimes enemies can make the best alliances" King Lancelynn knew what she meant and it was time for him to do something he never thought he would do.

Weeks would pass, but King Lancelynn finally made it to Kingswatch. It was a neutral city in the mountains. A citadel to be exact with a large library and those who kept records much like Lenntis. But the records that the monks kept at Kingswatch were different. They were the official records and timeline of meetings between kings. From peace treaties to secret plots, it held the records and history of the deeds of Kingswatch. This was the perfect place to meet with his new alliance for the Oracles of Erinnity. King Lancelynn of Anntheia arrived first and was led up the stone mountain path to Great Stone table that sat on the Alter of Kingswatch. An hour went by and King Jornnus Barrenn of Belmere was led up the same path to the great stone table. He was escorted to his seat by one of the monks and given a glass of wine. King Jornnus responded when he saw the king of Anntheia. "Why did you ask me here? This is not about some treaty with Anntheia is it?"

King Lancelynn replied. "No and I would not dare say the real meaning of this meeting in a message by raven."

A monk brought a large bound book to the table and opened it to a blank page. He asked King Lancelynn. "What is the topic of this meeting between kings for the official record?" King Lancelynn replied. "For the reformation of the Oracles of Erinnity."

This shocked King Jornnus and replied in kind. "You cannot be serious. This organization has long been dead and I have no interest in joining this ancient order."

King Lancelynn said. "If you listen to me for a few minutes then you might change your mind." So, King Lancelynn told King Jornnus about the girl with magic and how the prophecy of the five was true. He explained that magic had come back and it would upset the balance of power. This made King Jornnus afraid. He was no different as a King, he would do anything to hold onto power. After King Lancelynn explained the events that had happened, he said. "So, it is finally here, the return of magic. How I wish this would have been just stories we were told as childen."

"Yes, but it appears to be true and you do not want magic in the world anymore than I do unless it can be controlled by people like us."

King Jornnus nodded. "That is true."

"A long time ago, our Kingdoms were not enemies, but shared one to goal, that no one would have more power than us including the gods."

"That is also true. Do you know for sure if there are more out there?"

"Yes, at least four magic users. We cannot let the prophecy of the five come true. Will you help me?"

King Jornnus thought for a moment. It was not an easy decision to make. "My people will never go for helping an Anntheian King."

King Lancelynn asked. "Do you want to see magic be widespread throughout the land or do you want to control the power of the gods and always remain in power because that is what's at stake. Reform the Oracles of Erinnity with me as our ancestors did and stop those with magic as well as those who protect them. Let power remain with Kings as it should be."

King Jornnus was reluctant, this as Anntheia after all. It felt evil to make a deal with them, but then he remembered this was just an alliance among Kings. The two countries could still hate each other. King Lancelynn was right, this was to keep power in the right hands. King Jornnus agreed and the alliance between the two kings was recorded in the Kingswatch book. There would be much more to do. There would be secret armies to form. These two kings who hated each other became allies in the Oracles of Errinity. Now they would work together to hunt down those with magic. The secret war had now begun as it had 100 years before when those who wanted power all for themselves rose up and killed their gods. What was past will be again, what was true then, will be true tomorrow, for the battle of good and evil in Annmar was here.

APPENDEX

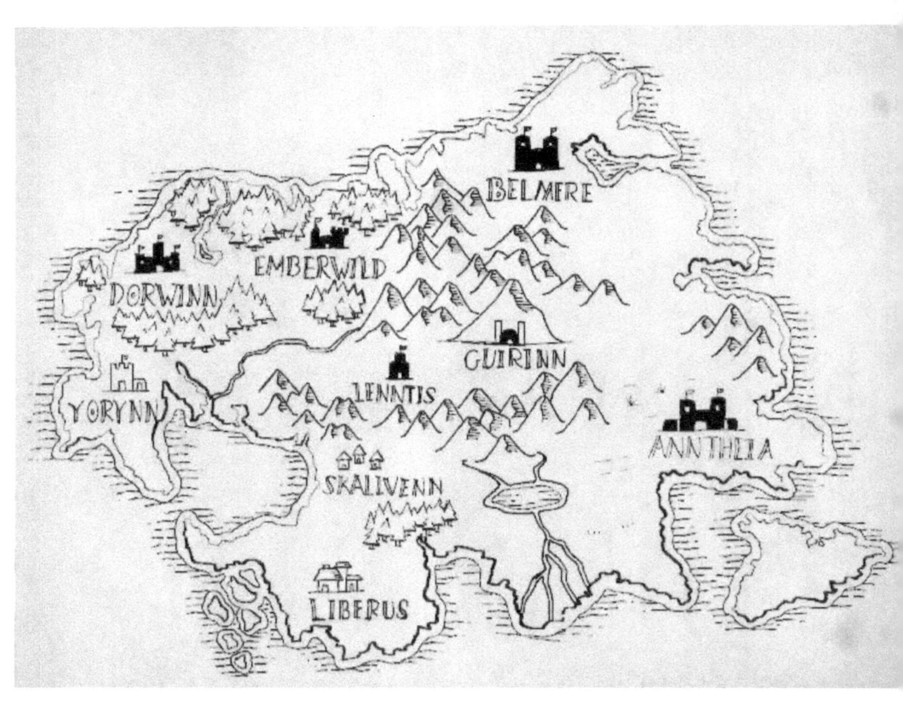

BELMERE
DORWINN
EMBERWILD
GUIRINN
YORYNN
LENNTIS
ANNTHEIA
SKALIVENN
LIBERUS

Kingdoms

Belmere

"By the blood of the old gods, we defend
what is ours and fight for those who cannot."

Belmere is the northernmost kingdom in Annmar. It resides in the northeast part of Annmar and has the coldest climate in Annmar. The kingdom is made up of Humans, although some Dwarves do reside in Belmere. Belmere has seven minor kingdoms made up of 7 royal houses. Belmere also has the second-largest army in Annmar. The citizens of Belmere are fierce and stern, made tough by the climate they live in. It is mostly cold, but Belmere can get hot in the summer months. Belmere is made up of mountains, forests, and hard flatlands. There are parts that are very beautiful and some that are very harsh. Belmere is known for being fiercely independent as a kingdom. Soldiers are known to be the toughest in Annmar, especially the soldiers from House Fensenn. The one thing that Belmere is truly known for is their Blacksmithing skills, especially swords.

Belmere is generally known for making the best swords in Annmar because of the minerals and ore found in the mountains of Belmere. The Bellmora Mountains have the best minerals and ore. Belmere does sell swords throughout Annmar, even to Kingdoms such as Anntheia. It is their number one commodity. The kingdom of Belmere has some uneasy truces with the Elven kingdom of Dorwinn and the Dwarven kingdom of Guirinn. Belmere's biggest enemy is the kingdom of Anntheia where tensions are often high since they share a border. The kingdom of Belmere may not be liked in some parts of Annmar, but they are respected for their honor and being true to their word.

One royal house is usually in control of Belmere and the senior male, first in line of that royal house becomes King of Belmere. When there is not a natural heir, the Lords of Belmere will vote and select a new king from one of the royal houses of Belmere. Wars have been fought because of this rule of law. The last time someone challenged for the throne was in 90 AG and it started a civil war. But Belmere survived and it is ruled by one king with 7 royal houses who still pledge their loyalty to the throne. No one has ever successfully invaded Belmere, invaders have been pushed back every time because Belmere has the toughest army when they are fighting together. And only Belmeriens know how to fight on the terrain in their country.

Royal Houses of Belmere

House Barrenn
House Fensenn
House Carstonne
House Annsier
House Mackwinn
House Hamsennd
House Searnonn

***** Surnames are based on the House a person belongs to. Those with different surnames are not of noble birth and some are usually bastard offspring with one of 5 surnames, Carac, Lamburnn, Ricon, Simonn, and Adkinn.**

Anntheia

"We are the light that shines
through the darkness of Anmmar."

Anntheia is the largest kingdom in Annmar. It is located in the Southeastern part of the world. Anntheia has multiple climates from warm and tropical in the very Southern regions with cold and winter-like conditions in the northern part, close to the border it shares with Belmere. It also has a variety of Landscapes from flat grassy trains to mountain ranges. Part of the kingdom contains thick dense forests and plush meadows like the elven kingdom of Dorwinn. With Anntheia being the largest Kingdom in Annmar, it also has the largest ports for trade thus making the kingdom have the largest economy in Annmar. The kingdom is divided by eight providences with each of those Providence is being controlled by a royal house. There are eight royal houses in Anntheia. The kingdom is seen as a symbol of elegance, especially its largest cities such as the capital, Wimbornn.

Anntheia also has the largest army in Annmar. The kingdom has 8 different Legions that take their name from the Providence from which they reside, with each Legion containing at least 50,000 soldiers. There was also the capital region, which guards the capital city and is made up of men from every Legion. The armies of Anntheia are well-trained and are considered the most professional of armies from fierce infantry units to heavy cavalry and larger, more devastating weapons such as ballista. Anntheia may not have the fiercest warriors in the world of Annmar, but the armies are usually considered the most well-trained throughout the land.

What was once a small kingdom has quadrupled in size within a hundred years since the fall of the gods and they are always seeking to increase the size of their kingdom. They do this through having small outposts in different parts of Annmar through treaties with other kingdoms or simply taking over other parts of the world and creating new borders. They are constantly at odds with the kingdom of Belmere. Anntheia is primarily known for having the richest economy, the largest army, and shipbuilding. All of the best-made ships are constructed in Anntheia. The kingdom also has the largest navy. The kingdom is viewed as the epitome of civilization and enlightenment. Anntheia wants to make the rest of the world in the very image of Anntheia.

Royal Houses of Anntheia

House Kesterinn
House Fairimier
House Hollowenn
House Duramonnt
House Alinnac
House Galliot
House Wynnwell
House Robintonn

*** Surnames are based on the House a person belongs to. Those with different surnames are not of noble birth, some are usually bastard offspring with one of 5 surnames, Edonn, Sadonn, Bloodshout, Gregornn, and Fulkspear.

Dorwinn

"Wisdom is the essence to living a long life."

Dorwinn is the Elven Kingdom in Annmar. It is located in the Northwest part of the world. A land with a mixture of climates from comfortably warm to mildly cold. It is considered the most beautiful part of Annmar with its rich green meadows, beautiful waterfalls, mountains, and lush landscapes. Some say the sun shines extra bright over Dorwinn. The Elves live long lives. Some say well over hundreds of years. They are considered the most intelligent of all beings in Annmar and their knowledge is considered unparalleled to all other races. They even have some of the largest libraries in the world that would even rival the great Citadel-Monastery of Lenntis who is known as the largest record keeper in the world. Elves speak their own language (Elven language), but also speak in the common tongue.

The kingdom of Dorwinn is made up of 6 royal houses. The Elves do not have a king but are governed by an Elven Council made up by the Lords of each royal house. The great capital city of Dorwinn is located in Taranonn. The Elves for the most part are considered a private race and do not often share their secrets outside of their Kingdom. They are more in tune with nature and can wield the metaphysical elements of nature. While it is not considered magic, it is deemed as power. For Elves have the ability to conjure natural elements for the use of medicine and weapons. It is these abilities that allow them to make powerful steel. Elven steel is considered sacred and as some of the most powerful Steel in the world, only rivaling the kingdom of Belmere. But the secrets and how they create their powerful steel are not shared, whereas steel from Belmere is traded throughout all of Annmar.

The Elves are also excellent warriors. Fierce and brave, they are known as the best archers in the world. But because of their skills with steel and making swords, they are also great Swordsmen. Fast and nimble, their armies have always been hard to defeat. But elves have also been known for their Naval skills. Their great ships, their ship-building skills rivaling that of Anntheia. While elves are not prone to war since they look for more peaceful solutions, make no mistake, elves can be one of the greatest enemies in war or the best ally because of their speed when it comes to their sword and archery skills. Dorwinn does not often align with other kingdoms as it keeps to itself, but when they do become an ally as in the case of Belmere, it is often in perpetuity unless the treaty specifies otherwise. Elves are known to be a wise and gentle folk with long life, but deadly and violent if need be when it comes to war.

Royal Houses of Dorwinn

House Mirarel
House Tyriall
House Anfalenn
House Volwinn
House Rhistell
House Thallann

***** Surnames are based on the House an Elf belongs to. All Elves belong to a Noble House. Half Elves will not have a noble name. The most common surnames for Half Elves are Ralnnnor, Jassinn, Alred, and Devdann.**

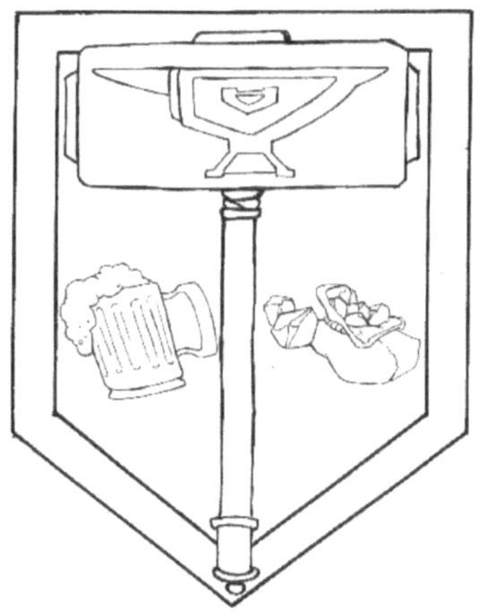

Guirinn

"Pride and anger are the jewels that make a kingdom."

Guirinn is the kingdom of Dwarves. The kingdom is located in the middle of Annmar within the Kerrodeenn mountains and borders three kingdoms, Belmere, Anntheia, and SKallvynn. The kingdom is a mixture of homes within the mountains and small villages. Guirinn has five royal houses with one of the royal houses being the ruling House of the Kingdom. The king or queen will always come from one of the royal houses until their line is distinguished and a new royal house becomes the ruler of the Kingdom. The capital city of Guirinn is Thoridunn and each royal house has their own capital city. Dwarves can be half or two-thirds in height compared to a human being. They may be short in stature, but they are also strong and capable Warriors.

Dwarves are known as the finest miners and tradesmen in the world. There blacksmithing skills are impeccable, rivaling that of Belmere. However, it is there mining and stonework for which Dwarves are truly known for in the world. Within the mountain ranges where the kingdom resides are some of the finest jewels and gold found in Annmar. This makes them one of the richest kingdoms. The finest jewels in all of Annmar usually come from Guirinn. The most prestigious hilts and pummels for swords are made in Guirinn because of the jewels that are placed in them. Also, because of their skill in stonework Dwarves are usually commissioned to help build castles in other kingdoms. Dwarves can always find work in Annmar

Dwarves do not naturally gravitate towards war. They believe in hiring out their trade and building commerce with other kingdoms. Because of this they for the most part remain neutral and whatever war they take part of is usually amongst their own kind, If they were to have an alliance it would probably be with Anntheia because that is where most of their business takes place. They have an uneasy truce with the kingdom of Dorwinn and Belmere.

When dwarves fight, their weapon of choice is usually an ax, a long hammer, or club. Dwarves are known to be stubborn folk, but they are very loyal to their allies and to a cause if they take it up. Dwarves can be boisterous in their celebration. That may have something to do with brewing some of the best ale in Annmar. The most common ale served in taverns throughout the world is brewed in Guirinn.

Royal Houses of Guirinn

House Morgor
House Thornnmer
House Snoddrik
House Grookheim
House Ellric

*** **Surnames are based on the House a person belongs to. Those with different surnames are not of noble birth and some are usually bastard offspring with one of 3 surnames, Ghof, Dhimm, and Starnn.**

Skallvenn

"A sword, ax, pike, or hammer
can make anyone honest."

Skallvenn is the kingdom of Barbarians (Example: Vikings). They are a violent and warring race that worship not only the god Anion, but many gods as well. Skallvenn has many terrains from the flatlands and forests to rivers and mountains It resides in the Southwestern part of Annmar. Barbarians are divided into twelve clans instead of small kingdoms. They do not have castles, but each clan has a capital city and has a large building or Great Hall that is their seat of government. Skallvenn does have a King and Queen. The king is selected by signs from the gods they worship or trial by combat if someone would challenge for the throne. The king may choose someone to fight in his place for trial by combat. The capital of Skallvenn is the town of Horvarkk. The largest building in Skallvenn is the Great Hall of Horvarkk, which serves as its seat of government.

Each clan is ruled by a Chieftain. Barbarians do not have royal houses. Chieftains or "the Chief" are chosen by the clan they rule over through a vote or trial by combat. Clan names are based on the animals and creatures in Skallvenn. Barbarians are only really known for war and the unusual sharp weapons they make. While Barbarians do know how to farm and have blacksmithing skills, they get most of their things through plunder. Barbarians will raid and pillage parts of their kingdoms. Barbarians have an incurable thirst for blood and gold.

Skallvenn is not a rich kingdom, but Barbarians can easily make a living beyond plundering other kingdoms by hiring out as soldiers. Because of their penchant for war. Barbarians make for great mercenaries. The king and lords of Anntheia hire Barbarians a great deal for their secret wars and for the uglier jobs in war. The clans of Skallvenn do war with each other as it is a rite of passage. They do not always get along, but will unite under a king's command. Barbarians do not have much use for politics, their politics is that of war. The most unique thing about Barbarians is each clan has their own language, but most Barbarians speak the common tongue.

Clans of Skallvenn

Ravennbeak
Crowthornn
Stormhounnd
Bearcrusher
Eagleclaw
Deerhornn
Wolfclaw
Badgerpikes
Snakehornns
Toadraiders
Ironntusk
Shadowrams

***** Surnames are based on what clan they are from. Barbarians are a part of clans, but can also have nicknames like "the black," "the executioner," or "the hunter."**

Yorynn

"No journey is complete without a good smoke,
a good ale, and the company of friends."

Yorynn is the kingdom of Halflings and Gnomes, sometimes referred to as the kingdom of Half-Folk. Gnomes, or the forgotten folk as they were sometimes known. They are small humanoids known for their eccentric sense of humor, inquisitiveness, and engineering prowess. Halflings are clever, capable opportunists. Depending on the clan, Halflings might be reliable, hard-working citizens, or they might be thieves just waiting for the opportunity to make a big score and disappear in the dead of night. Halflings adventurers are typically looking for a way to use their skills to gain wealth or status. Gnomes are more craftsmen and love building and making things, whether it's out of wood or farming. Both groups do co-exist together, but not necessarily in the same village. Yorynn does not have small kingdoms or castles. They do not have royal houses or lords. Yorynn is made up of villages with their own unique name, but the kingdom does have a capital city, called Dermwist where the elected King of Yorynn rules. He is chosen from one of the magistrates who rule over a village.

Gnomes and Halflings do not have much to do with the outside world as they mainly keep to themselves. Halflings deal more with the outside world through trade and commerce, but also because they are opportunists, some engage in criminal activities as well. Halflings make the best burglars and can be pretty crafty thieves, but mostly they deal in trade. Most Gnomes and Halflings from Yorynn are peaceful. They are mostly farmers and craftsmen. Gnomes are great crafters of musical instruments. The finest in Annmar. Halflings are great tailors and make the finest silks in Annmar. The one thing that Yorynn is truly known for is tobacco farming. The finest herb and tobacco is grown in Yorynn. That is their main commodity. Gnomes and Halflings do not involve themselves too much in the affairs of the world unless it's through trade and commerce. Most do not venture outside of Yorynn unless they are the adventurous type or take part in trade and commerce as well as criminal activities.

Yorynn generally gets along with all other kingdoms and has good relationships with them because of trade and commerce. Because of this, Gnomes and Halflings generally do not take part in wars, but because some halflings can resort to criminality, they can be used for stealth activities such as being spies or even assassins. They can get in out of without being noticed and because they are folk who are largely ignored by other races. Halflings have been employed as spies by other kingdoms, mostly Anntheia. But mostly the inhabitants of Yorynn want to be left in peace. The land is some of the most beautiful and all of Annmar. Because it shares a border with Dorwinn, it has some of the same beautiful landscapes from rolling green meadows to enchanted forests. And just like Dorwinn the climate is not too hot or cold. The temperature is almost perfect. Yorynn strives to be a peaceful place and that is why its citizens work hard to maintain the trade of tobacco, its main commodity, instead of seeking war.

Clans of Yorynn

Hallbim
Gimdinn
Tukmier
Wegrinn
Frimzock
Klimgrest
Wolvroot
Baknnecks
Rabnnooks

*** Surnames are based on the village they are from.   The village names are their surnames.

The Emberwild

"Magic lies within the secrets we keep, for only those who are worthy will know our true heart."

The Emberwild is the most secretive place in Annmar. It is the kingdom of the Fae or Faerûn (fairies). They are mystical creatures that live in the thick forest known as The Foxxwood. The Emberwild is located between the kingdoms of Dorwinn and Belmere. The forest area between the kingdoms is the Emberwild. Not much is known about the Faerûn, they remain mysterious on purpose. The Emberwild is a natural defense from the outside word and the Fae's villages reside deep in the forests and high up in the trees, making them hard to find. Fae can live on the ground and in the trees. In fact, there are cities in the trees, including a hidden city called The Cohnnwood reserved for Fae, Elves, Gnomes, and Halflings. The outside world rarely ventures into the Emberwild and Fae mainly keep to themselves, while being very suspicious of other kingdoms.

This just leads to their mystique in Annmar.
Fae can be as tall as a human being or small as a tenth of their size. But all Fae have beautiful luminescent wings, which allows them to fly. They are the only race in Annmar that can fly. No one knows what godly power gave the Fae that ability. It is another one of their mysteries. Faerûn are capable warriors. They are fast, which makes them good swordsman, but their true strength lies in their archery skills and because they can fly it makes them deadly especially from long distances. Fae do not fight in the wars of other races. Their wars are among themselves. Fae do not have royal houses. The Emberwild is made up of ten villages along with the secret city. But the Emberwild does have a capital city called Bramblemoon where the king resides. There is a king or a queen that rules over the Fae, chosen through prophecy by the oracles in the Faerûn kingdom. They choose who will best serve the Fae at that time and place.

The climate of the Emberwild varies from warm to cold. There are great snowfalls that come to the Emberwild since it borders Belmere. But the Fae are in tune with the weather as they are with all living things in their kingdom. The Fae are the one race more in tune with nature, even more so than the Elves. Since Faerûn are for the most part a mystery to the rest of Annmar, they are however, known for one thing. It is the one commodity they trade

with other kingdoms. Wood. The Emberwild has the strongest
wood in Annmar. The strongest bridges, buildings, and cities in the
trees are built with wood from the Emberwild, especially wood from
the Foxxwood forest. And while many do not venture into the
Emberwild, there is one city that is the center for most of their trade.
It is Roseloch, which is located on a lake along the Marasonn River
that separates the kingdoms of Dorwinn, the Emberwild, and Yorynn
from the rest of Annmar. Roseloch is a vibrant trade center for mostly
wood and other goods, and its main entry point into the Emberwild
and the world of the Fae.

Clans of The Emberwild

Mosswick
Littlestonne
Fernnspark
Brightmeadow
Lemonhornn
Firegust
Silkglade
Shimmerthistle
Greennpuff
Quickriver

*** **Faerûn (Fairy) don't have Surnames, they have first names
and say where they're from. Example: " Willow of Firegust."
But Fae also have common surnames like, Plumgloss, Sunstarr,
and Woodglenn. These are Fae that do not belong to a village.**

Liberus

Liberus is a trader's town that is not under the rule of any kingdom. It is the largest market center and port in the western part of Annmar. It also happens to be the second largest port in Annmar next to the Ship's Haven port of Anntheia. Liberus started out as a smuggler's port even before the fall of the gods. There are many places along the western coast that smugglers still bring in their goods to avoid port taxes by other kingdoms. The town was created in 40 AG by a smuggler's consortium who wanted to build some rule of law instead of seeing ships get robbed all the time. It was built with the idea that all could take advantage of the profits of bringing in goods to Annmar instead of paying high taxes and a percentage of the sale in other ports like Anntheia. The man who started it all was a merchant, but also more of a pirate than anything else. His name was Odinnel Ymbertt. A governing council was created with a Magistrate at the head of the council.

Liberus has always been a source of contention for other kingdoms as all of them would like to control the trade that goes through Liberus. But the town brings a lot of goods into Annmar and every kingdom does business with Liberus. Some refer to it as a necessary evil. Even when the town has been attacked and burned to the ground, it has always been rebuilt and trade has continued through Liberus. The town has also tripled in size over 60 years since it was created. All are welcome to trade-in Liberus and it does not require port taxes, just 10% of the value of their cargo that the merchant intends to trade, which is still cheaper than a port that will charge port taxes and 20% of the value of cargo passing through the port such as in Anntheia.

Smugglers still try to bring in their goods bypassing even Liberus by using some of the hidden ports around the town and that is why Liberus have Rangers who patrol the area. Liberus does business with all kingdoms and does not seek to have enemies even though some kingdoms view Liberus as an enemy. In order to maintain peace with other kingdoms, Liberus will trade all goods with all kingdoms. Those who trade in Liberus do so on good faith that they will get a fair deal and have their cargo protected from thieves and pirates. And more importantly, that they have the freedom to prosper as merchants. That is the philosophy of Liberus. In fact, the name of the town is a word for freedom. Liberus is also known for the special alcohol drink they distill, called Ruminn, from a sugarcanne molasses that is only found in that part of Annmar. It's the number one commodity that comes from Liberus and is heavily traded throughout Annmar.

Lenntis

Lenntis is the oldest Citadel-Monastery in Annmar. It has the largest library in Annmar as well. Lenntis contains all the recorded history of Annmar and has been around for over 1,000 years. It is located in the center of the world, high in the mountains between the kingdoms of Guirinn, Skallvenn, and the Emberwild. A Citadel- Monastery is a fortress that protects a huge library and a place of worship. The Monks that live there worship the 5 gods and maintain their secrets especially secrets of their power   Because they are also record keepers and keep the history of Annmar, Monks also keep the written history and stories about the 5 gods so that none in Ammar will forget them and who created the world.

A Monk's sole purpose is to record the history of Annmar, but more importantly to record the deeds of lords and kings. The actions of lords and kings effect history more than anything. Lenntis is a neutral site in Annmar. Lenntis takes no part in wars. Lenntis takes no sides so part of the Monk's job is to record the deeds of all races in Annmar in order to have an accurate account of their actions in history. And because Lenntis is neutral, all treaties and alliances are signed there; at a place called Kingswatch. Even secret alliances because there must be a record of everything. The Monks at Lenntis keep meticulous records from history to prophecies and even legends. Now, while some history from the war of the five gods has been lost, Lenntis has the most accurate records of what happened about the fall of the gods and the beginning of the first age since the fall.

Monks are not just recordkeepers, they are also warriors, although they rarely fight. Their fighting skill is a form of what is known as martial arts along with exceptional skills in archery and swordsmanship. They become Warriors to protect the history of Annmar. The Monks of Lenntis rarely leave the Citadel- Monastery, but sometimes they travel to complete special tasks that are essential to preserving the history of Annmar. Lenntis is also known for one more thing besides recording the history of Annmar. The monks also make a special kind of wine that is traded throughout Annmar. While other kingdoms ferment their own wine. The monks at Lenntis make a special blend that is in much demand and can be expensive. It is how they earn money for the upkeep of the citadel-monastery. The wine is called Allistarr Wine, named for the brightest star that shines over Lenntis.

Providences, Towns, Capitals, and Shrines

Belmere

TOWN	DESCRIPTION
Blackburnn	Capital of Belmere
Craydonn Rock	Seat of House Barrenn
Bannburgh	Seat of House Fensenn
Dornnwich	Seat of House Carstonne
Runnswick	Seat of House Mackwinn
Sliverkeep	Seat of House Annsier
Reddwater	Seat of House Hamsennd
Hullhornn	Seat of House Searnonn

Dorwinn

TOWN	DESCRIPTION
Taranonn	Capital of Dorwinn
Galaronn	Seat of House Mirarel
Elnnaril	Seat of House Tyriall
Kullerinn	Seat of House Anfalenn
Yesanith	Seat of House Volwinn
Halifarinn	Seat of House Rhistell
Nelldor	Seat of House Thallann

Anntheia

PROVIDENCES	DESCRIPTION
Irraginn	Location of House Kesterinn
Accuriann	Location of House Fairimier
Burkharm	Location of House Hollowenn
Exertinn	Location of House Duramonnt
Gillamornn	Location of House Alinnac
Miramurnn	Location of House Galliot
Oldihann	Location of House Wynnwell
Redonnia	Location of House Robintonn

TOWN	DESCRIPTION
Wimbornn	Capital of Anntheia
Draycorninn	Seat of House Kesterinn
Jongvale	Seat of House Fairimier
Eldiham	Seat of House Hollowenn
Accritonnus	Seat of House Duramonnt
Fohmskirk	Seat of House Alinnac
Killtharnn	Seat of House Galliot
Miristonne	Seat of House Wynnwell
Grimmsbynn	Seat of House Robintonn

Anntheia's legions are names after the providence from where they come from. Anntheia has 8 legions of soldiers.

Yorynn

VILLAGES	DESCRIPTION
Dermwist	The Great Hall and Capital of Yorynn
Hallbim	Village with a Greal Hall of Law
Gimdinn	Village with a Greal Hall of Law
Tukmier	Village with a Greal Hall of Law
Wegrinn	Village with a Greal Hall of Law
Frimzock	Village with a Greal Hall of Law
Klimgrest	Village with a Greal Hall of Law
Wolvroot	Village with a Greal Hall of Law
Baknnecks	Village with a Greal Hall of Law
Rabnooks	Village with a Greal Hall of Law

Guirinn

TOWN	DESCRIPTION
Thoridunn	Capital of Guirinn
Klogholm	Seat of House Morgor
Nozmore	Seat of House Thornnmer
Jokorinn	Seat of House Snoddrik
Dormholl	Seat of House Grookheim
Uminndike	Seat of House Ellric

Skallvenn

CLANS	DESCRIPTION
Horvarkk	Capital of Skallvynn
Ravennbeak	Village with a Great Hall of Clan Law
Crowthornn	Village with a Great Hall of Clan Law
Stormhounnd	Village with a Great Hall of Clan Law
Bearcrusher	Village with a Great Hall of Clan Law
Eagleclaw	Village with a Great Hall of Clan Law
Deerhornn	Village with a Great Hall of Clan Law
Wolfclaw	Village with a Great Hall of Clan Law
Badgerpikes	Village with a Great Hall of Clan Law
Snakehornns	Village with a Great Hall of Clan Law
Toadraiders	Village with a Great Hall of Clan Law
Ironntusk	Village with a Great Hall of Clan Law
Shadowrams	Village with a Great Hall of Clan Law

The Emberwild

VILLAGES	DESCRIPTION
Bramblemoonn	Capital of The Emberwild
Mosswick	Village with a Great Hall of Law
Littlestonne	Village with a Great Hall of Law
Fernnspark	Village with a Great Hall of Law
Brightmeadow	Village with a Great Hall of Law
Lemonhornn	Village with a Great Hall of Law
Firegust	Village with a Great Hall of Law
Silkglade	Village with a Great Hall of Law
Shimmerthistle	Village with a Great Hall of Law
Greennpuff	Village with a Great Hall of Law
Quickriver	Village with a Great Hall of Law

Neutral Cities

Liberus

Trader's Town not under the control of a kingdom. Second Largest Trading Port in Annmar.

Cohnnwood

Secret city in the trees for Elves, Half-Elves, Fairies & Halflings. Located in the Foxxwood Forest.

Dragonnshead

Neutral city for Sellswords and banished Barbarianns. Located in the west off the coast north of Liberus. The town sits off the coast of The Gleaming Gulf and has a small port.

Island of Oakheart

Home for the Rogues of Hamlinn. The island is located north of Belmere. The Rogues of Hamlinn are a group of or small army that hires out to the highest bidder. They are mercenaries.

Rosefall

Religious City where all faiths are welcome. Rosefall is near Lenntis. It is located north at the edge of the mountains between Guirin, The Emberwild, and Belmere.

Shainnleia

Temple where Shadowguards train. Shadowguards are a Secret Order that protect magic users and magical secrets.

Shrines & Temples

Shrine of Nydar

The place where Eras died and the power of the gods disappeared. It is the place where magic will return.

Shrine of Ellisar

The place where the gods first arrived. It also the birthplace of magic and the power of the gods. It is where life was created. Ellisar is A Citadel – Monastery for Magical History and is taken care of by the Druids.

Kingswatch

The neutral site where king's meet. The alter is located at Lenntis at the top of the mountain where Lenntis is located.

Temple of Folwimm

A sacred temple of the gods. It is the Temple for the God Eras

Temple of Vulmmer

A sacred temple of the gods. It is the Temple for the God Dresda

Temple of Simimarr

A sacred temple of the gods. It is the Temple for the God Cimis

Temple of Darthoridann

A sacred temple of the gods. It is the Temple for the God Anion

Temple of Thailia

A sacred temple of the gods. It is the Temple for the God Gennier

Military Ranks

Annmar Military Ranks	Military Rank Equivalent	Insignia
Field Marshum	5 Star General	
Sea Marshum	Admirant of the Fleet	
Admirann	Admiral (Navy)	
1st Genneral	4 Star General	
2nd Genneral	3 Star General	
3rd Genneral	2 Star General	
4th Genneral	1 Star General	
Capitaunn	Sea Captain (Navy)	
Commander	Colonel	
Commander	Naval Commander	
Magerus	Major (Army)	
Magerus	Lt. Commander (Navy)	
Captainn	Captain (Army Only)	
Cennturius	1st Lieutenant	
Master Sargenn	(Master Sgt. & Sgt. Major)	
Sargenn	Sergeant	

Corpus	Corporal	
Privamenn	Private	
Legionnaire	Member of A Legion	
Guardian	Bodyguard	
Sentinel	Regular Guard	

Acknowledgements

First, I'd like to thank James Chapman for the wonderful artwork provided in the book including the cover. I could not create this vision of the Annmar Chronicles without you. Next, I'd like to thank Audra Farris and Carol Felder for helping edit this book. And last, but certainly not least, I would like to thank Marius Donnelly and the staff of Trinity Hall Irish Pub for always providing a great place to get some writing done. This Irish Pub will truly be missed and I don't think I will ever find a place like it.

9 781932 996784